BODIES OF PROOF

A LEGAL THRILLER

JAMES CHANDLER
LAURA SNIDER

Copyright © 2025 by James Chandler and Laura Snider.

All rights reserved.

No part of this book may be reproduced in any form or by any electronic or mechanical means, including information storage and retrieval systems, without written permission from the author, except for the use of brief quotations in a book review.

Severn River Publishing
www.SevernRiverBooks.com

This is a work of fiction. Names, characters, businesses, places, events and incidents are either the products of the author's imagination or used in a fictitious manner. Any resemblance to actual persons, living or dead, or actual events is purely coincidental.

ISBN: 978-1-64875-661-0 (Paperback)

ALSO BY THE AUTHORS

Smith and Bauer Legal Thrillers

Justice Bites

Bodies of Proof

The Final Appeal

By James Chandler

Sam Johnstone Legal Thrillers

Misjudged

One and Done

False Evidence

Capital Justice

The Truthful Witness

Conflict of Duty

Course of Conduct

Reasonable Suspicion

By Laura Snider

Ashley Montgomery Legal Thrillers

Molly Sand Must Die

To join the reader list and find out more, visit

severnriverbooks.com

For Hannah, Abigail, H.S., M.S., and W.S.

PROLOGUE
SHEP

Sunday, May 30

Not all dogs are lucky.

The phrase *you lucky dog,* which Shep sometimes heard from humans, didn't always make sense. The neighbor—a Shih Tzu named Fancy—spent most of her time outside on her human's lap getting brushed.

Shep hated it when his human brushed him.

Fancy must be miserable. Plus, her name was Fancy and she wasn't fancy at all! She had a short nose and snorted when she breathed.

Shep was the luckiest Border Collie in all of Iowa because his human worked dog hours. She was home all day to play while he was awake and worked at night while he slept. Leslie—that was his human's name—even let him sleep in her bed! The bed was big and soft and better than a floor or a couch—and it came with Leslie cuddles and smelled like her!

Leslie was a nice human. She was very thoughtful, and every day they followed the same routine. Shep woke Leslie by touching his wet nose to her cheek, then she'd roll over and put a hand over her head. Shep would then hop over her and press his nose to her cheek again. She'd roll over, he'd jump over. And so on and so forth until Leslie was giggling and hugging him.

He was the most loved Border Collie anywhere! He was a lucky dog.

Today started no differently than any other day. Shep woke Leslie up, they ate breakfast, watched some women yell at each other on the square box with pictures, and then Leslie stood, stretched, and asked, "Do you want to go for a run?"

Oh boy, did he! Shep could run and run and run. And Leslie was training for a half marathon—whatever that was—which meant she went running every single day and brought him with her.

Shep jumped off the couch, soared through the air, and landed on the linoleum floor with a *thunk* and a slide. The floor was always a little slippery under his paws. He followed Leslie to the front door, where she slipped on her shoes and fitted him with his harness and leash. When she cracked open the door, he forced his nose into the small opening, then shoved his whole body through before she had time to open it. He knew he should have waited—a "good boy" would have waited—but he wasn't always a good boy.

It was a hot, sticky day and he started panting almost immediately, but that was okay. They always took the same trail, with an entrance at the end of their street. The trail was graveled, and it had thick woods on one side and a small, muddy stream on the other. Sometimes Leslie would let him wade in and drink the water, but not today. Today she made him stick to the trail. He pulled on the leash, trying to get Leslie to move faster, until they were finally in the woods and under the shade of the giant trees. They proceeded along the trail, and he could hear Leslie's breaths growing labored behind him as he led the way.

The smells! There were oh so many! That was what he loved the most—well, that and knowing that Fancy never got to run the trails with her human. Deer, squirrels, mice, birds, rabbits, possums, raccoons . . . They all lived back here. They would hide in the underbrush until Shep and Leslie got close and then they'd dart away. Shep always wanted to chase them, but Leslie scolded him when he tried.

This morning, Shep noticed a different smell—one he didn't immediately recognize. It was a strong smell, one that made him sneeze. He felt the hair on his back standing on end and he slowed his run. What was it? It smelled like that stuff that Leslie sometimes sprayed on herself before going out, but not as fruity or pretty as her smells, which also made him sneeze.

Leslie seemed to notice it too. She grew tense behind him. He could feel her body behind him growing rigid, her steps timid. He slowed to match her pace, then sped up because she started to speed up. There was a sudden heavy shuffling from the trees, and then Leslie made a sound of surprise and jerked on the leash. Shep turned to see a large human behind Leslie. The person wore all black and held something around Leslie's neck. He was pulling her backward and she was holding onto the leash. The human was putting something over Leslie's nose and mouth, and it was making her eyes do a fluttering thing that Shep did not like.

Shep bared his teeth, something he rarely did, and crouched lower to the ground. The hair on his back rose and a growl rumbled from his throat.

"Go on! If you know what's good for you, you mangy mutt, you'll stay back."

The human in black was a man.

Shep didn't like men. He charged the man, intent on biting him so he would let Leslie go. He wanted to sink his teeth into the attacker's soft skin and rip, rip, rip. He managed to get ahold of the man's boot before everything went black. Shep felt a searing pain, then a falling sensation. He felt his body losing its power, his four legs buckling beneath him. There was a gentle tug at his collar, then nothing.

When he opened his eyes, the air was much hotter and the blazing ball in the sky was in a completely different position. He stood unsteadily, then shook his head to try and rid himself of the pain.

He walked in circles and sniffed around in the woods, but Leslie was gone. The other human had taken her.

He was alone.

He wasn't a lucky dog anymore.

1

ADAM JENKINS

Monday, May 31

"The most difficult, most time-consuming crime to solve is murder," Special Agent Adam Jenkins said to the class of rookie law enforcement professionals. As an experienced agent for the Iowa Division of Criminal Investigation, he was tasked from time to time with teaching a class at the state's law enforcement academy.

A young woman in the front row tentatively raised her hand. She wore a police uniform from a small town in northeast Iowa. Jenkins marveled at her youth; at his age, rookies in their twenties seemed like kids. "I—I thought the perpetrator in most murders was usually the spouse? If that's true—"

"That is true," Jenkins agreed. "We always look at the spouse and others close to the victim first. But right now I'm talking about random murders—the ones where we can quickly rule out the usual suspects. The kind where we have DNA, but nobody to compare it to; where we have fingerprints, but none on file in the CODIS system. These crimes often take years and years to solve, and sometimes—maybe more often than not—go cold. This kind of crime is the most difficult to solve."

"So what you're saying is that murderers should kill random people and they'd get away with it?"

Jenkins turned in the direction of the speaker, a young man in the front row. He had light brown hair, blue eyes, and was heavily muscled in a way that told Jenkins he spent hours looking at himself in mirrored fitness centers. Physically, he clearly had what it takes, Jenkins thought. The more important question, of course, was whether he had strength in any of the ways that mattered.

He stopped talking and sighed. Try as he might to summon the enthusiasm, he was finding that coming back was getting more difficult as the years went by.

"Seriously? This isn't advice on how to commit crimes; it's a class on how to solve them. Do I really need to point that out? I mean, I thought it was a given, seeing that you are all in the law enforcement academy." He gestured to the classroom of eager young recruits. "You know, maybe Captain America here"—he took a step closer to the younger man—"ought to quit while he's ahead." Jenkins crouched down so he was eye level with the kid. "With *his* analytical skills, every criminal will go unchecked."

The class laughed.

Jenkins stood and turned to see his boss, Gerome Thomas, standing in the doorway, holding a cup of coffee and shaking his head. Thomas was the Special Agent in Charge of the major crime unit that covered Jenkins's district. For once, he wasn't frowning, so Jenkins assumed he hadn't taken it too far.

This time.

Thomas gestured toward Jenkins with his coffee mug. "We need to talk. Now."

Jenkins did a quick rewind of the events of the past few days, searching his memory to see if he could recall doing (or not doing) something that could have resulted in his placement at the top of Gerome's shit list.

"You all do some reading from your handbooks," Jenkins said to the class as he made his way to the door. "What's up, boss?" he asked once he and Thomas were in the hallway and out of the students' earshot.

"We've got another one," Thomas said.

"Kidnapping?" Jenkins said.

Bodies of Proof 7

Thomas nodded. "A waitress went out for a run before her shift. Leslie something or other. She never showed up for work. She apparently runs the same route every day at the same time. Right before her shift, like clockwork."

Jenkins shook his head. Routine was one of the biggest threats to safety—especially for single women.

"Maybe she's out with her boyfriend or something," Jenkins offered. "She could be tired of punching the clock and wanted to have a little fun. Isn't that what Cindy Lauper said? 'Girls just want to have fun?'"

Thomas's frown deepened.

"Sorry," Jenkins said. "Just trying to lighten the mood a bit."

There was a short pause while Thomas eyed Jenkins. "Well, don't," he said curtly. "I've got the boss on my ass and the press is starting to sniff around." He sipped from his cup and then continued, "According to friends and co-workers, this gal was known to take her dog with her. A Border Collie named—" He paused and looked down at a notepad. "Shep. The dog was found near the courthouse in downtown Franklin, unsteady on his feet, wobbling around like a New Year's Eve drunk, dragging a leash behind him."

"Weird."

"The local vet, Dr. Minsk, checked the dog out. She says she can't be sure what happened, but she thinks the dog was conked on the head with something. Probably lost consciousness for a while—concussion, you know?"

Jenkins nodded. "Any idea where the victim was running before she disappeared?"

"Same place she ran every day. A secluded trail along Soldier Creek."

Jenkins caught his breath. "That's where—"

"Exactly." Thomas nodded. "The same trail that we think Rebecca Calloway was running when she was abducted. And one more thing: the pooch had a small figurine tucked into its collar."

Jenkins reflected on the past year since Rebecca's apparent abduction. Law enforcement still had no idea what had happened to her. Despite the creation of an interagency task force and the expenditure of thousands of man hours searching, they had no body and only a single clue: a music box found in pieces on the ground adjacent to the trail. The crime scene had been searched, and despite the team's best efforts, they had located all the parts to the little bauble except for one.

"Don't tell me—"

"A tiny ballerina."

"Aw, shit!"

Some in law enforcement had quietly surmised that Rebecca had simply decided to leave for reasons known only to her. It happened. Her family, of course, had insisted she would never run away. While the case had not been closed officially, in the absence of both a body and hard evidence of a crime, many in the law enforcement community had concluded that Rebecca had simply decided to move on with her life and the abandoned music box was unconnected to her disappearance. Jenkins had never really bought into that; he was a girl dad with two daughters in their twenties. They were adults, certainly, but they still needed their dad. He talked to his girls at least once a week, sometimes once every few days. The idea that anyone's daughter would voluntarily leave her family, never to be heard from again, was inconceivable to him.

And he'd never believed the music box was unrelated. He didn't believe in coincidences.

"So we've got a second victim," he concluded.

"That's what I'm afraid of." Thomas sighed heavily. "I need you to head over to Franklin now and lead the investigation before the local cops screw it up."

It might be too late, Jenkins thought. Franklin's police department was among the poorest performers in the state. For sure, some of the officers in Franklin were decent—a few were even good at their jobs—but they were poorly led, and there were two or three officers he could name who didn't care about anything but a paycheck.

When a resounding bang came from inside the classroom, he peered through the doorway and saw several students chuckling. He cleared his throat, and the room went silent, everyone pretending to focus on their handbook.

He turned to Thomas. "What about the class?"

Thomas's gaze shifted to the room full of new, rambunctious, overly enthusiastic recruits. He'd been in their midst decades prior. "I'll finish up," he said.

"Thanks, boss."

"I don't need any thanks. I need you to catch this guy."

"We don't know for sure that it's a guy," Jenkins offered.

Thomas rolled his eyes and shook his head but didn't reply. There was nothing to say; they both knew that the abduction of women was a crime almost exclusively committed by men. Most people considered men the natural protectors of women, but the truth was they weren't protecting women from some unknown, incalculable threat—they were protecting them from *other men*.

Walking to his car, Jenkins reflected briefly on this turn of events. On the one hand, he was all too thankful to be off teaching duty. On the other hand, this crime would likely be a bitch to solve. Truthfully, in the absence of a lucky break, it might never be solved. And on top of everything else, he was supposed to be retiring soon—and the last thing he wanted was to retire with crimes unsolved on his watch.

But it was time to go.

His years dealing with major crimes had eroded his soul—or so his ex-wife had told him. And although she was dead wrong about a lot of things, he couldn't entirely dismiss her opinion on that. Seeing the worst of humanity day in and day out for decades was not conducive to living in peace and serenity.

He opened the door to his state car and adjusted the mirrors, wincing upon seeing his reflection. It wasn't the lines on his face or the age in his eyes, it was the knowledge that in his heart he knew full well he didn't want peace. Instead, he wanted to wage a full-on campaign against whatever sonuvabitch was hurting these women. He wanted justice. Later, maybe—and only if he could find justice for Rebecca and now Leslie—he might consider the pursuit of peace.

En route to Franklin, he calculated his pension in his head and wondered how hot it was in Arizona this time of year.

2

ALLEE

Monday, May 31

Beeep. Beeep. Beeep. Allee Smith's alarm blared, piercing through her dream.

She awoke from a deep sleep with a gasp, sat up, and out of habit ran her eyes quickly from corner to corner of the tiny bedroom, confused as to her whereabouts. But the moment passed quickly. She wasn't in prison anymore. She wasn't in jail. She wasn't on the streets. That life was behind her.

She took a few steadying breaths, then reached for her phone and turned off the alarm. She stared at the screen, blinking rapidly, feeling her eyelids scrape across her dry eyes—a constant symptom of spring allergies in rural Iowa. The phone's lock screen was a picture featuring Allee with her friend Whitney and her boss Marko. It was taken the day the trio had purchased a food truck and christened it Justice Bites. In the photo, they stood together, arms interlocked, grinning like lunatics. None of them had any idea how it would work, she recalled—or perhaps it was just her who hadn't understood the amount of work the business would require.

And it was Allee who seemed to be sacrificing the most to keep it afloat.

She turned her left arm to read a tattoo scripted along the back of her forearm. It was a line from one of her favorite books, *The Strange Case of Dr.*

Jekyll and Mr. Hyde, and read, *I am the chief of sinners, I am the chief of sufferers also*. During her five-year stay in Mitchellville, Iowa's only women's prison, Allee had fallen in love with classic horror novels. That, and her determination to never return, were the sole positive outcomes from five years behind bars.

She looked again to her phone. Above the photo was the time: 3:02 a.m. If she was going to get her baking done, she needed to leave, but her eyes were drawn again to the photo, where she stood with her coworkers in their makeshift food truck/law practice.

The food truck was glorious. Painted a flat black, with the words *Justice Bites* on the side panels in large block lettering. Beside the words was an image of Lady Justice with scales in her right hand. In lieu of the traditional sword, in her left hand she held a soft pretzel. Her blindfold was skewed so that one eye was revealed, as if Lady Justice was peeking.

Allee remembered her initial unbridled thrill as the business got underway. Everything had seemed like such a gift at the time, a new chapter in a newly sober life. But she had soon discovered the wisdom in what more than one old-timer in recovery had warned her about: sobriety was stressful.

Stress is a part of life, Allee reminded herself. She had known it since she was a child, forced to grow up quickly thanks to her mother's boozing and the endless parade of men who would leer at Allee when her mom wasn't around or paying attention. As a teenager, she'd lock her bedroom door at night and use substances to try to cope with her fear, shame, and disappointment. As a result, healthy coping skills were stunted, and even after she'd reached adulthood she continued to turn to drugs, resulting in her conviction, incarceration, and finally parole for possession of methamphetamine.

She rubbed her eyes, exhausted. She'd get so much more done if she didn't have to sleep, and an eight-ball of meth could fix that for a week. But she also knew that a single dalliance would result in her return to the life of chaos she had led previously, and would end with her again behind bars.

Allee pressed her palms to the mattress and forced herself into a sitting position. She stretched, stood, and then trudged down the hallway toward the kitchen. The floorboards creaked beneath her feet. The house was silent, which was normal at this hour. Allee's roommates, Whitney Moore and her six-year-old son Arlo, would be asleep for at least another hour. She'd been doubtful at first, but rooming with them had proven to be a welcome relief. For one thing, it meant Allee was never alone, left to her own devices, able to dwell on bad thoughts for hours on end. And although she hadn't spent much time around kids before this, she had discovered that little Arlo brought a joy to her life she hadn't expected, and exposed a tenderness in her that she hadn't known existed. The three of them lived a quiet, peaceful existence, for the most part.

The only issue was Leo, Whitney's soon-to-be ex-husband. He showed up every other weekend to get Arlo—which would have been fine if he had just shown up to retrieve Arlo, but that wasn't what happened. Instead, Leo would feign the need to discuss something about Arlo and maneuver to get Whitney alone so he could beg her to give him another chance. Inevitably, that would lead to an argument, whereupon Allee would take Arlo outside to play, away from the shouting.

Allee had grown up in a home with adults constantly shouting, screaming, and threatening violence. She knew it had done nothing for her. She would not blame her addiction entirely on her childhood, but she had learned in treatment and from twelve-step meetings that the unhealthy methods of coping she had developed were a natural response to that kind of upbringing. Now, as a convicted felon, she battled every day to cope with life on life's terms using newfound skills and focused on maintaining her sobriety one day at a time. As of today, it had been six years and five days since she had gotten her last fix—a remarkable achievement, she knew. But she understood there was no cure for addiction and that the desire to use would always hold space in her thoughts. Thus, her desire to shield Arlo— part of a promise she had made to do anything she could to keep him from following her path.

Creeping down the hallway so as to avoid waking them, Allee tried to focus on something else. The bad news was that today was Monday, meaning the weekend was over. The good news was that Leo wouldn't be back for another two weeks, so there was no immediate need to worry about what might happen. *One day at a time,* as her prison counselor had phrased it. *Try not to worry about the things you cannot control.*

Bodies of Proof 13

Whitney had left a light on in the hallway. It cast the narrow space in an eerie greenish-blue glow. Allee made it to the kitchen, where she saw the stove light was on, illuminating a small corner of the room. She flipped on the overhead light and walked quickly to the refrigerator, feeling the backs of her slippers dragging on the tile flooring.

Each square of tile had a large, flower-like object in the middle of it, in shades of orange, red, and off-white. The cabinets were dark, flimsy wood. There was no kitchen island, only countertops and cabinets that stretched along the walls in an L shape, giving the kitchen an outdated look that was almost vintage enough to be deemed stylish.

She opened one of the two refrigerators in the little house. This one was stocked with business inventory and was bereft of common items: no condiments inside the door, no sodas in the drawers. Each rack was filled with tin pans of cinnamon rolls. The other refrigerator, which stored the little family's food, was nearby in the attached garage.

Allee removed the first pan and placed it on the kitchen table, then removed its foil covering and tossed it in the trash. She repeated the process with the other two trays.

As always, Allee had stayed up late into the night to make the dough and cinnamon mixture. She'd then flattened the dough and spread the cinnamon mixture over it before slicing each into rows, rolling them into circular pieces, and placing them on the tray to cool for the night. They would now rest at room temperature for sixty to ninety minutes so they could rise. Meanwhile, she'd make the frosting. Fatigued, Allee was operating on autopilot. She'd followed this same routine every day for the past year. Occasionally, Whitney would help her, but most of the time, Allee worked alone. Making cinnamon rolls was demanding and labor-intensive; sometimes, she flirted with the idea of removing the cinnamon rolls from the Justice Bites menu altogether. In fact, at one point she had grown so tired of making them that she had raised the price to ten dollars per roll—an astronomical price in rural Iowa—but to her astonishment it made no difference. Customers complained about the price, which only added to Allee's frustration, but they continued to sell out within the first hour.

The tattoo running along Allee's left wrist to the tip of her index finger caught her eye. *Loneliness will sit over our roofs with brooding wings.* It was a quote from Bram Stoker's *Dracula*, her favorite book, and resonated with her because she was lonely sometimes even when surrounded by other people.

Like right now.

As she worked, she reflected on her new life. She would be tired, she knew, even if running Justice Bites was her only job—which it was not. For about a year now—since her boss Marko Bauer had gotten busted for driving drunk while he was defending Allee's cousin on a possession charge—she had worked as his driver and as the investigator for his one-man law firm in addition to her duties as baker.

The law firm was as much a part of Justice Bites as the cinnamon rolls. It was a mobile firm, headquartered in the Justice Bites food truck. Whitney served as Marko's office manager, fielding calls on her cell phone, keeping the firm's books, and maintaining his schedule. The truck went where the law firm needed to go. Each day it sat outside a rural Iowa county court-house. Which courthouse in which county was entirely dependent on Marko's schedule, but wherever they went, Marko met with new and existing clients at a folding table under an awning outside the truck. Justice Bites had been an immediate, unqualified success due in large part to Allee's cooking. She sold out of food wherever they parked, serving Marko's clients, courthouse employees, and local denizens. It was her calling, and seeing the looks on her customers' faces almost—almost—made it all worthwhile.

At six o'clock she heard little feet padding down the hallway. A moment later, Arlo came into the kitchen. He yawned and rubbed his eyes as he trudged over to the table.

Allee smiled at the little boy. "Good morning, weirdo," she said. It was part of their routine.

"You're weirder."

Allee glanced at the handmade tattoos running along her arms. He had a point. "Weird is good. If everyone was the same, the world would be boring."

"We're not boring."

"No. We aren't."

Arlo lifted his head and took a long sniff of the air. "Whatcha makin'?"

Bodies of Proof

This, too, was a routine.

"Cinnamon rolls."

"I want one."

Allee cut the smallest of the rolls in half and placed it on two separate plates. "You can have half of one. Your mom says I must limit your sugar. We'll share it." She spun around, holding one plate balanced on the palm of each hand.

"Deal," Arlo said, a smile spreading across his lips.

She placed his plate in front of him and the other in front of an adjacent chair. Sitting for the first time all morning, she savored her creation while watching him enjoy his. He devoured it in seconds, then licked the crumbs from the plate. If Whitney were awake, she'd scold him, of course, but not Allee. She wasn't his mother, and she would let him do what he wanted within reason.

Whitney, Allee knew, would not be awake for another thirty minutes. When that happened, the chaos would begin. Arlo would need to get ready for school and go to the neighbor's house to wait with her until the bus arrived. Allee and Whitney would have to load Justice Bites with the fresh cinnamon rolls and check to make sure they had everything they needed for the day. Once all that was done, they'd drive down the street to where Marko lived.

As Allee watched Arlo and thought about the day to come, a renewed sense of fatigue descended over her. How long could she keep this up? She had once hoped that things would get easier, but it had been a year now and the reality was that the everyday workload was the same. One day she would break. Nobody could bend that far without eventually snapping.

3

ADAM JENKINS

Monday, May 31

An internet search would tell a person that Franklin, Iowa, was a two-hour drive from Iowa's law enforcement academy in Des Moines, but today—with the use of flashing lights—Jenkins made it in half that time. He was not a permanent instructor at the academy; he was a special agent in Iowa's major crimes unit, but crime often ebbed and flowed. Of late, central Iowa had been in a significant ebb from a major crimes standpoint and Jenkins was bored, so he had volunteered to contribute some platform time. Not that he was complaining; boring in his line of work meant people were not hurting each other. It was good for humanity.

But it wasn't good for him.

Accordingly, he'd filled some empty hours teaching. As an expert in law enforcement, he had plenty of experience and knowledge to pass on to new officers *if* he could effectively communicate what he knew. And he had tried —he really had!—but for whatever reason the ideas he had in his head for lessons never really translated to classroom learning. Over time, he had begun to realize that deep down he hated teaching. For that reason, he was grateful to be back on the road today, headed toward the only thing he'd ever been really good at: investigating and solving major crimes.

He parked outside the Franklin County Courthouse and checked his watch. It was still a good thirty minutes before the courthouse opened at eight o'clock, so he had his pick of spots. He had hoped to meet with the local cops, drive to the scene, and get started immediately upon his arrival in Franklin, but for whatever reason he'd had trouble getting in touch with anyone in the Franklin Police Department who could help him. Sometimes that happened with small-town departments; they'd request assistance from the major crimes unit and then reverse course, declare their competence, and express their unwillingness to share information with an outside agency. Inevitably they would come around, but sometimes it wasn't until after the loss of valuable time. Jenkins could only hope that today's delay wouldn't hinder the investigation too much.

He stepped out of his vehicle and walked toward the law enforcement center. It was a large brick building with evenly spaced windows and no adornments. It looked out of place next to Franklin's ornate courthouse. The entire complex had been constructed as part of a traditional small-town courthouse square. Local businesses, once bustling with shoppers, now sat boarded up, with signs indicating their availability for sale or rent. For Jenkins, the sad spectacle was representative of how society viewed justice: once central to the town's existence, it was now an afterthought for a busy populace with their mind on other things.

In Franklin, the law enforcement center housed the sheriff's office, police department, and jail, each occupying its own floor. The front door of the center was unlocked, so Jenkins went inside and took the stairs to the second-floor police department. A middle-aged woman sat at a desk at the top of the stairs behind bulletproof glass. She had short, curly hair and thick-lensed glasses. She was focused on a computer screen and did not acknowledge him as he approached.

He cleared his throat.

She ignored him.

What is with this woman? Time was the most precious commodity in investigations, and Franklin officials had already wasted too much of his. It was not an exaggeration to say that wasting precious seconds now could be the difference between life and death for the missing girl.

"Excuse me," Jenkins said, trying but failing to keep his tone conciliatory. "I'm Special Agent Adam Jenkins. I'm here to see Captain Shaffer."

"Oh." The woman's body shifted toward him, and her gaze met his. Her nametag said *Carla*. "You must be here about the missing girl."

"Yes, Carla, I am."

"That poor dear," Carla clucked. "I play bridge with her mom, you know. She comes from a wonderful family."

"That's why I'm in a bit of a rush," Jenkins said. "Will you let Captain Shaffer know that I'm here and it is urgent?"

"Oh yes, of course." She picked up the receiver of a landline phone and shifted her body back away from him as she pressed several buttons. He could hear ringing, then a gruff voice answered.

"What is it?"

"Umm, Captain? This is Carla." She spoke softly into the receiver, cutting a worried glance toward Jenkins.

"I know who the hell it is, Carla! You're the only person at the front desk. What I don't know is what you want! Help me out, would you?"

"Yes. Sorry, Captain. Special Agent Jenkins is here to see you."

"Why the hell is he here so early?"

She looked toward Jenkins helplessly. "I'm sure I don't know, sir. Do—do you want me to ask?"

"No."

There was a long silence. "So, what do you want me to tell him?" Carla did not seem like the type to allow empty space to fill any vacuum in conversations.

"Tell him I'll get to him when I get to him."

"Okay," she said. She held the phone to her ear for another beat, then slowly lowered it and placed it on the cradle. She turned to Jenkins, a forced smile pasted on her lips. "Captain Shaffer says he'll be with you as soon as possible."

"Great," Jenkins replied through gritted teeth.

They were wasting time, and thereby violating one of the golden rules of police work, but there was also nothing he could do about it. If Shaffer wanted to play power games and make him wait, he'd have to wait.

Once an asshole, always an asshole, Jenkins thought.

He and Shaffer had a long history. They'd started in law enforcement at the same time, graduating in the same class from the academy. For unknown reasons, Shaffer had taken an immediate dislike to him, and had openly competed against him day and night, on duty or off. Fortunately, he was so far above Shaffer skill-wise that he'd never paid the guy much mind —until he was assigned to look into a scandal stemming from a defense attorney's claims that Shaffer had planted evidence. He'd been unable to verify the claims with certainty, but closed his investigation convinced Shaffer was dirty. How he'd ever been promoted to captain following that debacle was beyond him; he would have de-certified Shaffer and removed him from the force. Instead, he'd been promoted.

How long is he going to take?

Jenkins's gaze shifted to a clock mounted on the side wall. A minute passed. There was a sitting area nearby with inexpensive furniture and decades-old magazines, but he didn't want to sit. He began to pace, and when the clock ticked forward another minute, he reapproached the front desk.

"Tell him I'm running out of time," he directed. He didn't wait for an answer before continuing. "This is supposed to be an emergency."

"That's what I said," Carla said, nodding conspiratorially toward her phone. "But the captain doesn't see it that way. I just texted him." She brandished her phone, pointing to the screen, then turned it back toward her and put on a pair of readers. "He said, and I quote, 'Stop bugging me about this. I will get there when I get there. It's not like we have a dead body, Carla.'"

Jenkins could feel his face warming, but he swallowed the retort before it left his mouth. It wasn't her fault. He could have done without the quote —that hadn't helped lower his blood pressure—but at least she was trying to be helpful. The problem was small-town departments and their characteristic lack of urgency. They knew their people, for sure. But sometimes that worked against them. In this case, no body didn't automatically mean the young woman was a runaway. Especially since this was the second disappearance in a year.

After quickly perusing the files, Jenkins was convinced the first girl to disappear, Rebecca Calloway, was dead by now. He hadn't worked her case

—in fact, his office hadn't been called for an assist. But he had read the file (such as it was). The lack of urgency—at least at the outset of the woman's disappearance—was, in Jenkins's opinion, largely responsible for the case being bungled so badly. A well-run investigation with an appropriate degree of urgency might well have resulted in law enforcement finding Rebecca alive. And now, in Jenkins's opinion, they were making the same mistake again—but this time, they were dragging him along for the ride. He was reasonably certain Shaffer had been forced to call for assistance by the police chief, or had called simply so he could blame someone else if things went badly. He was about to insist that Carla contact Shaffer again when noise from outside caught his attention. Someone was laying on their car horn and shouting.

"What's going on?" Jenkins said, making his way toward the large window in the seating area.

"Don't worry about them," Carla said with a chuckle. "They do that every day."

Jenkins looked outside to see two food trucks parked across from each other in the courthouse square. One was red, white, and blue with the words *Freedom Burgers* scripted on its side. The other was black with white lettering that read *Justice Bites*.

"Justice Bites," Jenkins commented wryly. "Great name."

Carla chuckled again. "It's owned and operated by a defense attorney, Marko Bauer, and a gal he defended a while back."

Fitting, Jenkins thought.

"I don't approve of the ownership, but they have the best food in town, hands down. It's probably the best food truck in Iowa," Carla said. "You should try it while you're here."

"I might do that," he said without conviction. It was none of Carla's business, of course, but he didn't make a habit of supporting defense attorneys or felons in any way. Turning back to the window, he watched a tall blonde woman walk around the Justice Bites truck while holding her middle finger up toward the Freedom Burgers truck.

Classy, Jenkins thought. *Welcome to small-town, cutthroat capitalism.*

4

ALLEE

Physically, Allee was behind the wheel of Justice Bites, with Marko and Whitney riding beside her. But mentally, she was isolated—alone in her thoughts, her mind whirring while their voices droned on, background noise against the internal battle raging. Her prison counselor had warned Allee that as a frenetic thinker, she needed to be aware of her tendency to shut out the world. The contents of her thoughts varied, generally depending on the time of day; this morning, en route to another twelve-hour day combining two distinct occupations, Allee was confronting self-doubt.

Prior to their purchase of Justice Bites, Allee had never managed a business or balanced a budget. She'd worked in plenty of kitchens as a line cook or sous chef, but those jobs focused on food preparation and presentation; she wasn't required to track receipts, pay bills, or determine the amount of food to order (which was turning out to be a lot harder than she'd thought). Unused food spoiled, and unserved customers went away not only unsatisfied but with their money still in their wallets. Efficient stock management, she was learning, could be the difference between a profitable or unprofitable day. A mistake either way was akin to lighting a stack of bills on fire.

The business is doing fine; stop worrying. But it wasn't in her nature to be carefree or to simply yield to whatever might happen. And who could blame her? She had spent the better part of her life allowing others to make decisions for her that didn't work out well. But even after gaining sobriety, she had failed time and again in various endeavors. The old-timers said to live one day at a time, but was it any surprise that she only saw potential potholes and pitfalls ahead?

The money thing was especially troubling. After all, she was a felon with access to business accounts. What would happen if she accidentally overdrew an account and couldn't pay it back for a while? Would anyone believe it was an accident? Of course not. The bank would assume the worst; they'd think she had written a check knowing the money was not in the account and would report her to law enforcement. That would start a chain reaction that could only end in shackles.

I need to go through all the bank accounts again tonight. They had taken out a line of credit—in Marko's name, of course—and opened a business checking account. She also had a company credit card with her name on it. Never in her life had she owned a credit card. It made her nervous as hell, because it felt too much like free money. Intellectually, Allee knew that nothing was free, but she also knew she had spent a lifetime making decisions on impulse.

It was probably the drugs. They changed people. She hadn't used in more than six years, but she was—and would always be—an addict and an addictive thinker. Her mind drifted to the tattoo running along the bottom of her left arm. *I am the chief of sinners. I am the chief of sufferers, also.* It was from *The Strange Case of Dr. Jekyll and Mr. Hyde.* The tattoo was crude, inked while she was incarcerated in Mitchellville prison, at the time wanting desperately to use, to do anything to take her mind off where she was and why.

At some point, she'd decided she needed a distraction, and she found it in books. The Mitchellville prison library wasn't large, and none of the books were new. But the collection was eclectic and featured a rather large horror section. In time she would learn the books she favored were old enough to be in the public domain and therefore cheap enough for the prison to add them to their collection. But regardless of why they were stocked, by good fortune and solely on a whim, one day Allee had pulled a dusty hardcover from a shelf and become enthralled on the spot. She fell

immediately and deeply in love with classic horror novels like *Carmilla,
Frankenstein,* and *Dr. Jekyll and Mr. Hyde.* Losing herself in the stories of
those unloved, misunderstood characters—"monsters," some said—was
crucial in her successfully serving her time.

"*Allee!*" Whitney's voice was sharp and shrill.

"What?"

"You missed the turn!" Whitney jerked a thumb over her shoulder, indicating the sign behind them for Highway 17.

"Aw, crap." It was where she usually turned, but not the only highway
that would take them to Franklin. "I'll keep going to take Highway 169
north."

"What's going on with you?" Whitney said. "You've been out of it since
you picked us up. Was Arlo trouble?"

"No."

As Marko's legal assistant, one of Whitney's many unpaid tasks was to
go over to his house in the mornings to make sure he was awake and ready
for the day. That left Allee alone with Arlo, and responsible for helping him
get ready. Sometimes it felt like they were coparenting two kids, not one.

"He went over to Adaline's without a fuss?" Whitney asked.

Adaline was their neighbor. She was in her sixties and retired. Her children were grown and out of the house and her husband had passed away a
year earlier. Heart failure, she had informed Allee (who hadn't asked).
According to Adaline, it had been a complete shock. She'd expected to
spend the remainder of her life growing old with him.

"Oh, yeah," Allee assured Whitney. "She had those waxy convenience
store doughnuts that Arlo likes so much. He took one look at them and
bounded inside without looking back." Allee did not understand children
in many ways, but she would never, ever understand their food choices.
Macaroni with powdered cheese? Waxy doughnuts? Frozen, crustless
peanut butter and jelly sandwiches? Children seemed to love foods that
came from boxes and bags, but why? It all paled in comparison to the real
thing, especially if Allee was making it.

"Okay," Whitney replied at last. "Good."

Allee turned north on Highway 169. From here, it was a straight shot to
Franklin; they'd be there in less than thirty minutes. She tried to focus on

Whitney and Marko's conversation. The law business was separate and distinct from the food truck business, but as the investigator she was still part of it. In fact, she was really the link between the two businesses—which made her resentful on occasion. They all profited from the food truck, but it was Allee who carried the load. Justice Bites was clearly an afterthought for both Marko and Whitney (not entirely unexpected), but she hadn't expected them to *ignore* Justice Bites, forcing her to shoulder almost the entire load while still being fully engaged with the law practice. She shook her head, trying to dismiss her resentment to better focus on the ongoing discussion.

"What do you know about my first client meeting?" Marko asked Whitney.

"A guy named James Innis. He's been charged with Operating While Intoxicated."

"Private pay or court appointment?" Marko asked.

"Private pay."

"Oh, good."

Despite her promise to herself, Allee bristled. "Do you have to say it like that?"

"Like what?" Marko asked.

"Like someone with money is so much better than a court appointment."

"They *are* better—"

Allee snorted.

"From a business standpoint," Marko continued. "And that's what we are running. A business."

"Right," Allee said irritably.

"Allee, it's business, not personal," Marko said. "You understand, don't you?"

Oh, she understood, all right. Marko was all about money, and from what she'd observed, his level of service was directly proportional to the amount of money he was getting from the client. Understanding was not her problem; it was acceptance.

"Don't get all worked up, Allee," he warned her. "We've got a long day ahead of us."

Allee gripped the steering wheel tighter. "I'm not," she forced herself to say. It wasn't just business to her; it was personal. *Very personal.* Marko could think what he wanted—she didn't really care. But it showed in the way he separated clients by financial category and dealt with them in each group. And she knew how it worked from the client side, as well: Marko had been court-appointed when he represented her, and he'd been court-appointed when he represented her cousin, Nate. His preference for private pay clients had been obvious, and made her feel like a second-class citizen. It was as if Marko thought poor people deserved a lesser defense.

"They're all clients," Allee insisted. "They should all be equally important."

"Well, they can't be," Marko replied. "We've gotta pay the bills. Now drop the attitude, because I'm going to need you to sit in on the meeting this morning, Allee."

Marko required Allee to attend private pay client meetings. It was one of the many ways those clients received better representation. Looking back, she recalled that Marko hadn't bothered to hire an investigator to work on her case, which had ended with her doing a nickel in Mitchellville.

"Seriously?" Allee protested. "It's just an OWI. You don't really need me."

"Yes, I do," Marko replied quickly. "This client needs to know up front that we have a team ready and willing to work for him. We need to impress him so that he will tell friends and relatives that our firm is the one they want."

"Whatever," Allee said. Wasting time on the meeting would seriously limit her ability to sell food, especially when Nate, her cousin and their only employee, hadn't shown up. Allee knew he would call in later today and claim he was sick, which happened more often than not these days. He wasn't actually sick, of course—not in the cold or flu way. He was sick in the head. Nate's struggle was between his ears, which, in many ways, was much, much worse.

"Love the enthusiasm," Marko said sarcastically.

Allee shrugged. She was barely containing her anger and was shy of the energy or the desire to muster feigned enthusiasm. "Then Whitney will have to cover for me."

Whitney groaned.

"Love the enthusiasm," Allee said to Whitney.

"I'm sorry," Whitney said quickly. "But you know I hate working the register."

Allee knew it well, because Whitney complained every time she had to step up. "You should only have to sell doughnuts and cinnamon rolls," she said. "We won't change to the lunch menu until eleven o'clock. I'll have to be back by then," she reminded Marko.

This was the way of their businesses these days. Everyone (except Marko, of course) was stuck doing work they didn't want to do.

Allee was still angry. "I've been thinking," she began while side-eyeing Marko. "Court appointments could also use an attorney who is ready and willing."

"I told you I didn't mean it like that, Allee," Marko snapped. "Leave it alone."

"Why did this James guy hire us, anyway?" Allee said, returning her focus to the road. "If he's got so much money, why didn't he hire one of the flashy Des Moines firms?"

Marko smirked. "Because I'm better than all those attorneys," he said without hesitation.

Debatable, Allee thought.

"I'm the best attorney in Iowa."

Allee swallowed a quick retort. "He has no way of knowing that," she said, striving not to roll her eyes. Marko lacked a lot of things—self-control, emotional maturity, and empathy, to name a few—but he had never lacked confidence.

"Our website says it, does it not?"

"Yes, it does," Whitney said brightly. Allee could hear her nails clacking against her laptop keys.

Whitney turned her computer so Marko could see the screen. "Here it is! See?"

Allee glanced from the road to see Whitney pointing to the screen. "Right here it says 'Iowa's best attorney.'"

Allee shook her head. *In the same meaningless way a crappy coffee shop says "World's best coffee."*

Bodies of Proof 27

Truthfully, it wasn't that Marko was a bad attorney—he was not. Instead, Allee saw him as an above-average lawyer who—if he cared enough—would be superb. But he didn't, so he wasn't. The problem wasn't intelligence, it was heart.

"Did he book his consultation through the website?" Marko asked.

Whitney shrugged. "I don't know, but I can find out." She clicked a few laptop keys. The truck cab was silent while they waited, the only sound the tires on the road and the roar of the wild Iowa wind beating against the windows.

"Here it is," Whitney said at last. "It looks like he came in through the website. He used the 'schedule a free consultation' button."

"Huh," Allee said. They'd had that button on the website for months, and until now it hadn't brought in any clients. They'd all chalked it up as a failure after weeks with no traction. Allee had almost felt sorry for Whitney, who had been really excited about the installation of that button, thinking it might bring in all kinds of new clients.

At last, Allee turned in front of the Franklin County Courthouse. The square was still and silent. As they drove around the courthouse, they saw the familiar cars parked out front. Angie from the auditor's office always arrived early. She was a nervous, flighty woman who always seemed to be trying to prove that she was working harder than everyone else, when in reality she was probably up in her office playing computer games.

The janitor's old truck was parked a few stalls down from Angie's sedan, and then there was a vehicle that Allee had never seen before. She studied it as she passed. It was parked in front of the courthouse, but in the slot closest to the law enforcement center.

Who is that? Nothing was open yet. The few remaining shops on the square were shuttered until nine o'clock, and the courthouse itself wouldn't be open for another ten minutes. *None of my business*, she reminded herself. She parked the truck sideways in its usual location between the courthouse and law enforcement center, occupying three parking spots. Allee parked strategically, positioning the "Place Order Here" window facing the street and giving her space on the square's grass to set up the tables and shade tent for hungry customers (and Marko's client meetings).

"All right," Allee said, shutting down the engine. "Let's un-ass this thing."

While Whitney and Allee got to work, Marko stood silently, watching as Whitney unhooked and began setting up the awning that spread from the side of the truck while Allee grabbed a long folding table and several chairs from the back.

The two women were finishing setup when another food truck turned the corner, blaring its horn obnoxiously and heading for a row of vacant parking spots across from Justice Bites. The truck was painted like an American Flag and had *Freedom Burgers* scripted on both sides.

"Dale," Whitney said, shaking her head sadly. "Why doesn't he give it up?"

As Freedom Burgers passed her, Allee gave the blue-eyed, bearded skinhead behind the wheel the middle finger, holding her arm in the air and tracking it along with his truck, thereby ensuring he would see it—and her. For his part, as he passed, he maintained a laser focus on her, challenging her. Then, raising a hand, he pointed a finger gun at her, then pulled the imaginary trigger.

Outwardly, Allee showed no reaction. At the same time, her stomach fluttered. He was doubtless a felon, but just the type to ignore the law prohibiting him from carrying. She needed to keep an eye on his ass.

"What is wrong with that man?" Whitney asked, concern evident in her voice.

Allee watched the truck for a few moments longer, then shook her head, forcing thoughts of threats out of her mind. "Who cares? Screw him."

"Hard pass," Marko said, coming to her side.

"He hates us," Whitney said.

"Tell him to take a number," Allee said. They were three misfits who had spent the better part of their adult lives as outcasts. It was going to take a lot more than dirty looks, finger guns, and blaring horns to run them off.

Apparently well-rested, Marko slapped the tabletop. "Our first client will be here any minute," he said. "Let's get to work."

5

JENKINS

"I see you've gotten a whiff of the local trash."

Jenkins recognized the gruff voice, and he turned to see Dennis Shaffer approaching. It had been years since they had seen each other, but Shaffer's beady eyes hadn't changed a bit, and as always his uniform was perfectly pressed. The only flaw in his otherwise inspection-ready appearance was what looked like scuff marks on the toe of a boot.

Trash. Jenkins frowned. He had spent his career traveling throughout Iowa investigating the most dangerous criminals the state had to offer. But he would never refer to anyone as *trash*. People were flawed, to be sure, and some were evil. But they were human beings deserving respect and dignity —frequently despite themselves. To dehumanize them in any way was a dangerous, slippery slope for a cop to embark upon.

"Nice of you to find the time to see me," Jenkins said, choosing to switch the subject rather than debate the merits of defendants. He knew the man well enough to know nothing he could say would influence Shaffer's view of humanity. "What happened to your boot there?" He didn't particularly care, of course, but knowing Shaffer as he did, he knew that pointing out a flaw in Shaffer's appearance would get under his thin skin.

"I'm busy. Can't stop everything every time a *special agent* shows up,"

Shaffer said with a shrug. "Not your concern," he added, looking at his boot.

"Considering it was *your* department that requested my assistance, I would have expected you'd be ready to get started."

"Yeah, well, I didn't want you here," Shaffer replied. "If it were up to me, you wouldn't be."

"That, I believe." Jenkins turned his attention to the window, watching as the people in the black truck sat down at a table beneath an awning they'd set up in record speed.

"The chief and sheriff are both antsy," Shaffer explained. "Two girls in two years doesn't look good for anyone."

"No. It doesn't." They hadn't asked for help with Rebecca Calloway's disappearance, and they'd dragged their feet making the call for this one. "What are your thoughts?"

"I don't see what all the fuss is about." Shaffer shrugged. "That Calloway girl ran away—I'm sure of it. And the Martin girl probably did too."

Well, that explains his delay in seeking assistance, Jenkins thought. It was the simplest solution, sure, but it didn't explain a lot of things, beginning with the second girl's dog showing up staggering downtown or that the two girls apparently disappeared from the same general location.

"I think you're wasting your time," Shaffer continued. "But it's an election year and that's got the chief's panties in a wad."

"The chief of police is appointed, not elected."

"Yeah, well, those who appoint him are elected, and Chief seems to think there is reason to be concerned."

Jenkins hoped there was more to the chief's concern than his upcoming election; his concern should be solely for the two young women and whatever horrors they had suffered and might continue to experience. "Then we better get down to business," he said. "Where's the crime scene? You want to take me there, or are you gonna have an officer do it?"

Shaffer gestured around himself. "You're looking at it."

"What?" Jenkins turned away from the window to give Shaffer a hard look. "You're joking." Shaffer wasn't smiling. If anything, his expression had grown colder. "Is this your idea of a joke? Who is gathering evidence?"

"There isn't any evidence to gather."

That was bullshit and Shaffer knew it. There was always evidence. Always. They just had to look for it.

"I told the chief that we found the dog. That's it," Shaffer said, his tone growing defensive.

"Where? Where did you find the dog?"

Shaffer moved quickly, stepping into Jenkins's bubble near the window. "The dog was wandering around over there." Shaffer gestured to the north side of the courthouse. "His leash was dragging behind him, and he was stumbling around like he had a few too many down at Olde Bulldogs."

Olde Bulldogs was a local bar and restaurant. It had been a long time since Jenkins was inside the place, but he remembered it as a tavern that passed for upscale in Franklin. Martinis with cheap liquor and two-for-one Happy Hours. Clean but inexpensive faux-leather seats. There was nothing really wrong with the joint, but it would never survive in a place like Des Moines. Not in its current state, pretending to be something it wasn't.

"Where was the abduction?" Jenkins was trying to contain his irritation. "If you know."

"On the running trail."

He turned to face Shaffer. "Tell me that you've at least secured the trail."

Shaffer shrugged. "I didn't see a point. I mean, I had my officers go through and check it out, but they didn't find nothin'. Nobody uses it anyway," he added, then paused briefly before finishing his thought. "Especially now."

Jenkins took a deep breath, resisting the urge to wrap a hand around Shaffer's neck. "Get someone down there and shut it down. Now."

Shaffer angrily retrieved his phone and began punching keys. After a few moments, he looked up. "Done, but not because you asked," he said, trying to maintain a degree of control. "I did it because we need to make the public think we are doing something."

At the very least. "Where is the ballerina figurine?"

"With the dog."

Jenkins sighed heavily. He lowered his head and pinched the bridge of his nose, trying to maintain his composure. "Why didn't you place the figurine in evidence?"

"Because it was with the dog. Preserve the scene, you know?"

Ridiculous. "Where is the dog?" Jenkins asked after a long moment.

"At the vet. They wanted to keep him for observation."

At least Shaffer had gotten that right. He'd half-expected him to say that he'd released the dog to roam free. "All right," Jenkins said. "Let's get going. Who have you assigned to assist me with the investigation?"

"Nobody." Shaffer smiled for the first time, but it was a sardonic, humorless expression that spread across his cratered face like a snake slithering through water. "This one is all on you."

Jenkins nodded and again turned to the window, his face hot with rage. Shaffer had to know that the investigation was already impaired, if not corrupted. And unless they were idiots, so did the sheriff and the chief of police. It was becoming clear they'd called DCI not to solve the cases but rather to cover their asses and so he could serve as the eventual scapegoat.

"Good luck," Shaffer said.

Jenkins didn't look away from the window, but he felt himself relax when he heard Shaffer turn on the heels of his heavy boots and depart. When the door to Shaffer's office closed behind him, Jenkins's anger began to subside, replaced by determination. He couldn't allow himself to be distracted by the mistakes made to date. What was done (or not) had been done (or not).

The good news was the dog had been found and was under the veterinarian's care. The vet had the ballerina figurine as well, which would normally be problematic from a chain-of-custody standpoint. But vets were doctors and doctors were smart; hopefully, this one would know enough to keep evidence in a safe place. Jenkins would need to get there soon, but first he would focus on the scene in front of him. As he understood it, the dog had been with Leslie when she disappeared. Or was taken. He couldn't entirely eliminate that possibility. Yet. Jenkins didn't know a lot about dogs, but he figured the animal must have been frightened. Why didn't he just go home—wherever that was? Why was he found wandering the square? Could he have found his way to the courthouse because he saw it as a familiar, safe place? Jenkins needed to determine if there was any connection between the dog, the girl, and this area. Maybe someone in one of the food trucks would know. *That's where I'll start*, he told himself with a nod.

Having made his decision, and just as he was about to start heading downstairs, a black sedan pulled up next to the Justice Bites food truck. It was sleek and expensive, a better fit on the streets of New York or LA than Franklin, Iowa.

Curious.

He'd start with Freedom Burgers to get the lay of the land before approaching Justice Bites.

6

ALLEE

It was nine o'clock sharp when the black limousine pulled into a parking spot next to Justice Bites. Allee had been watching the clock on her phone, fully expecting the client to be late for his appointment. Rich people valued their time only. But to her surprise, the shiny black Mercedes came to a stop right as the clock moved from eight fifty-nine to nine double zero.

"He shouldn't be driving," Allee muttered.

Marko shrugged.

They were seated at the small table beneath the food truck's canopy. Allee placed her phone next to her laptop computer. The laptop's screen was open but dark, and she could see her reflection in its blackness, her eyes narrowed, her mouth pinched. She'd never had much of a poker face. Marko sat alertly next to her with a legal pad and a pen, bright-eyed and bushy-tailed in his sobriety.

While they waited, she allowed herself a quick look at the truck. It wasn't new, it wasn't perfect, but that beautiful black beast meant everything to her. It was the only thing she'd ever built, the only thing she'd created. Vehicles had always provided her a sense of freedom, but this one also held the hope of financial security. She wasn't quite there yet, but she could see the promise of it. Whitney, Allee knew, was somewhere inside the truck, covering for her, filling orders for coffee and pastries. Allee would

Bodies of Proof 35

rather be filling orders than listening in as Marko met his new client; they had agreed to put some profits into the purchase of a new doughnut fryer a week ago and she'd only had a few chances to use it. She'd taught Whitney, but she wasn't entirely sure Whitney had understood.

Whitney will be fine for an hour, Allee told herself. *Probably.*

"He isn't driving," Marko said, pulling Allee out of her thoughts.

"What?"

"James Innis." Marko nodded to the vehicle. "He isn't driving."

As Allee watched, a man got out of the passenger seat. Calling him a man was a bit of a stretch. He was a boy, really, who didn't look a day older than nineteen. His limbs had the thin, gangly look of youth. His hair was dishwater blond, short on the sides and longer on top, combed carefully off to the side.

"Is he old enough to drink?" Allee asked. Their client had been arrested for operating while intoxicated and was apparently enough of a celebrity to merit news coverage of his foibles. She placed her finger on the mousepad of her laptop. It sprang to life with the short news story still on her screen.

"Teenage son of business tycoon arrested on suspicion of operating while intoxicated."

Tycoon was also a bit of a stretch, in her opinion. She had done some quick online research into the Innis family. They owned a corporate farm consisting of several thousand acres of land throughout Franklin County. They also owned several ethanol plants throughout Iowa. The family was rich, but to Allee the word *tycoon* was reserved for the Rockefellers, Musks, Waltons, and the ultra-wealthy of their ilk.

But, then again, what did she know?

Allee watched as Innis ducked and leaned back into the vehicle to say something to the driver, then straightened and closed the door. He paused for a moment with his eyes closed, his back straight, his head held high, and his nose in the air. Was this something he was taught at a boarding school, or what? It looked like he was smelling the air. For what? She didn't know. Perhaps he'd caught a whiff of cinnamon and sugar wafting from Justice Bites.

At last, his eyes opened, wide and wild. His head moved quickly, like a bird's might. His eyes met hers and she shivered as a jolt of anxiety ran through her. *Danger. Danger.* Her body tensed as every nerve ending kicked in, deciding whether to flee or fight.

This is ridiculous, she told herself. He was a child. A rich, probably pampered kid, whereas she'd been to prison and had known how to handle herself long before that. She'd spent her time around drug dealers, convicts, and drug addicts. This boy couldn't be dangerous. Not to her. She steadied herself, her mind drifting to the tattoo on her left collarbone. It was a quote from Frankenstein: *Beware; for I am fearless, and therefore powerful.*

"James Innis, I presume," she heard Marko say as he rose.

Innis's gaze settled on Marko for the first time. "That's me." His voice was strong, confident for a young man in the way that only someone who had been given every advantage could master. He strode around the vehicle to meet them in person. Allee remained seated until Marko's hand encircled her bicep. He squeezed and pulled her to her feet.

"Stop it," Allee hissed.

"Stand up," Marko ordered through clenched teeth.

Innis made it to them and stuck his hand out. It wasn't aimed at either Marko or Allee, so she allowed Marko to take the younger man's hand.

"Marko Bauer." He pumped James's hand up and down enthusiastically, then nodded to Allee. "And this is my investigator, Allee Smith."

Allee didn't say anything. She didn't smile. She didn't extend her hand.

Marko nudged her with his foot. *Fine,* she thought. She shook Innis's proffered hand. His palm was soft and uncalloused, his handshake weak. "Nice to meet you," she heard herself say.

"Where'd you get all the tats?" Innis asked.

She hated the abbreviated word *tats.* It sounded lame, a slang term that was supposed to sound hip, but in Allee's opinion it fell short—and was only made worse coming from a rich kid's mouth.

"Nice black T-shirt," Allee countered.

She was deflecting. She was not interested in telling him anything about her. While it was true they'd both found themselves wrapped up in the justice system, they were not the same. This guy had been born with the proverbial silver spoon in his mouth and had squandered his obvious advantages, whereas Allee was raised in a poor, one-parent family. Her mother was a chronic alcoholic who rarely remembered she had a daughter, and when she did, it was generally to complain that Allee was a burden. Allee had busted her ass and—despite a number of setbacks—fought for everything she had. It wasn't much and it didn't matter, because no matter what she had done or would do, a guy like Innis would still make it out of the situation better than Allee or any of her former friends.

They were not the same.

"I always wear black," Innis replied, looking down at his shirt. "I have a million of these in my closet."

"A little overkill?"

A sardonic smile shot across Innis's face. "Overkill," he said with a chuckle. "I guess that's a fitting word."

"What's the point of it?" Allee said.

Marko nudged her with his foot, this time far harder than he had the last. It was a warning. He wanted her to be kind, to be gracious, but Allee had no intention of treating this dork any differently than she would anyone else who crossed her lines. Marko didn't mind her sarcasm with court-appointed clients, so he could get used to it with this little rich boy.

"I don't have to waste energy choosing what to wear each day."

"The Steve Jobs method," Allee remarked, her tone flat. "How original."

Allee had read the book *Jobs* while she was in prison. It had been a tattered copy, missing a few pages here and there, but she'd gotten the gist of it. Steve Jobs was a wild, unpredictable man. He'd used drugs, like Allee, but he also had an unimaginably creative mind. And money. Another example of money and power buying freedom. He wore a trademark black turtleneck, and the book said he did it for the same reason Innis was now claiming.

Innis shrugged. "I don't know; I just want to keep my life simple." His expression did not change as he spoke. His facial features were even, his skin smooth, his cheeks still rounded with youth. He was objectively attractive, but there was an emptiness in his green eyes that made Allee uneasy. Something in him caused something deep in her to stir anxiously.

"Shall we get started?" Marko asked.

"Yes." Innis turned his attention to Marko, and as he did so, Allee's heartbeat began to slow.

"Have a seat." Marko gestured to the chair across the table from him.

"Sure." Innis turned to his driver and made a circle gesture, and the vehicle slowly backed out and turned onto the road. "He'll drive around until I'm ready for him to pick me up."

The limo took a half loop around the courthouse and stopped on the other side, parking where the driver could still see Innis. Why? Did Innis think he needed protection from them? The engine remained idling. From what Allee could tell, the driver looked to be close to her in age, in his early forties. His hard jaw, thick forehead, and the deep lines in his cheeks and forehead told a story of stress and strength. Allee suspected that the two of them had been some of the same places and done some of the same things. It was odd and disconcerting to see a kid telling someone like him what to do.

What a waste of gas, Allee thought.

"To give us privacy," Innis said aloud, perhaps reading her thoughts.

Unsolicited, Innis reached into his pocket and produced a large wad of cash. He slapped it down on the table.

"That's ten thousand dollars." Innis beamed with undeserved pride, as if he'd worked for the money himself. Which he didn't. *There is no way,* Allee thought.

"My retainer for operating while intoxicated is five thousand," Marko replied quietly, although he didn't look or sound offended by the amount.

"That just means you'll work that much harder for me," Innis said. It wasn't a question; clearly, he fully expected Marko and Allee to focus their attention on him at the expense of other clients. Allee, of course, wanted to tell the arrogant prince to piss off, that they worked hard for everyone regardless of their financial status. She hoped Marko would show some spine and speak up, but she knew better. Marko wanted the money.

"Well then, we'd better get to work," Marko said.

7

JENKINS

Jenkins approached the Freedom Burgers food truck. He could tell the truck's interior lights were on, but the ordering window was still closed.

Are they open yet? Maybe not. For most people, burgers were not a breakfast food, and it was nowhere near lunchtime. But the truck was here —why come just to park and not sell anything? Why not just come later? Surely the preparation and cooking of burgers couldn't take much time, and it wasn't like downtown Franklin was so busy that the owner wouldn't be able to find a parking spot later in the morning.

He approached the window and peered in. He could see a man wearing red pants and a blue polo shirt with stars moving around inside. The outfit matched the truck perfectly. Jenkins knocked on the window, watching the man kneel beside some kind of machine. The man stood, turned, and marched to the window. Seconds later, it flew open, banging against the side of the truck.

"What do you want?" he asked. He had flinty blue eyes, a long beard, a shaved head, and a tattoo peeking out from beneath his polo shirt. The portion that Jenkins could see looked to be a globe with bird talons—probably the lower half of a Marine Corps tattoo.

Jenkins displayed his badge. "I'm Special Agent Jenkins with the Iowa Division of Criminal Investigation."

"Oh." The man raised an eyebrow, a hint of a smile forming at the corners of his lips. "Dale Cameron." He extended a hand, and Jenkins shook it. "I'm the owner and operator of this lovely lady." He patted the side of his truck like one would a horse.

"Do you sell anything this early in the morning?" Jenkins asked.

"I didn't used to, but then they came along," Cameron said, nodding in the general direction of the Justice Bites truck. "Now I sell coffee and breakfast pizza."

"What kind of breakfast pizza?"

"The only kind worth eating. Eggs, sausage, and bacon—man food."

"Okay," Jenkins replied doubtfully.

"If you want sissy, sticky pastries, you'll have to buy from the felons."

"I'll have some coffee and a slice of pizza."

"Good man," Cameron said approvingly. He turned and made his way to the back of the truck, where he remained for a few moments. Jenkins could hear him moving around until he returned with a plastic plate holding a sad-looking slice of pizza and a Styrofoam cup with steam wafting from the top. He placed the items on the ledge in front of Jenkins. "That'll be five dollars and fifty-seven cents."

Jenkins opened his wallet and counted out a five and a one. He handed it to Cameron.

"You want change?"

"No thanks." Jenkins took a bite of the pizza and almost choked. The eggs were slimy and the sausage cold, but the bottom of the pizza was blazing hot. *How is it possible to get so many things wrong at one time?*

"So, what brings you to town?" Cameron asked. "I'll bet you're investigating them, am I right? Are they putting drugs in their food? They are, aren't they?" The questions were asked rapidly, giving Jenkins no time to respond. "I knew it had to be drugs; they have people lined up, coming back day after day," Cameron mused. "There's no way they'd choose that trashy truck over mine unless they were getting a little something-something to go with their cinnamon rolls—am I right?"

"Umm, no . . . I'm not aware of any reports of anything like that," Jenkins said, running his tongue gingerly over the scalded roof of his mouth. Judging by the garbage Cameron called pizza, Jenkins had a pretty

Bodies of Proof

good idea why people were choosing Justice Bites—and it had nothing to do with drugs. He forced himself to swallow the foul, half-chewed bite in his mouth, then washed it down with a quick swig of bland coffee. He tried to focus his attention on Cameron rather than contemplate the potential pizza-borne illnesses he might have just swallowed.

"I'm wondering if you know anything about a dog that was wandering around here yesterday."

Cameron's brow furrowed. "The dog? Oh, yeah. I know about the dog—if you're talking about Leslie Martin's little black-and-white monster."

"Monster?"

"The little bastard always growls at me," Cameron said. "I tried to pet him once and he tried to bite me!"

"I guess that's why they say not to go around petting strange dogs."

"Who says that? I can pet whatever dog I like."

"Right," Jenkins said without conviction. Petting other people's dogs was a great way to lose a finger, of course, but he wasn't there to discuss animal safety. He was there to discuss Leslie's disappearance. "Tell me what happened yesterday."

"I was here doing my thing—you know?" Cameron began. "That little dog came wandering up on the square here, wobbling around like he'd finished a bottle of whiskey. He's got kind of a bushy tail, right? Well, that tail of his was tucked so tightly under him, you'd think he'd just had his balls cut off."

"And then?" Jenkins asked, encouraging Cameron to continue.

"I'd never seen him without Leslie before, you know? But yesterday he was by hisself, and he was dragging a leash. I thought it was weird, 'cause that dog sticks to her like glue."

"Did anyone approach the dog?"

"No. The dog went straight to their truck," Cameron replied, nodding toward the Justice Bites truck. "She—"

Jenkins followed Cameron's finger and saw a woman with a bright blonde pixie cut sitting next to a man in a suit at the folding table under the awning.

"She saw the dog and started petting him."

"Who is she?"

"She's the felon."

Jenkins took a deep breath. "Does she have a name?"

Cameron either didn't hear or ignored the question. "She's all tatted up with prison tattoos," he said. "What kind of woman would do that to her body? It's disgusting."

Jenkins pointedly stared at Cameron's arm. "It's hard to say."

Cameron got his point. "I'm a man," he snapped. "And for your information, this is a tattoo for the Marine Corps. It means something."

"I'm sure her tattoos are frivolous and completely without meaning," Jenkins replied calmly. "Especially if she inked herself."

"Right," Cameron said with a quick nod of his shaved head.

Cameron's failure to recognize sarcasm was no surprise. "You still haven't told me her name. Do you know it?"

"It's, uh, Allee. I only know 'cause I heard someone call her that."

"So, from what you've told me, it sounds like that dog went right up to Allee. Do you know why?"

"Maybe he thought she was his sister!" Cameron cracked. He sobered quickly when Jenkins didn't smile. "Yeah, I do; Leslie walks that dog down to get food from that truck every day for lunch or breakfast. She never comes here even though I know her mom and dad—I went to high school with him; we played JV football together, for Chrissakes!" he exclaimed. "That's why I know they gotta be selling drugs outta that truck. No way Leslie would choose them over me. We're almost like family, you know?"

A dysfunctional one, to be sure. Jenkins had two daughters, both grown and off on their own; he wouldn't want either within ten feet of Cameron, and he'd rather see them eat gas station sushi than this guy's pizza.

"She works at Olde Bulldogs," Cameron continued. "As a bartender. And she lives in one of the lofts above the courthouse square." He looked around, his gaze scanning the top floor of the buildings around them. "I don't know which one, though."

Sure you don't. Jenkins nodded, silently encouraging Cameron to keep talking.

The tactic worked, and Cameron spent the next minute or so gossiping about people he saw daily on the courthouse square. Finally, he ran a hand over his bald head and asked, "So, are you going to question the felon?"

Bodies of Proof   43

"If you are asking whether I intend to *talk* with *Allee*, well . . . Yes. I will." It was none of Cameron's business, of course, but Jenkins knew full well he needed to talk to her—and anyone else who worked at the Justice Bites food truck. Since the dog had apparently gone straight to their truck, they were probably the people who reported Leslie missing and might have information he needed. But before he did that, he needed to tweak Cameron.

"I'm going to be asking everyone this question, Dale, but where were you yesterday when Leslie went missing?"

Cameron's eyes widened for a split second, then narrowed. "Me?" He placed a hand on his chest, a touch of defensiveness creeping into his voice. "I ain't sure that's any of your business."

"I'm just trying to get a handle on who was where when. You under-stand," Jenkins added, knowing Cameron would not.

"I was here."

That was a crap response. Cameron has no idea when Leslie disappeared; no way he can offer an alibi. He's winging it. Jenkins waited for a beat before following up. "Is there anyone who can verify that?" he asked. "Maybe a regular customer who purchased something from you?" *And who wasn't later hospitalized for some sort of stomach problem?* he thought, watching Cameron for a tell.

Cameron crossed his arms in front of himself. "I think I'm through talking to you."

Good enough. Cameron had said plenty already, whether he knew it or not. He knew the girl, where she lived, where she worked, and he was familiar with her daily routine. He resented her choice of food, and he had answered Jenkins's questions regarding his whereabouts defensively and—more importantly—without asking *when* Leslie had disappeared.

"Thank you," Jenkins said. "I'll see you later."

"Hey, don't forget your pizza," Cameron said, handing Jenkins the slice. "How is it?"

Jenkins thought quickly. "Like nothing I've ever had before."

Cameron's face brightened. "Great to hear! Tell your friends about me, would you?"

"You can bet I will," Jenkins promised. He turned and began walking toward the black truck with the image of Lady Justice on the side, blindfold skewed, holding scales in one hand and a pretzel in the other. To Jenkins, she looked mischievous, like she was ready to start all kinds of trouble. Of course, if Cameron was to be believed—and that was a big *if*—Allee was a lot like this caricature of Lady Justice.

8

MARKO

"How do we start?" Innis said, rubbing his hands together. "I've never done this before." He sounded like a sophomore who had just received his first invitation to a coveted party.

Marko nodded in what he hoped the kid would see as a knowing way. "I usually begin by going over the minimum and maximum consequences of—"

"No," Allee said, sharply interrupting Marko. "First he has to sign a fee agreement."

Marko pursed his lips, annoyed by the interruption. He hated it when she was right. But she was right. Fee agreements set out the parameters of the representation, and ensured all parties understood the ten thousand dollars—*Holy hell, ten thousand dollars!*—was designated solely for representation of him on the operating while intoxicated charge. That meant if Innis—like a lot of criminal defendants—was to be arrested or charged with some new offense, they were in agreement *now* that he would have to pay an entirely separate retainer later.

If only I could be that lucky, Marko thought. "Fee agreement. Right. Let me just—" He grabbed his phone and began typing a text message. "I'll just have Whitney get started on that while we continue our meeting."

"Whitney is busy in the truck." Allee looked pointedly at the truck window. Marko followed her gaze to where a line of people waited for service. "I'll be happy to switch places with her so she can work on the fee agreement," she added hopefully.

"You're needed here," Marko said. They'd been over this once already. He needed Allee's help as an investigator. The law firm came first, the truck second. He thought they'd made that clear long ago. Apparently, Allee was going to need some reminding. "Whitney can finish up with the customers and then draft the fee agreement next. As long as we sign it before James leaves, we should be fine."

"Great," Innis said. A wide grin split across his face. It was slightly maniacal—far too gleeful for the situation.

A twinge of something—angst?—settled deep in Marko's chest. Ten thousand dollars for one case! If they did well, Innis would tell his little frat brothers, and the referrals from rich parents would roll in! They'd all start turning to Marko when their sons picked up a public intoxication or harassment charge. The firm would be set. All they needed to do was keep their eyes on the prize, which meant keeping Innis happy.

"As I was saying," Marko continued while reaching over and sweeping the stack of cash toward himself, "let's start by going over the minimums and maximums of the offense." He stuffed the wad of bills into his breast pocket. He wouldn't dare count it in front of Innis—rich people frequently found money distasteful, and he didn't want to offend his new star client.

"Do you know my mother?" Innis asked.

"Your mom?" Marko repeated, thrown by the sudden shift in topic.

"Yes," Innis replied levelly. "She's a terrible woman."

"I'm sorry to hear that," Marko replied. He felt Allee's foot tap his own. Perhaps she was right. "Look, if you two have something to work out, then perhaps instead of a lawyer you should see a therap—"

"Do you know her?"

"No," Marko admitted. "I don't know either of your parents. I know nothing about your family."

"Then maybe that's where we should start," Innis said.

Now Allee's knee bumped Marko's under the table. He snuck a quick glance at her, and she gave him one of her *I told you so* looks.

She was right. Again. "I don't see what your family has to do with an

Bodies of Proof 47

operating while intoxicated charge," Marko said. "We should focus on the offense and then work our way backw—"

"See, there's where you're wrong, Marko," Innis interrupted. "My mother *is* the whole problem."

"In a larger context, that may well be true," Marko allowed. "But there is no such thing as an 'It's my mother's fault!' defense to an operating while intoxicated charge. The jury would laugh you right out of the courtroom."

"They'd better not."

Not sure what you'd do about it, Marko thought. In the five minutes he'd spent with Innis, he was becoming increasingly certain he'd made a mistake in agreeing to represent him. Innis was going to be a royal pain in the ass. They still hadn't signed the retainer. "Maybe—"

"My mother is a control freak," Innis said simply.

Marko sighed inwardly. *Yeah, well, aren't we all?* Apparently, Innis wasn't going to let it go. But at least he could bill it.

"When she'd get upset with me, she'd tell me—"

"Your mommy problems are not our problems," Allee interrupted. Her tone was sharp, her words clipped.

Marko stiffened. It wasn't Allee's place to speak to clients like that— especially private pay clients! On the other hand, he was dreading hearing whatever Innis had to say. As a matter of law, there couldn't be a connection between a bad mom and an operating under the influence conviction. Even if Innis's anger at his mother had led to the drinking—and there was a lot of that going around—it still wouldn't provide a legal defense. Thus, there was no point in discussing it. They weren't Innis's therapists; they were his legal team.

"You sound an awful lot like my mother," Innis replied at last. He was looking toward Allee, but his gaze was so empty it caused a shiver to run up Marko's spine.

Marko's attention was drawn to a man rounding the corner of Justice Bites. He was older than Marko, and looked over his shoulder as if he was about to do something he didn't want observed. As he cleared the corner, he stepped quickly to a trash can, dropped something in, and smiled.

While Marko, Allee, and Innis watched, the older man walked directly to their table, stopping a few feet away.

"Hello there," he began amiably. If Marko had to guess, he would say the man was somewhere in his mid to late fifties, with graying hair and deep creases around his mouth and eyes. He was a cop. It was apparent in the way he walked, the way he moved into an area that was clearly not meant for him without a second thought. "Are you all the owners of this food truck?" He gestured to Justice Bites.

Marko half-expected Allee to jump and say, "Yes, that's me! I'm the owner!" in an effort to avoid their meeting with Innis. Instead, she seemed to freeze; while he watched, she stiffened and went silent. She must have caught on to the cop vibe as well.

The last thing Marko needed was a cop interfering with this deal. "Who's asking?" he asked, standing. He did not extend a hand.

Jenkins flashed his badge and put it back in a pocket. "Special Agent Jenkins with the Iowa DCI."

No kidding. "I don't know if you noticed," Marko said as he gestured to the table, "but we are in a meeting."

Jenkins nodded in understanding. "This will only take a second," he replied.

Marko side-eyed Allee and could see her openly glaring at Jenkins. They wanted Jenkins gone, but they were on public property. He couldn't force the issue; unless Jenkins left of his own accord, he, Allee, and Innis would have to finish their conversation inside the cramped Justice Bites truck. He watched as Innis slowly spun in his seat, turning completely around so he was facing Jenkins.

"We're not interested," the younger man said.

Jenkins ignored him and spoke to Marko. "I'm here about the dog."

"Nobody gives a damn about a dog," Innis said, his voice oddly devoid of emotion. "And I'm on the clock, so if you think you need to talk to my lawyer, you can wait until I'm done."

Jenkins's smile didn't reach his eyes. "Ah, it's *that* kind of meeting," he said. "I'm sorry. I'll order something from the truck and then be back over when it looks like you're about done—how's that?"

Marko wasn't convinced Jenkins was sorry about anything. He started to reply when Innis cut him off.

Bodies of Proof   49

"We'll be finished in thirty minutes," he said, then looked to Marko and raised an eyebrow. "Isn't that right?"

Marko shrugged. "Sure. Sounds about right."

As Jenkins turned toward the food truck, Marko hurriedly typed a message to Whitney and hit "send" before he reached the ordering window. Seconds later, he heard Whitney say, "Hello there. What can I get you?" She was preparing to take Jenkins's order when Marko heard his message arrive. "I'm sorry, sir," he heard her say. "It's my boss. I need to do something for him real quick."

Whitney had been wrongfully accused of a crime a year earlier. He'd met her when he was appointed to represent her after he'd had his own run-in with local cops. She'd been a teacher before being falsely accused of a sex crime by a student, torn from her family, and incarcerated. Having lost her career as the result of the allegations, she was every bit as suspicious of law enforcement as Allee and Marko were.

The three sat in uncomfortable silence until Whitney emerged from the truck with a printed copy of a fee agreement. Marko gave it a cursory read, then went over it with Innis. When both he and Innis had signed the agreement, Marko shrugged. "We'll talk again soon," he said. "We can't speak freely when we've got cops breathing down our necks."

"I'll call tomorrow," Innis promised.

"I'll make time for you," Marko said, trying not to sound as resigned as he felt. He'd been around long enough to know that high-paying clients—like beautiful women—were often high maintenance, and their need for attention was directly proportional to the fee. He wasn't accustomed to hand-holding, but he was probably going to have to get used to it if he was going to run a highly successful on-the-road defense firm. Might as well start right now.

9

WHITNEY

Whitney took a deep breath when at last the line of customers dwindled to a spare few. The morning's *rush*—as brief periods of high-volume sales were referred to in the industry—was today a flat-out *crush*. In truth, she had never intended on spending this much time behind the till in the food truck, and early on it hadn't been a problem: lines were short, customers few, and because on many mornings they sold only a few items, Allee could easily bounce back and forth between meetings with Marko and serving customers. But Allee's skills were amazing, and their sales grew exponentially. Once word had gotten out about Allee's cinnamon rolls, everything changed. Sales of the cinnamon rolls fueled sales of everything else as Allee expanded the menu, meaning they all had to put in time taking orders and running the till. But then again, that was why they started the business in the first place.

Are they almost done with that meeting? Whitney wondered. She leaned out the window to see Marko and Allee seated at the folding table. The young man across from them sat straight as a soldier with his head held high, which was odd for a boy his age. She'd been a teacher before the Price boy accused her of raping him. She'd been arrested, taken from her family, and ultimately acquitted—but only after he admitted he'd made the whole thing up. Despite the acquittal, she could never go back to teaching; she'd

Bodies of Proof 51

never feel safe, so she started working with Marko and Allee when the opportunity came along. But her new occupation didn't mean she'd forgotten what teenage boys were like. She knew a thing or two about them, and they didn't sit up straight.

A man approached the table from the general direction of Cameron's food truck. Whitney tried not to look at the monstrosity with its garish stars and stripes. In her opinion, America's flag was a symbol, a way to honor the country, not a design choice.

I wouldn't do that if I were you, Whitney thought as the man continued toward the table. Marko was protective of his time with clients; should the man interrupt them, Marko was sure to blow a gasket.

Her gaze wandered to Cameron's truck. He was at the window with binoculars, watching the man's movements. There was no need for binoculars, of course—the food trucks were across the street from each other. But Dale was nothing if not dramatic. That man took everything to extremes.

She turned back to see what the older man was up to. As she watched, he looked behind himself surreptitiously, then tossed something—was it a slice of pizza?—into the trash before approaching Marko, Allee, and the younger man. *You fool!* she thought.

She was watching Marko when she was interrupted.

"Excuse me." It was a man's voice, albeit a soft one.

"Oh, sorry," a startled Whitney said. She hadn't seen him approach. She pulled herself back inside the truck and straightened, trying to act as if she hadn't been eavesdropping. Her effort failed.

"Enjoying the entertainment?" the man asked.

"Something like that." She could feel her face reddening with embarrassment.

"This is where that dog turned up yesterday, isn't it?"

"Yes. Word gets around fast." Whitney had been the one to call the cops and report the situation. She knew immediately that something horrible had happened. Leslie did not leave her dog behind, and that dog would never leave her. And she rarely kept him on a leash when she came down to order from the truck. She used to joke that she couldn't make Shep run away if she tried to, so when he staggered up to Justice Bites dragging his leash, Whitney made the call.

"Yeah, well, Leslie used to babysit my kids," the man explained as Whitney watched him closely. Something about him made her uneasy. "That was when she was younger, of course, and before she got herself a real job at Olde Bulldogs."

"Oh, yeah?" Whitney asked halfheartedly.

"Yup. My kids are devastated by her disappearance, to be honest."

He didn't look old enough to have children, and she didn't think she'd seen him before—she would have remembered the scar on his cheek. "Is there something I can get you to eat?" she asked, trying to sound cheery. Whitney had no desire to discuss Leslie or her dog. She'd done her part when she called the cops, was connected to that horrible man—Shaffer, was it?—and listened while he bad-mouthed Leslie.

"She probably just took off with some guy," Shaffer had said.

"She wouldn't leave her dog," Whitney had insisted. "And she's not like that—but it would be okay if she was."

It was yet another example of how nobody valued women. She was shocked when Marko had later informed her that Shaffer was now a captain in the police department. He'd led the team that had arrested Whitney a year earlier and had physically torn Arlo from her arms. He'd been a jackass then, and he hadn't changed a bit when she'd called yesterday. He'd acted as though she was a bother—like she'd been interrupting his very busy schedule, when she knew damn well he probably spent most days playing poker with deputies rather than responding to actual crimes. According to Allee, rumor had it that Shaffer had a touch of a gambling problem, made worse by the new casino being built in town. Whitney didn't doubt it for a second.

"I'll take a cinnamon roll, I guess," the man said, pulling Whitney from her thoughts. "And a cup of coffee."

"Coming right up." Whitney turned, grabbed a disposable cup, and filled it with steaming coffee from a carafe. She popped a lid on the cup and moved over to the food warmer, where she used a set of tongs to grab the remaining cinnamon roll and place it in a to-go container. She turned, set the items on the ledge in front of the man, and keyed the order into the register.

"That'll be thirteen dollars and fifty-seven cents."

Bodies of Proof
53

"Thirteen dollars?" The man sounded exasperated. "That's outrageous!"

The question confirmed her belief she'd never seen this man before—at least not here. First-time customers usually groused about the Justice Bites prices, but returning clientele never did.

"Your choice." She shrugged. "This is the last one. Would you rather give the person behind you a chance to purchase it?"

The two customers behind the man watched eagerly as he weighed his decision.

"Well, uh, I dunno," he said uncertainly.

"Morning, Rosie," Whitney said to the red-cheeked, round woman standing next in line. "This is the last cinnamon roll. We've got a complaint about the price. Do you want to buy it?"

"I most certainly will!" Rosie said with enthusiasm.

"The last one?" a short man behind Rosie exclaimed. "Again? Damn it! I've been trying to get my hands on one for three days." Whitney knew his name was Charles; he was a custodian in the courthouse. He wasn't lying, either—he'd been there every day, and every day they'd sold their stock by the time he made it to the head of the line. "I never can get here on time."

"Ten minutes earlier, that's all you need to be," Whitney said.

"Yeah, well . . . I hate getting up and around in the mornings," Charles grumbled.

"There you have it," Whitney said to the man, gesturing to Charles and Rosie. "You don't like the prices, others are more than willing to pay them."

"I think I'll keep it," he said. He handed over the cash and Whitney placed it in the register while Rosie and Charles groaned aloud.

She watched as the man departed with his prize. "Sorry, kids," Whitney said apologetically. Her phone buzzed in her pocket. She grabbed it and glanced at the screen, thinking it was Leo, her ex. She had primary custody of Arlo, their six-year-old son, so she couldn't ignore any messages. If Arlo was sick at school or had forgotten to bring his lunch, she had to solve the problem.

The message was from Leo.

We need to talk. Give me another chance. I know I screwed up. I'll be better.

Not talking about that, Whitney typed. *It's over.*

The response was quick and vehement.

You can't throw our life away just because I made a mistake.

Leo hadn't made a *mistake*. Instead, he'd refused to believe her when she'd been arrested. He'd refused her requests to bring Arlo to visit her, leaving her to languish on her own. It was unforgivable. She could not get past the betrayal even if she tried. They needed to move on with their own lives and learn to co-parent.

Watch me, she replied. She was considering whether to add anything else when Rosie spoke up.

"Do you have doughnuts left?" she said, pulling Whitney's attention away from her phone.

As Whitney lifted a metal cover to see what food remained, a man approached the food truck. "I'd like to talk to you," he said. She realized it was the same man who had just interrupted Marko and Allee's meeting with their client. Now he was at her window, interrupting her conversation with a customer.

What was with these men and "needing to talk to her?" They needed to get in line like everyone else. Her phone buzzed in her pocket again. She groaned and grabbed it, ready to explode on Leo, but it wasn't Leo this time —it was Marko.

I need you to draft a fee agreement. $10,000 flat fee for representing Innis in an OWI. Do it before you serve the customers. And he's a cop.

Fine, she sent back, then sighed and pocketed her phone. She was getting tired of men telling her what to do—especially men who were perfectly capable of performing the task on their own. Marko had the fee agreement form on his computer. All he had to do was type Innis's name in the client line, $10,000 in the paid retainer line, and OWI for scope of representation.

"You." She pointed at the older man who had interrupted Marko and Allee's meeting and was now over here bothering her for who knew what reason. "Get in line." She turned to Rosie and Charles. "Can you give me a minute? I'll be right back. Marko needs help with something."

They groaned but didn't argue. They understood the rules of Justice Bites. All repeat customers did. The law came first.

10

JENKINS

Jenkins leaned against the truck while he waited. He suspected that attorney had put her up to something to dissuade—or at least delay—her talking with him. Defense attorneys were always playing mind games. All the good ones were tricksters by nature; they had to be. They were almost always outmanned, outgunned, out-resourced, and working to defend a guilty party. It was no surprise that they enjoyed messing with authority—especially cops.

With his back to Justice Bites, Jenkins allowed his eyes to wander to the Freedom Burgers food truck. He should be able to see Cameron at the window. He'd been there earlier, watching the competition through binoculars. Jenkins had seen Cameron watching him as well when he had crossed the street to talk with the Justice Bites crew. Cameron's surveillance was weird—obsessive even, like the nosy neighbor on a 1970s sitcom. Peeping and surveillance had seemed funny back in the day, but surveillance was in reality always unsettling, especially when the person doing the spying was a middle-aged man and his fixation was on a staff of women.

There were no customers waiting in line at Freedom Burgers. *No great surprise there.* The breakfast pizza was terrible; if the burgers were anything like that, he'd rather eat sushi from a gas station—and he couldn't stomach sushi on his best day. Based on what he'd seen so far, he should be able to see Cameron snooping on his neighbors. Cameron's alibi—"I was working at the food truck all day"—was flimsy at best. Given the lack of customers, it would have been easy for him to slip away for long periods of time.

"All right," the woman said from inside the food truck. "Who's next?"

Jenkins turned to see her in the window, smiling down at the customers. He'd deemed her nice-looking before, but her smile completely transformed her face. He'd heard people describe someone as having a smile that lit up the room, but he'd never understood the phrase.

Not until now.

She assisted two customers and then turned to Jenkins. "You don't look like you're here for the cinnamon rolls," she said. The smile was gone and her voice was no longer welcoming. On the other hand, she wasn't exactly cold either. Hers was an attitude of studied indifference.

"You've got that right," he said, approaching the window. "And from what I heard, it's a good thing, since you're sold out."

She held up an index finger. "That reminds me." She stepped away from the window and again disappeared from Jenkins's line of sight. He could hear a rustling sound inside the truck, then the back door slamming shut. A moment later she came around the truck with a large poster. "Can you hold that?" she asked.

He did as requested, watching while she pulled four strips of masking tape from a small roll and, with his help, proceeded to tape the poster to the side of the truck. She stepped back, hands on her hips, and admired her work. The sign read, *Cinnamon rolls sold out. Try the doughnuts.*

"Does this happen often?" he asked.

"Every day," she replied. She stepped forward and pressed the top corners of the poster to ensure it was secure before turning around to face him. "Thanks for the help. I'm Whitney, by the way." She extended her hand, and he shook it.

"Adam Jenkins. I'm a special agent with the Iowa Division of Criminal Investigation."

"Ahhh," Whitney said with a nod. "That's why they sent you to me."

"Why?"

"They hate cops." She nodded, indicating Marko and Allee.

Bodies of Proof 57

He looked to the pair, and decided they were still talking to the new client. "And you?" To his surprise, he felt his pulse quicken, as if her answer would somehow make any difference. *What the hell?*

"I've got my opinions about some of the cops around here," she said quickly. "That Captain Shaffer, for one."

You and me both, he thought.

"But the rest . . . they seem like men and women doing their jobs, just like me."

Jenkins nodded approvingly. She had lovely eyes.

"I see you've met Dale," Whitney said, nodding toward the Freedom Burgers food truck. "He's a prince, huh?"

"Yeah," Jenkins said, following her gaze. "Where is he now?"

"Not sure." She shrugged. "But I can tell you he won't be gone long. He'll be back with another plan to sabotage us."

"What do you mean?" Jenkins asked. He turned and met her gaze.

"He spends all his time spreading rumors and lies about us, trying to run off customers," she said. Her eyes were on him, unblinking. "If he spent half as much time figuring out how to make his food edible as he does trying to get people to stay away from our truck, he'd probably be up to his ears in customers. But instead . . ." She sighed and shrugged, leaving the sentence to die without breaking her gaze.

Jenkins felt his ears getting warm. He gave up and looked down, then refocused. "You don't put drugs in your food, then?" he asked, a smile tugging at the corners of his lips.

"No," she said with a chuckle. "That's a new one. Is that what he told you?"

"Something like that."

"Well, I can assure you we don't do that." She shook her head, bemused. "So, now that you know you can eat here and still pass your next drug test, what'll you have?"

Jenkins nodded to the sign. "I see the sign," he mused. "You sure you don't hold a few back for special customers?"

"Like cops?"

"Or old guys with a sweet tooth." He immediately regretted referring to himself as old.

"We do not." She shook her head, and he watched her hair brush across her shoulders. "But we do have other pastries and a damn good cinnamon coffee."

Jenkins nodded and smiled and again forced himself to break eye contact with her. He was well past his prime—at the tail end of middle age, really. This woman wasn't interested in him, and he shouldn't be interested in her. He had a job to do. He took a deep breath. "I'll take some coffee. Then I'd like to talk to you about what happened yesterday."

"Thought you might," Whitney said with a nod. She turned and made her way back to the truck.

He couldn't resist. "Might what? Have coffee or ask questions?"

"Both," she called over her shoulder.

While she was gone, he berated himself. *Get it together, man. This isn't high school. You're not here to flirt.* Who was he and how had this woman distracted him so easily?

A moment later, Whitney placed a steaming cup on the counter. "Be careful," she advised.

"How much do I owe you?"

She waved a hand dismissively. "It's on the house."

He grabbed the coffee and placed a five-dollar bill on the counter. Department policy prohibited accepting gifts without reporting them, which was a major pain in the ass. And it was a bad look, especially from someone potentially involved in his investigation. At this point, he had no idea where this thing was going. As far as he knew, Whitney could be involved in Leslie's disappearance.

"So, if you want to know about yesterday, I take it that you want to talk about Shep," Whitney said, leaning on the counter.

"Is that the dog?"

"Yup. Leslie's Border Collie," she affirmed. "How is he?"

Jenkins shrugged. "I don't know yet. I wanted to get some information from you folks before I headed to the vet."

"What do you want to know?"

"Everything," Jenkins said, taking out a pen and notepad. He pulled a recording device from his pocket and held it up. "Do you mind if I record our conversation?"

Bodies of Proof

He watched her as her weight shifted and her smile disappeared. "No," she said, appearing uncertain.

Huh. Why the sudden change? Was she nervous? Whatever. She'd agreed to answer some questions, and she wasn't under arrest, so he didn't have to read her Miranda rights.

"Everything okay?" he asked. "You seem . . . unsure."

"I am," she said. "Last time I was questioned by cops I got arrested."

Years earlier, he would have hoped she wasn't involved. But he'd lost hope long ago.

11

WHITNEY

What happened? One minute this old cop was making googly eyes and flirting with her, and the next he was looking right through her like she was a suspect or something. The cops she had dealt with before—like Shaffer—were all brawn and no brains. Was this how it was with cops who were good at their jobs—cozy up and then switch tactics, leaving a person frazzled and wrongfooted?

He pressed a button on the recording device and spoke directly into it. "This is Special Agent Adam Jenkins with the DCI. It is"—he paused to glance at his watch—"1023 hours on Monday, May 31st. I am here with Whitney . . ." He stopped the recorder and looked up at her. "I didn't get your last name."

"Moore. It's Whitney Moore."

He started the recording again and said, "Moore." He placed the device down on the ledge in front of Whitney.

She looked from left to right. "I just want to say I've only got a minute. Customers will start showing up again soon. Most of the courthouse staffers take a break around ten-thirty or ten-forty-five. Many of them come down here to get a snack."

"That's fine," he said, seemingly unfazed. "I'm looking for a missing girl. Her—"

Bodies of Proof

"Woman," Whitney interrupted.

"Pardon me?"

"Leslie is nineteen," Whitney replied tersely. "She isn't a *girl*. She is an adult woman." *If I'm going to start this interview wrongfooted, you're going to be off balance as well.*

"Right, yes." He cleared his throat. "Woman."

Whitney stood still, blinking several times. This was his interview; she saw no need to fill empty spaces with words.

"Were you the one who reported her missing?"

"No. I reported that I'd found her dog. I don't know who reported her missing."

"Right," he said, appearing to make a note. "The dog. Tell me how that happened."

"Well, I was working"—she gestured to her surroundings—"and Shep came wandering up here. He was wearing his harness and leash like he always did when Leslie took him for a walk. I knew something was wrong right away. That dog would never run from her. Never. She used to joke that she couldn't make Shep run away if she tried."

He again made a note and then looked up expectantly.

"I came out and knelt beside him," she continued. "He was shaking and wobbly on his feet. That's not like Shep. I'm not sure I can fully explain it. He just wasn't acting like his usual self, so I called the police and said I found a dog. They sent me to some newbie cop to report something they called 'dog at large.' I told them I'd take care of Shep, and I did. I called Dr. Minsk right after ending the call with dispatch."

"How did you know something was wrong? I mean, couldn't the dog have just gotten out?"

"I told you. He wouldn't run away. Not for any reason. Then there was the harness and the leash. The dog didn't put those on himself. It was incongruous."

Jenkins was looking at her blankly.

"It didn't make sense," she said. "I was an English teacher," she offered to explain her use of a word he clearly didn't understand.

He smiled. "Did you notice anything else about—" He cleared his throat and glanced down at his notepad. "Shep?"

"No. What else would I be looking for? I mean, he's a dog."

Jenkins shrugged.

"Look, Officer—"

"Agent."

"Agent . . . uh . . ."

"Jenkins."

"Agent Jenkins, I couldn't imagine anything *that* bad had happened to her. I thought she'd maybe sprained an ankle or something on the trail, or that maybe she was suffering from heat stroke. It's been humid as all get-out around here lately."

"Hmm." He pursed his lips like he didn't believe her. "I'm wondering how you know Leslie and her dog so well?"

"They come to the truck almost every day—they have pretty much since we opened. And Leslie is a former student of mine. She came the first time to tell me that she'd supported me through the, um . . ." She swallowed hard, hating to bring up a subject she was desperately trying to put in her past. "False charges. Then she bought a cinnamon roll, and the rest is history."

"A runner who eats cinnamon rolls? Doesn't that kind of defeat the purpose?"

"Of which? Running or eating cinnamon rolls?"

He laughed.

She narrowed her eyes. "Not all runners are health nuts," she explained. "Some runners do it so they can eat whatever they want." She patted her flat stomach to emphasize her point.

"And was Leslie a health nut or a run-so-I-can-eat type?"

"I don't know. We never specifically talked about it, but I think the latter. She certainly didn't eat like someone who was counting their calories."

He made another note and nodded his understanding. "You taught English?"

"I did. I left a year ago. I won't go back."

"What happened?"

She was irritated with herself for having told him about her teaching career. "Ask Shaffer about it," Whitney snapped.

"I will, but I'd rather get your side of the story."

Bodies of Proof 63

"There is only one side. The record is clear. A kid made false accusations about me; law enforcement believed him without discussing it with me; I got arrested and my life was almost ruined. That's it. End of story." That wasn't it, and that wasn't the end of the story, of course. That wasn't even the worst part. She hadn't even mentioned a very public arrest, or Shaffer ripping her little boy from her arms, traumatizing them both. She had skipped the part about a month in jail, her husband abandoning her and refusing to let her see—let alone cuddle—Arlo. Then there was the ugliness of a divorce that was carried in the local paper and now his constant apologies—apologies that had gone beyond obsessive and were now bordering on controlling and psychotic.

The opening and slamming of the food truck door startled Whitney. Jenkins put his notepad and pencil in his pocket.

Seconds later, Allee stepped into the truck. Seeing Whitney at the window talking to Jenkins, she seemed to make a quick decision.

"The interview is over," Allee said, crossing her arms and glaring down at Jenkins.

Jenkins openly appraised her. "You must be Allee Smith."

Allee grunted.

"If you have a few minutes, I'd like to speak with you, as well."

"And I'd like you to get out of the way," Allee said. "You're scaring our customers away."

Whitney looked around. It was odd that they hadn't had any patrons since the questioning started. While things generally slowed once the cinnamon rolls were gone, business didn't usually come to a complete halt.

"I understand," Jenkins said. Whitney didn't think he did. She watched as he turned away. "I've got other witnesses to get to," he added. "I can come back later."

"Or not at all," Allee said to his back.

He stopped, turned, and flashed a tight smile. "Or I drag you over to the station for questioning." Whitney watched as Allee and Jenkins stared at each other. Apparently satisfied he'd made his point, he again turned and walked away. As he did so, Whitney released a breath she hadn't realized she'd been holding. As she continued to watch the cop—who was old enough to be her father—he stopped at Marko's table and appeared to focus on something for a long moment.

Marko was now sitting across from a different client, one Whitney assumed was court-appointed because he'd released Allee. While Jenkins stood nearby, Marko was looking around and shaking his head, clearly irritated at another interruption. Whitney craned her neck in an attempt to hear what was being said.

"What do you want?" she heard Marko ask.

"I'm wondering what that is," Jenkins replied, pointing to an object Whitney couldn't see.

It wasn't a question, so Marko didn't answer—at least not loud enough for Whitney to hear. When he didn't answer, Jenkins reached into his pocket, pulled out his phone, and snapped a picture of Marko, his client, and the table. Then he turned and strolled away, whistling as he walked, holding his now-tepid coffee in one hand and his phone in the other.

"What the hell was that all about?" Allee asked Whitney.

Whitney shook her head. "He was asking about Shep."

"Who?"

"The dog that I called the cops about yesterday," Whitney replied.

"Can you imagine?" Allee began. "You go to cop school or whatever and you finish your career asking people about dogs." She shook her head. "Come on, Whitney," she said. "We've got a line forming. You pour the coffee and I'll handle doughnut duty."

Whitney complied, but without much enthusiasm. Something was going on—that cop was handsome, but he was no dummy. She didn't know exactly what, but whatever it was, it was bad.

And she suspected they had just become involved.

12

JENKINS

He was enjoying talking with Whitney and was getting some helpful information, but her co-worker—the one Cameron had called Allee—had swooped in and ended it with the finality of a guillotine blade. *Thwap*, and it was over. From the looks of her, Allee had spent some time in custody, and judging from the tattoos covering her arms, she'd done a little time in Mitchellville, as well. Some women got tattoos to try and look tough, of course, but this Allee chick was the real deal.

He walked away from them, moving slowly and hoping that maybe Whitney would assert herself and insist on finishing the interview. In their few minutes together, he'd sensed chemistry and tried to use it to his advantage. But perhaps he'd come on too strong, been too eager. He'd been guilty of that throughout his career and his personal life. His ex-wife used to say he was like a broken record, spinning and skipping, doomed to make the same mistakes over and over again.

The attorney was sitting with a different client now. This one was the opposite of the preppy kid in the black T-shirt. He was much older, with long, scraggly hair that was thinning at the top. His skin was the sallow yellow that usually indicates liver issues.

"What do you want?" Marko snapped. He was glaring at Jenkins with narrowed eyes.

Jenkins flashed a sardonic smile. He may have worn out his welcome with Allee and Whitney, but this Marko guy hadn't been welcoming to begin with. Most defense attorneys would at least fake pleasantries in their dealings with cops—not this guy. Jenkins had done a quick internet search earlier, and found little to commend the guy—especially given the very public drunk driving conviction he had gotten. Shaffer had been the arresting officer. That must have been interesting. So this Marko guy was apparently a drunk in addition to being a jerk. Not unusual; in Jenkins's experience, a lot of defense attorneys drank heavily. He took the measure of Marko and decided to tweak him. He liked to think of himself as the bigger man, but sometimes he couldn't. This was one of those instances.

He took his phone out of his back pocket, raised it, and began walking around the Justice Bites food truck, snapping pictures and acting as if he was investigating something. In the corner of his eye, he could see Marko's client becoming alarmed. "Wh-what's he doing?" the client asked.

Marko stood. "What the hell are you doing? I'm trying to work here!"

Jenkins ignored him. Marko could piss and moan all he wanted, but there was nothing he could do to stop him. They were in a public place; Jenkins was standing on a public road. He could take as many pictures as he wanted, and snoop around outside the truck as much as he pleased. Ignoring Marko's protests, he continued to act as if he had a plan until he tired of the game, pocketed his phone, and made his way to his car, knowing full well all eyes were on his back.

His next stop would be the running trail where it was believed Leslie had been assaulted. From what he understood, the trailhead was about a quarter mile up the road. He drove in silence. Minutes later he exited the vehicle and looked around. No signs marked the trailhead, but yellow police tape stretched across an opening in the brush where a crushed rock pathway met the pavement. The tape was stretched across the opening, looped around the branches of trees on each side. A sign attached to the tape warned the public that the trail was closed.

At least Shaffer got that done, Jenkins thought. He lifted the tape enough to make his way under it, then replaced it and started walking. He could clearly hear the vehicles traveling nearby. But the sound of human activity faded as he made his way further into the dense timber, until he only heard

Bodies of Proof   67

his own footsteps on the gravel. The trail was secluded, and a sense of fore-boding swept over him.

Why would any woman run alone here? Jenkins wasn't a runner, but surely these women must have known the world was a dangerous place, that there was safety in numbers? A vision of a young, attractive woman running in tights with earbuds in place and music blaring came to mind, followed by that of some damned creep lying in wait. Jenkins shook the image from his mind and felt for his sidearm. An unsuspecting woman, weakened from exercise and deaf to the world, stood no chance.

He had unconsciously slowed his walk when he saw something on the trail several yards ahead of him. In and amongst the fallen leaves and twigs on the path, an object of some sort appeared to be lying in pieces. Approaching carefully, he stopped, looked at the sky in frustration, and sighed. *How in the hell could any law enforcement officer fail to take this material into evidence?* He knelt and placed his evidence kit next to him, then began taking photographs. When he was satisfied he had documented the scene, he carefully labeled and bagged each tiny item. While he couldn't be sure, it appeared something—a toy, perhaps?—had been crushed and scattered on the trail. Whether it had anything to do with Leslie's disappearance, he couldn't be sure and might never know. He stood and was ready to continue down the trail when he spotted a smear and a spot of dark, dried liquid in the leaves on one side. *Blood!* He again knelt and photographed and collected the evidence before placing it in small, labeled bags.

At last, he continued down the trail, eyes glued to the path. Finding nothing of evidentiary value, he stood and looked at his watch. He was about to head back when a flash of color perhaps a hundred feet off the trail caught his eye. He knew instinctively something wasn't right, and he debated whether to follow his training and call for backup or follow his instincts and investigate further.

He lifted his phone and took a photo from where he stood. Then he switched his phone to record and began the trek through the thick foliage. Branches grabbed at his clothing and leaves slapped him in the face. He chose to hold the phone, recording every second, rather than protect himself from the forest. As a DCI agent, he did not have a body camera. Those were for beat cops and he hadn't been one for years. Usually, this sort of investigation belonged to the local police, but Shaffer had made it abundantly clear that Jenkins was on his own. So, here he was, making do with what he had. Though he doubted he would be alone in this investigation for long if his instincts were right. As he continued to force his way through thick brush in the direction of the flash of color he had seen, the birds and animals that had been making noise fell silent, and the only sounds were his grunts and the snapping of twigs under his feet. Further in, the smell of damp leaves gave way to a familiar odor. He felt the hair on his forearms and the back of his neck standing, and he once again considered calling for assistance.

Fifteen feet later, he forced himself through an especially stubborn tangle of brambles. Pulling at his clothing to loosen it, he stepped into a clearing and froze. He was face to face with what used to be Rebecca Calloway. She'd been missing for a full year, and many of her features were missing as the result of animals and weather, but he was certain it was her. He'd seen her on the news and in case files. He'd seen her face on flyers in grocery stores and on telephone posts with the words "missing" and "reward." The long, curly brown hair was the same length it had been when she was reported missing, her skin fair but ashen. Her body was posed.

He stopped recording and called Shaffer.

Shaffer answered on the first ring. "Giving up so quickly? I told you it was bull—"

"I found Rebecca."

"Oh, good, I'll let her parents know that they came to the city council complaining about us for no reason. The anniversary, my ass. The anniversary of her running off with—"

"She's dead."

Shaffer was silent for a long moment. "How do you know that?"

"She's hanging from a tree."

"Shit."

"Right about where Leslie Martin probably was when she disappeared."

Shaffer groaned.

"I'll call my forensics team," Jenkins said. "But you need to get the medical examiner and some officers over here to secure the scene."

Bodies of Proof 69

"Done."

For once, Shaffer wasn't fighting him. Unfortunately, it took the body of a young woman to get his cooperation.

"I'm on my way," Shaffer added.

Jenkins hung up, texted the forensics team the facts, and sent them his location. Then he turned his attention back to the young woman. She was hanging, but not in the way Shaffer probably envisioned it. The rope was not around her neck; rather, it was around her wrists, which were bound together above her head. Her elbows were separated by a thin piece of wood. Her legs hung down straight with her toes pointed toward the ground. She was dressed in a light pink leotard with sequins and a matching skirt. She had disappeared while out for a run, but she—or someone—had changed her outfit before her body's discovery.

She hadn't been a ballerina in life, but she was in death.

13

MARKO

"What is that?" Marko asked, indicating the small, round object on the table near his client. "Is it yours, Jack?"

Jack Daniels was a long-term court-appointed client. He was an alcoholic—which was probably fitting with a name like Jack Daniels—but to add to his problems, he was also a meth addict. One addiction was bad enough, but two meant certain trouble. Marko knew a thing or two about alcoholism—he was early in recovery himself—but he'd never gotten too deep into the drug scene.

"No," Jack said, shaking his head vigorously. "Ain't never seen it before."

"Then where did it come from?" Marko asked. He hadn't helped Whitney and Allee set up the table, but he'd watched them do so. "It wasn't here when I met with the client before you," he said accusingly. He picked up the box and examined it. It could be a stash box, of course—lots of addicts kept their drugs and paraphernalia in small containers that meant something to them—but this didn't look like something Jack would utilize. He was more of a Crown Royal bag type of guy. As Marko turned the small box in his hand, he saw a ballerina painted on the side. She was sitting down, tying her shoes.

"Well, it wasn't me, okay?" Jack snapped.

That cop was interested. Why? "Yeah?" Marko lifted an eyebrow. "It looks expensive. Something you came across in your travels, maybe?"

When Jack merely shrugged, feigning a lack of interest, Marko turned the box over in his hands, looking for a way to open the thing. He found a tiny button on the side, pressed it, and watched as its top sprang partially open. Marko lifted the lid to the fully opened position, whereupon a tiny plastic ballerina turned on a spindle and a familiar song played. Marko scoffed. The ballerina fit the music box—her twirling and dancing was just as one would expect, but the music was all wrong. Marko was not a music buff, but he knew the tune. "Is that 'Ding-Dong! The Witch Is Dead?'"

Jack shrugged again. "I don't know, dude, and I don't care. Are we going to talk about my case?"

"Yeah," Marko replied. "We will—just as soon as you explain what the hell this is, and why that cop is interested in it." He leaned in and brandished the box, holding it close to Jack's face.

Jack was focused on the tabletop.

"Did you steal this?" Marko pressed.

Jack lowered his head like a puppy being scolded, but remained silent.

"Jack, I'm your attorney. Tell me what's going on. Remember: if you report a crime that has already occurred to me, I can't say shit. I'm bound by attorney-client privilege. So whatever you've done, you can safely tell me."

For a long moment, Jack said nothing. Then he looked straight into Marko's eyes. "I didn't steal it," he said at last, his voice gruff from years of overusing alcohol and cigarettes. "But it isn't mine, okay?"

Marko did not believe him for a second. "No sweat," he said. "If it's not yours and you don't want it, then I'll just toss it. It's trash, right?" When Jack didn't respond, Marko drew his arm back and tossed the little box into the courtyard grass some distance away.

Jack flinched.

Marko studied his client, waiting for the outrage to emerge, but it never did. As an addict and alcoholic, Jack was generally restless, irritable, and discontented to begin with, and since he owned few possessions, Marko had expected tossing the little box would get a rise out of Jack. *Maybe he is telling the truth for once,* Marko thought.

"Can we talk about my case now?" Jack asked again.

"Sure." Marko turned to his laptop and hit the space bar, causing it to spring to life. He typed in his password—*Marko!is!the!best!1234*—and pressed "enter." He had wanted his password to be 1234, but Whitney and Allee wouldn't allow it. They made him pick a sentence, which was annoying, but according to them using a sentence provided better security.

He navigated to his client management software and typed "Jack Daniels" into the search bar. A lengthy list of Jack's cases appeared on his screen. There were at least twenty case numbers. The word *closed* was displayed beside all but one. Marko hadn't studied the case before today, in part because this was their first meeting, and in part because he wasn't too interested. All the online file contained was the criminal complaint, which by law only required enough information to convince a judge there was probable cause a crime had been committed and Jack had committed it. In practice, criminal complaints usually contained very little information of use to defense counsel.

Clicking on the open case number, he waited while the facts relevant to the charge populated the screen. The charge was Harassment in the First Degree. Marko looked at Jack, who was again staring at the table. Most of Jack's prior charges were drug and alcohol-related—things like public intoxication, urinating in the street, criminal trespass, or shoplifting from a liquor store. Marko scanned the document, stopping near the bottom where the officer had written his narrative. As expected, it was brief. "The Defendant threatened to kill the victim when she refused to serve him." Marko found the location of the alleged offense. It was Olde Bulldogs restaurant.

"What were you doing at Olde Bulldogs on Saturday, May 29?"

"Trying to get served."

"Alcohol?"

"Uh, yeah," Jack replied sarcastically. "It is a bar."

"Who was the server?" The alleged victim's name was not in the report.

"Nobody served me. That was the problem."

"Did you have money?"

"Of course! Why else would I be there?"

Marko knew Jack rarely had money, and he knew better than to ask how he got the money. He might have stolen it, extorted it, or found it—but it wasn't wages from a traditional job, that was for damned sure. With Marko's clients, it was frequently the case that the less he knew, the better. This was one of those occasions.

"So, who was working that day? Who refused to serve you?"

"I don't know her name. It's that girl everyone is talking about."

Marko typed "Leslie Martin Franklin" into the Google search bar. There were hundreds of search results. He clicked on the top one, a local news article titled "Missing Runner or Runaway?" The article contained a picture of Leslie Martin, likely pulled from her Facebook account. She had wavy, shoulder-length dark hair that framed her face and accentuated her bright blue eyes.

He turned the laptop so Jack could see the image. "Is that who wouldn't serve you?"

"That's her."

Marko turned his computer back around and fought the urge to groan. Jack would soon be a person of interest in the disappearance of a young woman.

14

JENKINS

Jenkins stood expectantly as Shaffer arrived with a fleet of law enforcement. One moment the forest was still and silent, the next it was crawling with first responders and law enforcement officers from multiple agencies. There were deputies, police officers, troopers, and firefighters. To Jenkins's horror, they immediately began marching down the trail, seemingly hellbent on destroying the sanctity of his crime scene.

"Stop!" he shouted.

After years in major crimes units, he knew how to run a crime scene. If Shaffer wouldn't take charge, he would. He began barking orders, and thirty minutes later, the area was cordoned off, the medical examiner had arrived, and the DCI forensics team was gathering evidence. Everything was in order when he turned and started to make his way up the trail and to his car.

Shaffer had appeared and was tagging along behind Jenkins. "Where are you going?" Shaffer asked.

"To investigate."

"But the investigation is here," Shaffer replied.

Jenkins heard the desperation in Shaffer's voice. Despite his position and rank, the man clearly did not want to be placed in charge of anything.

"No, it's not," Jenkins replied. He turned to face his former classmate.

Bodies of Proof 75

"This is handled." He gestured to all the people working around him. "They know their roles and they're working on their tasks. They don't need me here micromanaging. We don't have time for that, so I'm going to start asking some questions."

"Of who?"

"Rebecca Calloway's parents, the veterinarian, and Leslie Martin's parents—to name a few."

"Why?"

"Because we have to find Leslie as soon as possible, or she is going to end up like that," Jenkins replied, pointing back toward Rebecca's body.

Shaffer shrugged. "She's probably already dead."

"Maybe, but what about the next one?"

"Say what?"

Jenkins shook his head in disgust. "You're kidding me, right?" he asked. "You saw Rebecca." He gestured again toward the clearing where he'd found her. "She was posed. Posed! What the hell does that say to you?"

"Her killer is a sick fuck."

"Well, there's that," Jenkins agreed. "But there's more to it than that. Only one kind of killer poses his victims. It ain't family members, and it ain't passion killers, like a boyfriend who got rejected. You've got a problem."

"*I've* got a problem?" Shaffer asked, alarmed. "Wait a minute! This is your case!"

"Yeah, I know. And it's not going to solve itself. I've got work to do." Jenkins turned and continued up the trail.

Jenkins could feel Shaffer following closely behind. "I'll help," he offered.

Probably the best thing you can do is stay out of my way, Jenkins thought, but he kept the thought to himself. He may not want help, but he needed it.

They continued up the trail in silence. "Where's your car?" Jenkins asked Shaffer when they reached the trailhead. The road was clogged with emergency vehicles, their overhead lights flashing red and blue.

"There. Why?"

"You're going to have to drive." Jenkins nodded to his unmarked car. It was boxed in by a state trooper and a sheriff's deputy. Shaffer driving would save a good deal of time.

"So I'm your chauffeur now?" Shaffer growled.

He really was an unhappy man, Jenkins realized. His every comment or thought was negative. "You wanted to help. You can drive, or you can get those guys to move their cars so I can get down the road."

Shaffer grunted, and they got into his vehicle, an SUV with Franklin County Police written on the side. He barely waited for Jenkins to shut the door before taking off.

"You know, regardless of what you may think," Jenkins said, clicking his seatbelt, "I'm not out to get you."

Shaffer side-eyed Jenkins as he drove. "You think you're better than us," he said. "All you Des Moines guys do." He took a sharp turn and Jenkins's stomach twisted. Getting in with Shaffer might have been a mistake. There was a fine line between some law enforcement and the criminals they investigated. Shaffer might well be one of them.

"I can't speak for other agents," Jenkins began, "but I don't think I'm better than you. To be honest, I don't think about you at all." He reached up and grabbed the handle above the passenger door as Shaffer roared around a corner. "But from what I've heard, I think I try harder than you. I think I care more than you. And effort and giving a shit usually yield better results." He closed his eyes as Shaffer passed a slow-moving hay truck on a blind corner.

"That's a fancy way of saying that you think you're better than me," Shaffer said. They drove the rest of the way in silence. Jenkins opened his eyes when Shaffer brought the vehicle to a screeching halt in front of a small ranch-style home on a quiet cul-de-sac. It was painted a medium blue with white trim and brown shutters, and featured a two-car garage. "This is where Patty and David Calloway live."

"Are they her biological parents?" Jenkins asked. Given the number of blended and broken families he dealt with, he'd long ago learned to make sure who-was-what before dealing with families in crisis.

Shaffer nodded. "Far as I know."

How can you not know that? Jenkins swallowed hard and got out of the vehicle. Notifying families of the death of a loved one—especially a child—

Bodies of Proof

was every cop's worst nightmare. Fortunately, he didn't have to do it often. As a DCI agent, he didn't usually get involved in investigations until after these kinds of notifications had already been made. But this one had been different from the start, and it would likely stay that way.

Shaffer led the way to the front door, knocked three times, and stepped back. They waited in silence. Jenkins could hear someone moving around inside. Barely audible to begin with, the sound grew louder. *Shuffle, shuffle, thump.* It repeated several times, then came to a stop near the door. A floorboard creaked.

"Who's there?" a woman called from inside. "Can't you see the sign?"

Jenkins had in fact seen the "No Soliciting" sign.

"We're not here to sell you anything, Pat," Shaffer said. "It's Captain Shaffer."

"Oh."

After a brief pause, the door was opened by a small woman. She had close-cropped gray hair and deep-set gray eyes with dark circles under them. Her concern was obvious; she leaned against the door, clinging to it like it was the only thing preventing the weight of the world from dragging her down.

"We need to talk," Shaffer said simply. Without her consent, he stepped past Pat Calloway into her home.

Jenkins wanted to protest. This was not how things were done, but he didn't want to chastise another officer in front of the public, so he focused his attention on Pat Calloway instead of Shaffer.

"I'm Adam Jenkins." He extended his hand. "I'm a Special Agent with the Iowa Division of Criminal Investigation."

"Patty Calloway." She shook his hand. Despite her small frame, her handshake was firm. "I'm glad they are *finally* taking Rebecca's disappearance seriously," she added, indicating Shaffer with her head. She motioned for Jenkins to come inside and shut the door behind him.

The house reeked of cigarette smoke. It was deathly quiet.

"She's dead, Pat," Shaffer called from the kitchen.

Jenkins was appalled. He could see Shaffer sitting at the kitchen table, holding an apple that Jenkins could only assume he had plucked from the large fruit bowl in the middle of the table.

"She's—" Patty began, but before she could complete the thought, her legs buckled, and Jenkins was barely able to catch her before she fell to the ground. He lowered her into a sitting position in an overstuffed chair as a sob tore from her throat.

"Help me out here!" Jenkins barked with a dark look toward a completely unfazed Shaffer. "Get me a cool cloth and a glass of water. Now!" For once, Jenkins was thankful that he'd been there to help notify the family. Without him, this poor woman would have learned of her daughter's fate from a cop lacking any empathy whatsoever. He crouched down next to her, letting her cry out the heaviest of the tears. He was standing beside her, helping her take a sip of water, when the front door flew open.

"You!" a man roared from the entryway. He held a grocery bag in each hand. His receding hairline held back a shock of white hair. Deep lines—probably the result of decades working in the sun—lined a florid face. "What the hell do you want? I thought I told you never to come back to our . . ." The man's voice trailed off when his gaze fell on Pat Calloway. He dropped the bags and rushed to his wife's side, then sank down next to her, ignoring Jenkins. "What's wrong, honey? Did he hurt you?"

Jenkins looked quickly to Shaffer, who took a bite of the apple, seemingly unmoved by the drama unfolding.

What is wrong with you? Jenkins wondered. He'd long deemed Shaffer incompetent and uncaring, but now, he was beginning to see him in a new, lesser light.

15

ALLEE

Not surprisingly, a flood of customers appeared within minutes after Jenkins left. People could smell a cop a mile away. For the next hour or so, Whitney and Allee struggled to keep up with orders; it seemed there were always at least five people waiting in line. They functioned well as a team, but just when it looked like they were finally starting to catch up, another three people would appear.

It wasn't unexpected, of course. It was lunch hour, and word of their food had gotten around—especially their Burglary Burritos and Trespass Tacos. Like the cinnamon rolls, they were customer favorites and sold out quickly. Finally, when one o'clock rolled around, the crowd tapered off.

Allee was cleaning up, bagging trash, and wiping down counters when Marko came to the window.

"You'd better get inside," she heard Whitney say before Marko could open his mouth. Allee saw her point to her watch. "You've got pretrial conferences right now."

"I know, I know," Marko said. "I can read a calendar."

Not when you're off the wagon, Allee thought. She wasn't the only struggling addict operating their small, strange businesses. Marko was a newly recovering alcoholic. Allee had a full six years of sobriety under her belt, but she still fought the constant call of dope. For his part, Marko wasn't at a year yet, and he continued to have hiccups. As a result, Allee and Whitney were constantly intervening, searching his stuff for hidden bottles and watching him for signs of slipping. Allee told herself that she really didn't care, except for the fact that if the law firm failed, Justice Bites might fail too.

"I want to talk to you about Jack," Marko said to Allee.

"Daniels?" Allee asked. "Now?"

"Yeah. He's charged with harassment first. The complaint says he threatened to kill that missing girl."

"Leslie?" Allee asked, then clenched her jaw. She expected he would respond in his usual flippant way. He hadn't known Leslie like she and Whitney did. They had developed a relationship over the past year. Leslie would come to the food truck daily, and they'd chat. That's how Allee had learned that Leslie shared her love of classic horror novels. Allee rarely met another person who had even read *Dracula*, let alone *Carmilla* and *Frankenstein*.

"Yeah, her," Marko said, his tone dismissive. "Listen, I need you to go over to Olde Bulldogs and speak with the staff. I wanna know if anyone else heard the argument between her and Jack."

"She argued with Jack?" Allee arched an eyebrow. *I don't think so. She isn't the argumentative type.*

"Yeah. On Saturday night, supposedly."

"The night before she disappeared, then."

"Yeah." Marko looked at his broken watch. Allee knew it would show ten minutes after two. "And he's charged with harassment first."

She paused, reflecting. She'd worked for Marko since he'd gotten his operating while intoxicated bust. Between that and her own experience, she knew that many crimes, like harassment, were tiered by the level of perceived severity and labeled first, second, third, with "first degree" representing the most severe allegation.

"What did he say to her?" Allee asked.

"He threatened to kill her. *Allegedly.*"

Allee clenched her fists for a long moment, then released them. She

Bodies of Proof 81

had to cut back on the emotion. They worked in small Iowa towns, and as a result they met and developed relationships with many locals through Justice Bites. This wouldn't be the first or last crime that involved someone Allee had gotten to know and liked.

"I need you to make sure nobody overheard their conversation."

"Why?" Allee asked.

"Because Leslie is gone. She can't testify that he threatened her. If nobody else heard it and there are no recordings, then the State will have to dismiss Jack's case."

Don't get upset, Allee reminded herself. This was his job, and this was exactly the kind of thing she was required to do as an investigator. Her role was to find holes in the State's case against Marko's clients so they could get them the best possible outcome. A dismissal would be exactly that. Emotions be damned.

Marko spun on his heel and started making his way toward the court-house, whistling. The tune was familiar, but it took a minute for Allee to place it. "'Ding-Dong! The Witch Is Dead.'"

"Well, that's nice," Whitney said, her tone flat.

"Yeah." Allee was at a loss for words.

"Sometimes it feels like we're on the wrong side, doesn't it?" Whitney asked. "But hey, at least he is taking more interest in court-appointed clients —right?"

Allee smiled briefly. Whitney was ever the optimist. She could see the silver lining in any shitty cloud. "Yeah," she agreed.

Before her five-year stint in prison, Allee had lived her life in chaos, running with a circle of people and doing things neither Marko nor Whitney could begin to imagine. As a meth addict, she had no real "friends." But she'd used with, slept with, fought with, and lived with meth addicts she thought were her friends. Together, they bought and sold drugs, stole, and damaged property. Looking back, it was clear that as a criminal she had naturally spent the better part of her life with criminals. But this was different. She and the addicts she hung around with weren't murderers or kidnappers—hell, nobody was ever sober or straight long enough to pull off something like that, let alone get away with it.

Whitney was right. It was good that Marko's interest in court-appointed clients had improved since their discussion that morning while she drove them to Franklin. But she couldn't help but wonder why.

What exactly had Jack done? Was it just an argument? What wasn't Marko telling her?

16

JENKINS

"Mr. and Mrs. Calloway," Jenkins began. He had waited patiently while David Calloway had talked soothingly to his wife, convinced her to move to the couch, and seated himself beside her. Despite the couple's obvious and understandable distress, he needed to get as much information as possible as soon as possible. Patty had been crying uncontrollably from the moment Shaffer had crudely broken the news to her. "I know this is a bad time, but—"

For the first time since his arrival, David's attention was drawn from Patty. He turned his head toward Jenkins but kept his arms around Patty. "Who are you? Why are you here?"

Bad news wasn't like wine; it didn't get better with age. "Mr. Calloway, I'm Special Agent Jenkins. I found your daughter, Rebecca, earlier today."

"Found," David repeated flatly.

Jenkins nodded. "She was not alive."

"Are you sure?"

"Dave," Shaffer began. He pushed himself up from the kitchen table and marched impatiently into the living room area. "We can't make this any better than it is. She's dead. Okay? Murdered."

As Jenkins watched, David's emotions turned from grief to rage. "I thought I told *you* to never come back?"

Shaffer shrugged. "I'm the law." He tapped the Franklin PD badge on his shoulder. "That means I can do what I—"

"Shut up, Shaffer," Jenkins interrupted. He waited a few seconds before continuing. "This is the Calloways' home. If they don't want you here, then you need to leave."

"But—"

"Go," Jenkins said quietly. His eyes met Shaffer's. "I'll handle this."

Shaffer hitched up his pants. "This is my town and—"

"No," Jenkins repeated. "You asked for my help. I am here. This is my investigation now."

"*I* didn't ask for anything—"

"Your boss did," Jenkins corrected himself. "Now go."

Shaffer stared hard at Jenkins for a long moment, seemingly undecided. Jenkins thought things might go sideways, but at last Shaffer shrugged and headed for the door.

"Wait for me in the car," Jenkins ordered.

Shaffer huffed something in response that Jenkins couldn't quite hear, but it sounded an awful lot like *my ass I will*. He'd deal with Shaffer later.

"I don't understand," David wondered aloud over the sound of Patty's crying. "Murdered? How?" Jenkins was watching David closely. His rage had settled with Shaffer's departure; he now seemed fully composed, aside from a slight tremor in his hands.

"We're not sure," Jenkins answered honestly. "We'll have to wait for the full autopsy. It's, uh, possible we could have a preliminary report as early as tomorrow."

"If you don't know how she died, then how do you know she was murdered?"

"Well, the, uh, position and condition of the body when she was found, for one thing."

Patty wailed aloud at Jenkins's mention of Rebecca's body. David hugged her tightly, then turned his attention back to Jenkins. "You found her?"

"I did."

"Where?"

Bodies of Proof 85

"Off to the side of a running trail not far from here," Jenkins began. "She was in the woods some distance from the trail itself."

"Oh my God!" Patty screamed.

Jenkins nodded sympathetically. "Look, maybe we should—"

"She's been gone for a year!" David exclaimed. "How could they not have found her?" He swallowed hard, not waiting for a response. "Was she . . . *gone* all that time?"

Jenkins waited for Patty's renewed wailing to be stifled by David's renewed hugging. "I don't know the answer to that question," he said. "I really think we should save this question for a later time." He looked pointedly to Patty, then back to David.

"What was her condition?" David insisted. "You must know if she was, er . . ." He looked down at his wife. She had wriggled from his grasp and was now curled into the fetal position on the couch with her hands covering her face. "You have to know," he continued, lowering his voice to barely above a whisper. "I mean, how do you know it was her if she had . . . decomposed."

"I'm not a pathologist," Jenkins said quietly. "I'm just a cop. But for the most part, she was in good condition," he explained, trying not to recall her missing face.

"So her kidnapper held her all this time," David concluded with a nod.

"I'm not a doctor, but it looked to me like she'd been alive until recently."

"What do you mean? If she was killed recently, then—"

"Mr. Calloway, I just don't know, and I don't want to give you false information. Speculation will only make things more difficult."

"Fine," David said.

Jenkins watched while David ran a hand over his balding forehead and then placed that hand on Patty. As he spoke, he rubbed small circles on her back. "Someone told me the cops are saying that Rebecca and that other girl's disappearances are related. Why do you think that? Maybe that girl did run away. Maybe she . . ." His voice trailed off. "How can you know it was murder? Maybe she ran off and then came back?"

Having read the police files, Jenkins knew that David and Patty had pressured law enforcement to do something about their daughter's disappearance for more than a year. Unfortunately, most of their pleas fell on deaf ears. The official position was that she'd probably run off. Over the course of the past year, David had refused to entertain the idea.

"She was posed, David," Jenkins said softly.

"Posed?" He blinked several times. "Like what?"

"Like a . . . ballerina."

"A ballerina?" David scoffed. "But my Rebecca was a tomboy—the furthest thing from a ballerina! She played volleyball and softball. I bought her a glove when she turned eleven. She is no girly-girl. I think you've got it all wrong. That can't be her."

"It's her," Jenkins said quietly.

"But she wasn't a ballerina!" David insisted.

"In my experience the, uh, *pose* isn't about her. It's about the, uh, killer." He was watching Patty.

"So, what now?" David asked. His words were without hope, as heavy as a body weighted down and sinking to the bottom of the ocean. "When can we have our little girl back?"

"Soon," Jenkins promised. "After the autopsy. I'm doing the best I can to move this investigation along. I think you can go ahead and start planning a funeral and wrapping up her affairs."

David nodded slowly.

"But if you don't mind, I do have some questions for you."

David nodded again.

"It seems like you and your wife have issues with Captain Shaffer."

"You're damned right, we do!" David replied quickly. "He ignored us from the moment Rebecca disappeared. I will never forget what that sonuvabitch told me when I originally reported her missing."

"What did he say?"

"He said, 'Dave, she's a waitress and a partier. I figure she ran off to Vegas to make more money.' He didn't say it like it was a theory or a supposition, either. He said it just like that. 'She ran off to Vegas,' like there was no room for debate or any other conclusion."

Jenkins wrote *waitress* on his notepad. It was another thing Rebecca and Leslie had in common.

"Then he insinuated that Rebecca was a prostitute," David continued.

Bodies of Proof 87

"My little girl! I lost it and told him never to come back here, never to talk to me or Patty again. I told him that when he dies, I'm going to live long enough to spit on his grave."

Probably have to get in line. "Where was Rebecca working when she disappeared?" Jenkins asked.

"Olde Bulldogs. She made decent tips, too."

Jenkins made another note. Olde Bulldogs was the same place Leslie was working when she disappeared. "Did she have any enemies?" he asked carefully.

"Not that I know of."

"Did she have a boyfriend?"

"Not when she disappeared."

"So, how about ex-boyfriends?" Jenkins followed up quickly.

"Maybe," David said. "Look, I'm her father, but she was a big girl, and I wanted to respect her privacy. She was a very private person. Especially with me. I think she had been seeing someone, but I don't know who. Hell, I don't even know if it was a man or a woman."

"Was it normal for her to be secretive about her relationships?"

"With me?" David nodded. "Yeah. Once she became an adult, she kept those things to herself. Not that I blame her," he added, then smiled as he reflected. "She was my little girl. If I'm bein' honest, nobody was ever going to be good enough for her. Not in my eyes. She knew that."

"Sounds like you gave her space," Jenkins began. "But you did say *ex*. What makes you think she might have ended a relationship?"

David shrugged. "For one thing, she stopped having plans on Friday nights—even spent some time with us when she wasn't working. You know, she didn't have a lot of girlfriends in Franklin anymore. After high school, they all went to Des Moines, Ames, or Iowa City for college. I think she felt left behind." He glanced down at his wife, then his eyes lifted to again meet Jenkins's gaze. "We had wanted her to go to college, of course, but she said she wasn't ready yet. One gap year turned to two, and then—" He cleared his throat. "Well, then she thought it was too late. Perhaps things would have been different if she'da left for school."

Jenkins didn't know what to say. He was no mental health expert, but that kind of *what if* thinking couldn't be healthy. David and Patty had just received the most devastating news of their lives. They would need time for it to sink in. He'd get more valuable information once the shock wore off.

"I should probably get going," he said, standing. "You've been very helpful. I've got some places to start." He tapped the notepad in his hand. "I'm sure I will have lots of questions in the future, but for now, I'll leave you to . . . your loss."

David nodded. Jenkins got his telephone number and then headed out the front door, expecting to see Shaffer waiting in the driveway with the car running. He was wrong. Shaffer was nowhere to be found. He shook his head and started making his way back to his car on foot. Shaffer had a lot of explaining to do. This was just one more thing Jenkins could add to the list he would file with the Franklin city council when this was over. At best, Shaffer was massively insecure and immature. At worst, he was purposely sabotaging what was now a murder investigation.

17

ALLEE

As Allee walked quickly down the back street, sweat soaking the back of her black *Beatles Abby Road* T-shirt, she cursed under her breath. She was just off the courthouse square, headed to a storage facility where she kept her pickup for use when she was in town. It took her five minutes to walk the three blocks west where she saw a large sign that said *Kum and Leave Storage*. It had once been bright red with yellow lettering, but the colors had long since faded to salmon and off-white. Some kid had spraypainted a C over the K. Allee guessed that transgression had happened so many times that the business gave up on repainting. She walked through the fencing surrounding the units and started down the rows of identical garage stalls just large enough to park a small car.

Which one is it? She hadn't used her truck much of late; there hadn't been a lot of investigations recently. She produced her key ring and flipped through the keys until she found a small red key with the number four etched into it. *Unit four it is.*

She quickly located unit four, inserted her key, and tried to turn it, but nothing happened. She jiggled the key. Still nothing. Puzzled, she stepped back, placed her hands on her hips, and glared at the lock. When her phone rang, she reached into her back pocket. The screen showed a number that she didn't recognize.

"Smith here."

"Allee Smith?"

She recognized the voice. "You called me. You should know."

"True." Innis's voice was smooth, unperturbed, confident in a way that was unusual for a young man, and almost fantastically annoying.

"How did you get my number?" When he didn't respond, she pressed the issue. "Did Marko give it to you?"

"Do you like *The Nutcracker*?"

What the hell kind of question is that? "You mean like ballet?"

"Of course?"

"I'm a recovering meth addict, as you no doubt know," she said. "I prefer men not in tights and slippers."

"I understand," Innis said with a chuckle. "It's not one of my personal favorites. My dad goes every December. He doesn't really like it, but—"

"What is your point?" Allee interrupted.

Innis laughed slyly. "I guess I don't have one."

This had happened before with other clients. "You do realize that I am paid in six-minute increments and the clock's running?" Allee asked. "And it's a twelve-minute minimum," she added.

"No problem," Innis replied. "What's your billing rate?"

"Fifty dollars an hour."

"Good for you."

It oughta be a hundred to pay me for dealing with—

"Well, I'm good for it. You probably recall that I paid Marko double the usual retainer," he said.

"I remember." She looked at her watch. "Look, your money may be infinite but my time is not, so how about you cut to the chase and tell me what you want?"

"Why are you at the Kum and Leave?"

Allee froze. "How do you know where I am?"

"Just a guess."

My ass. She looked around, concerned. A shiver ran up her spine as a bead of cold sweat trickled between her shoulder blades. Where was he? Did his father own the storage unit? Was he watching her through security cameras—or worse, a rifle-mounted scope?

Bodies of Proof

"Don't get all worked up," he said soothingly. "I'm not going to hurt you."

"Oh, you can bet that," she snapped. She had been molded and hardened through years of tough living in jail and prison. Firearms aside, she had no reason to be afraid of a pipsqueak like him. "What. Do. You. Want?" She wasn't going to repeat herself.

A long silence followed—one she did not attempt to fill. After a full thirty seconds, he spoke at last.

"What did that cop want?"

"What are you talking about?"

"That cop who was talking to you earlier," he replied levelly. "At the food truck. What did he want?"

"That's none of your business."

He waited a few seconds before replying. "I'll pay you to tell me."

She scoffed. "Dude, not everything is for sale."

Again, there was a moment before he spoke. "Did you tell him anything about me?"

She'd had just about enough of this. "Why would he be asking about you?"

"No reason." He paused again. "But did you? Did you say anything about me?"

"No." *You dipshit.* "Of course not. One, I don't know anything about you, and two, I work for Marko, so I'm bound by the same attorney-client privilege as he is."

"Oh." She could hear his smile through the phone.

"Why?" she asked.

"No reason."

"Is there something I should know?" *Two can play this game.*

"No."

Allee shook her head. "Is that all?"

"For now."

"Great." Allee hung up and went back to jiggling the key, trying to get the storage unit to open. As she did, her mind replayed the phone conversation. Innis was strange, no doubt. *Maybe he's just lonely*, she thought. Money couldn't buy love. In the limited conversations she'd had with Innis, he'd already mentioned both of his parents, and not in flattering terms. She jiggled the key and twisted again. Finally, it turned and the lock released. Grabbing the handle, she twisted and lifted the garage door. Her old truck sat inside. She'd had the vehicle since she was a teenager. It wasn't fancy. It didn't even have power locks, but it still worked.

Focus on Jack Daniels's investigation, she told herself. She could worry about Innis later.

18

MARKO

"I want to work off my charges."

Marko sighed heavily. He was sitting across from Clint Woodford, a client who spent a lot of time in legal trouble—a so-called "frequent flyer." They were in an attorney-client room in the courthouse, meeting for Woodford's pretrial conference. The room was basic with bare, off-white walls and only three pieces of furniture: a beat-up square table and two blue plastic chairs.

Marko sighed again. "You're telling me you want to snitch."

"I'm not a snitch," Woodford said quickly, leaning in closer to Marko, as if doing so would make him both hear and understand.

Marko flinched. Woodford was an atypical meth addict; most were emaciated and frail, but not this guy. He was a bull of a man with round pink cheeks and a protruding belly.

"I want to work off my charges," Woodford repeated.

Marko pressed a couple of keys on his laptop. "You are charged with possession of methamphetamine, third offense. It's a felony, but you're looking at a nickel, max."

"You've told me that already," Clint said.

"The prosecutor is offering probation."

"I don't want probation."

Marko sighed a third time. *Of course you don't.* "All you'd have to do is stay straight and meet with your PO once a month. You know as well as I do that meth only stays in your system two or three days, and you'll know when your probation appointments are coming up. All you gotta do is make sure you don't use a few days before. Piece of cake."

"I don't want probation."

"Fine." Marko slammed his laptop shut and sat back. "I'll humor you. How do you want to 'work off' the charge? And I'm telling you right now if it involves ratting out any of my other clients, I'll have to withdraw as your attorney."

"I'm not snitching."

Marko ignored him. "And I'll remind you, if you piss on a dealer, you are going to have a helluva time buying product in the future."

"It's not a dealer and I'm not snitching."

"Then what is it?"

"It's about someone I know." He looked left, and then right. "And them girls that went missing."

Marko sat quietly, watching the big man closely. Woodford knew damned well they were in a soundproof room; there was no need for secrecy aside from a desire to create a dramatic effect. "What girls?" he asked impatiently, crossing his arms. "There's a lot of girls around here."

"The ones what's missing."

Marko sat up straight. "Are you telling me you have information about Leslie Martin and Rebecca Calloway?"

Woodford nodded, but said nothing.

"Well, what've you got?"

Woodford looked around the empty room again. "I know a guy," he began. "Someone who works at that restaurant they both worked at, Olde Bulldogs."

"And?"

Marko knew the place well; he frequented the restaurant back in his drinking days, as it was one of the few in town with a fully stocked bar. More than once he'd bellied up to the Olde Bulldogs bar to do a little day-drinking, downing Old Fashions until he'd run out of time, money, or both. Reflecting on those afternoons made his mouth water. For Marko, booze

Bodies of Proof 95

was an obsession; it occupied his mind and soul to the exclusion of all else. Even now, with months of sobriety to his credit, he'd found nothing that could fill the void.

"Dude's name is Oliver Prince," Woodford said at last.

"I know Oliver well," Marko said. He'd spent every afternoon with him for years. "What about him?"

"He knows some strange shit that had been going down in that joint even before Rebecca and Leslie disappeared."

Marko pressed a hand to his gut. A year earlier, he, Allee, and Whitney had unraveled one of the most bizarre and twisted restaurant crimes in Iowa history. Marko had been stabbed and nearly died in the process. He had no interest in getting involved in anything like that again. "I'm not interested in whatever's going on in that place," he said. "I had enough of the restaurant business with the shit that went down in The Yellow Lark. If they're doing some weird shit over at Olde Bulldogs, find yourself a different attorney to—"

"It has nothing to do with the restaurant," Clint said. "It just happened there."

The worst of the nonsense that happened at The Yellow Lark wasn't part of the restaurant, either. It just happened there.

Marko looked at his watch. "Look, I've got stuff to do. Tell me what you want me to know, and I'll decide if it's worthwhile."

Woodford nodded in acknowledgement, took a deep breath, and began speaking. "Oliver said there was this guy that started coming in regularly about a month before Rebecca disappeared. Young guy. Wouldn't sit in any section but Rebecca's and he'd leave her notes. Creepy notes."

"I'm listening," Marko said, his attention piqued.

"He stopped coming after Rebecca disappeared."

Could be a coincidence. "What did the notes say? Did he keep them?" Marko asked.

"You'll have to ask Oliver."

"You said you had information on both girls. Rebecca disappeared a year ago; what could any of this have to do with Leslie? You said the guy stopped coming in after Rebecca disappeared."

"And that's true—right up until about a month ago," Woodford replied quickly. "Oliver said this guy was doing the same things with Leslie, like coming in every day, insisting he get seated in her section, leaving notes and stuff. He even showed me one."

"Were you in the bar?"

"Whattaya mean?"

Marko pinched the bridge of his nose and paused for a beat, trying to rein in his irritation. "You're on pretrial release, Clint. You aren't supposed to be in a bar."

"I wasn't drinking," Woodford replied. "And it's also a restaurant."

"But you were in the bar area." Marko took a deep breath; this was getting him nowhere. "Look, never mind. Just stay out of the bar area."

"Do you think it will help?" Clint asked. "With my charges, I mean."

"What did the note say?"

"I've got a picture of it." Woodford unlocked his phone and scrolled through his images, then stopped and clicked. An image populated the screen, and he turned it so Marko could read.

The note was written on a napkin. It said, "The world is a *Carnival of the Animals*, but I will free you soon."

"Carnival of the animals? What the hell does that mean?" Marko asked.

Woodford shrugged. "I told you it was weird shit."

You were right about that. "Why is Carnival of the Animals italicized like that?"

Woodford shrugged again. "I didn't write it," he said, pocketing his phone.

"Who was this given to? Leslie or Rebecca?"

"Rebecca."

"Hmm," Marko said. Rebecca had disappeared more than a year ago. It could have some value, but at this point the cops would be far less interested in information about Rebecca than Leslie. Unless, of course, Leslie turned up dead, too. But if all he had was Oliver's word and a note Oliver said was shown to him by Rebecca...

"So, do you think it will help?"

"Maybe," Marko said. "But the prosecutor is going to want to know why you and Oliver didn't report it a year ago."

Bodies of Proof 97

"The bar," Woodford replied, placing a large hand on his chest. "You said it yourself. I'm not supposed to be there."

Marko smirked. "Right. And what's Oliver's excuse?"

"He doesn't roll with cops. Plus, he didn't think it was important. He thought it might be some sexual thing. People are into weird stuff."

He might be right, Marko thought. "Send me the picture of the note and I'll reach out to the prosecutor."

"Done." Woodford retrieved his phone and poked at it with an enormous forefinger.

Seconds later, Marko's phone buzzed; he saved the image in his photographs. As he was about to put his phone away, it buzzed again with a text from Allee.

That Innis kid creeps me out.

What did he do? Marko typed back.

We'll talk later. I am OMW to Olde Bulldogs.

Good, Marko typed. *I have some information for you.*

About Olde Bulldogs?

You could say that.

Great, Allee wrote. She added an emoji appearing to sigh in exasperation.

My thoughts exactly. He stepped out of the meeting room and called Allee. She picked up after the first ring.

"What's this I need to know about Olde Bulldogs?" she asked. It sounded like she was in her truck. He could hear the tires on the road, the groan of the old engine. He was surprised the thing still ran at all.

He quickly explained his conversation with Woodford.

"Why did he wait until now? Rebecca has been missing for a year. Do you really think McJames will let Woodford use the note to proffer?"

"No," Marko said honestly. "But I've got to try."

Daniel McJames was the local prosecutor. A tall, red-headed man with a hot temper, he was in his late thirties—about the same age as Marko—but that was about the only similarity between them. Marko was always pushing boundaries, whereas McJames was a rule follower and enforcer.

"All right," Allee said. "While you do that, I'll see what I can dig up over at Olde Bulldogs. But I'm focusing on Jack Daniels's case first."

"That's fine."

"I know it's fine," she snapped. "I wasn't asking permission."

Marko shook his head in irritation. "Get to work." This was the way things worked between them, and he'd grown used to it over time. Allee had saved his ass literally and figuratively on multiple occasions. Accordingly, he tolerated much more from her than he would from anyone else. He glanced down at his gold Timex watch; it was still broken. "We've got a few hours before we have to head back to Ostlund for the evening."

"What's that?" Allee asked. It didn't sound like she was talking to him anymore.

"What's what?"

"Never mind," she said. "I've got to go. I'll see you later."

She hung up, and he was left staring at the phone. Few people would leave their boss in the dark like that, but he had learned not to dwell on it. Besides, he had work to do. He pocketed his phone and turned his attention to the court's chambers, where McJames would be waiting to discuss Woodford's pretrial conference.

Convincing McJames to proffer would not be easy.

19

JENKINS

"This is bullshit," Jenkins said aloud as he walked the mile back to his car. He wasn't at risk, but it was the principle of the thing: Shaffer had left another officer alone during a call, thereby violating an officer's foremost duty. The sun was unrelenting; sweat soaked his clothing, and with each step he could feel his anger rising. He retrieved his phone and dialed the police department's non-emergency line.

"Franklin Police Department, this is Carla," a cheery voice answered.

"Carla, it's Special Agent Jenkins." He tried, but recognized he failed to keep the irritation out of his voice.

"Oh, yes, how are you?"

"Not good, Carla, not good."

"Why not?"

"I need to talk to the chief of police."

"Oh, okay. He's busy right now, but I can leave him a—"

"Interrupt him. This is important."

"Yes, sir. One moment."

Elevator music filled the line as he waited for Carla to transfer the call to the chief. A few moments later, a gruff, tired voice came through the line.

"Hank Brown here."

"Chief Brown," Jenkins began, then paused to gain his composure.

Might as well dive right in. This was not a time for niceties. "We need to talk about Captain Shaffer."

Chief Brown sighed. "What'd he do now?" His already-tired voice shifted to one of resignation.

Jenkins told him about the call to Rebecca Calloway's house, Shaffer's treatment of the Calloways, then his abandonment of a fellow officer.

"Where are you now?"

"I'm walking back to my car."

"What? That man—"

"How is he the captain? He doesn't have the brains or the patience to supervise a wet sponge, let alone other officers."

"That's . . . let's just say it's complicated."

"Yeah?" Jenkins said. "I've got time to listen." By his estimation he had at least another half mile before he reached the trailhead.

"He knows things that, if released, would lead to a lot of trouble for me. It's an election year. Two of the city councilpersons are up for reelection in hotly contested races. If I do anything to make them look bad, it could be over for me."

Jenkins's jaws clenched. He took a deep breath before responding. "Lemme get this straight, Chief. You won't do anything about Shaffer because he is extorting you—is that right?"

When the chief didn't respond, Jenkins continued. "Tell me, did he catch you cheating on your wife with a secretary or something?" Still no response. It was as good as an admission.

"You've got to be kidding me," Jenkins said aloud. It was the most unoriginal story of all time. Silence stretched between them, stoking Jenkins's anger as he walked through the Iowa heat. "So instead of doing your job, you're gonna let Shaffer screw up investigation after investigation, harming countless people. Am I hearing that correctly?"

"That's why you're here," Chief Brown said quietly. "I need you."

"And what if Shaffer's actions quash our ability to find the person or persons who kidnapped Rebecca and Leslie, and murdered Rebecca?"

Jenkins imagined the color draining from the chief's face. "Do you have reason to believe they will? I mean, is it that screwed up?" he asked.

"I don't know! Right now the best I can say is that he is a crooked cop, a sociopath, and a guy who is apparently extorting his boss. I've been told he has a habit of planting evidence on people he doesn't like, and from what I've seen, I can't say that he's done anything right during these investigations. I don't have anything on him, but I damn sure wonder how a captain of police can have so little interest in the disappearance of two women. It'd make a lot more sense if he had something to do with their disappearance, I'll say that."

"Jesus, Jenkins! What do you mean?"

"I mean his refusal to do any investigating or to preserve any of the potential crime scenes—that's beyond simple negligence. Hell, a rookie one week out of the academy would do a better job of preserving evidence than he has. His treatment of the Calloway family would make a perfect how-not-to training video. And he knew both victims, right?"

"Well, it's a small town, Jenkins," Brown replied. "We all knew—know—knew the victims."

"Yeah, well, he's either completely ineffectual or intentionally incompetent," Jenkins observed. "I go back and forth between deeming him not in compliance or maliciously compliant." He could see the car up ahead a couple of hundred yards. "Neither bodes well for a police captain. I'll never understand why you elevated him to that role."

Brown was silent for a long moment. When he spoke, his voice sounded small. "Jenkins, I'm in a lose-lose situation here."

"I get it," Jenkins replied bitterly. "And you chose to lose in a way that harms other people. I know exactly your situation and exactly who you are." He hung up before he could say more. There was nothing worse than a spineless law enforcement official. Shaffer was bad, but it was Brown who empowered him, and in Jenkins's mind that made him the more dangerous of the pair.

He was wiping the sweat from his brow with a soaking wet handkerchief when an old, beat-up Ford truck slowed beside him. At first, he ignored it and continued his march. But when it matched his pace, he took a look and recognized the driver as Allee from the Justice Bites food truck. She leaned across the bench seat and rolled the window down. It lowered in jerky motions common with a hand crank.

"Out for a walk, Agent Jenkins?"

He made a face. "You're hilarious—ever think of doing the comedy circuit?" he replied. "If you are going to gloat, best move along. I'll be back at my car in a minute, and I'll have a pack of K9s and handlers here so fast it'll make your head spin."

"I'm clean," she said. "Isn't time something you shouldn't be wasting? Shouldn't you be out looking for Leslie?"

"Yeah, I should be, but—" A burst of anger shot through him, and he forced himself to let it pass. "Shaffer," he finally explained.

"Say no more." Allee leaned over and popped the lock to the passenger door. "Get in. I'll take you where you need to go."

Normally, he wouldn't accept a ride from a convicted felon and potential fact witness in Leslie's disappearance. But he remembered how Shaffer had referred to Allee as trash, and he decided that anyone who was trash in Shaffer's book was more likely to prove valuable.

20

WHITNEY

How long is she going to be gone? Whitney wiped her brow with the upper part of her forearm. The food truck was Allee's business, not hers. Sure, she'd agreed to help when needed, but lately, she'd been spending way more time dealing with customers than Allee or Marko. *This is not what I signed up for.* She'd signed on to help with the law practice, not to be in food service. She looked at the handful of customers still in line and sighed heavily. Fortunately, they were running low on supply. In another half hour or so, she'd be able to shutter the serving window and post the "Sold Out" sign out front.

"How can I help you?" she asked a young woman.

"I'd like a cinnamon roll," the woman replied.

Whitney pointed to the sign they'd put out that morning. "We sold out in the first hour," she said. "What else could I get you? A Pro se Pretzel? A Burglary Burrito?"

"Pretzel."

Whitney turned toward the warmer. "With or without salt?"

"Without."

Whitney grabbed the last unsalted pretzel, set it in a small box, and turned back to the register, placing it on the shelf in front of her. "That'll be five dollars and twenty-seven cents." She collected the money and made change, then thanked the customer and sent her on her way, thinking to herself that the last thing the woman needed was another five hundred calories at this time of day.

She turned her attention to the next customer, and immediately recognized him as James Innis, one of Marko's clients from earlier that day.

"If you want to talk to Marko, he's not here," she said.

"You remembered me."

"Part of my job," she answered noncommittally.

"Still," he said. "I'll have one of those."

She boxed a pretzel without asking him what kind—she had the feeling it really didn't matter.

He handed her a card. She ran it through the reader and handed it back to him. He accepted the card and slipped something into her hand at the same time. It was a small, folded slip of paper.

"What is this?" she asked, holding it between her thumb and index finger.

"Open it after I'm gone."

Whitney narrowed her eyes. "Why?"

He flashed a smile and waggled his eyebrows.

She blinked several times in rapid succession. Was he flirting with her? She was at least fifteen years older than him.

"Thanks for the pretzel." He backed up, holding the box and eye contact. As he did so, the black limo he'd arrived in earlier that day pulled up behind him. He held her gaze for one last moment, then turned and hopped into the backseat.

What a weirdo. When the car had left the parking lot, she looked down at the small paper. It was thick cardstock, slightly larger than a business card. *What the hell?* The last time she'd been handed a note she was in junior high. There was only one way to find out. She unfolded the paper and read, "You are living a modern-day *Cinderella* story, but this isn't any *Midsummer Night's Dream*."

"What on earth?" Whitney asked aloud. *What could it mean?* As a former English teacher, she was thoroughly familiar with each work, of course. *Cinderella* was a novel—well, a novelette, really—while *A Midsummer Night's Dream* was a play that had been written centuries earlier. Each had

Bodies of Proof

been adapted hundreds if not thousands of times over the years. He was messing with her. Well, she'd dealt with hundreds of boys, and she knew a prank when she saw one.

She tossed the card in the trash can.

"Can I get some help here?"

The man's impatience was clear, and Whitney got back to the job of taking payment in return for Allee's food.

21

MARKO

Marko popped his head back in the attorney-client room. "I'll be right back," he said to Woodford, who was twisting his hands together nervously.

"Are you going to talk to the prosecutor?" he asked.

Marko had represented Woodford more times than he could count, but he'd never seen him like this. The big man couldn't sit still; he squirmed in his seat and wouldn't meet Marko's gaze.

"You okay, man?" Marko asked.

"Yeah. Why wouldn't I be?"

"I'm not sure," Marko replied, staring pointedly at Woodford. "But I damned sure better not be walking into that office to meet with McJames, trying to sell him a pack of lies," he added. "You gotta know that if I am, it's gonna bite *you* in the ass, not me."

"They aren't lies."

"Good enough," Marko said with a shrug. "It's your funeral."

He closed the door, but not before he thought he heard Woodford say something along the lines of, "Or yours." He was tempted to rush back in there and confront his client but knew it wouldn't do any good. He understood his clients, and he knew that pressing Woodford would only result in him clamming up. Besides, he'd warned Woodford that his plan could

Bodies of Proof 107

backfire. That's all he could do as an attorney. He provided advice; the client got to choose whether or not to follow it.

He made his way down the ornate hallway, keeping away from the gold filigree railing. The courtrooms were on the third floor of the courthouse, and there was a large atrium at the center of each floor. A year ago, he'd been standing in this very same hallway, talking with Allee and her cousin, when Whitney's brother had appeared out of nowhere, sprinted past them, and leaped over the railing to his death. Since then, Marko had been painfully aware of how easy it would be for someone to sneak up on him and shove him over. As a defense attorney dealing with desperate and mentally ill people, he knew there were some who would love to do the honors. Knowing this, he stayed close to the outside wall when he was on the second and third floors of this building.

McJames would be waiting for him in the judge's chambers at the end of the hallway. A large window was built into the door to the chambers. Approaching quickly, Marko could see McJames inside, pacing and talking on the phone.

That's odd. McJames usually sat in one of the chairs, tapping his foot impatiently while he waited, ready to pounce on Marko the moment he came through the door and complain about him taking too long.

Today, when Marko opened the door, McJames looked up, then spoke quietly into his cell phone and hung up. "Thanks for actually being on time today," he said sarcastically.

Marko indicated the broken Timex watch that had once belonged to his father. "A broken clock is right twice a day."

"What does that mean?"

"Not sure," Marko replied. "Just felt like the right thing to say."

"Whatever." McJames clapped his hands. "Clint Woodford—will he take my offer?"

"Not exactly."

"What does that—" McJames was cut off by his phone ringing. "I have to take this." He stepped away from Marko and answered, walking toward the law library for privacy.

Marko rocked from heels to toes, waiting. And waiting. He had a thought and smiled wryly. *This must be what McJames usually feels like.* He didn't mind making McJames wait—he kind of enjoyed it, really—but it wasn't fun to be on the other end of things.

"You could take a seat, you know," Delilah, the court attendant, said. Her desk was nearby, and it was her job to keep track of the pretrial conferences. She was a frigid-looking woman who favored clothing two sizes too large and mismatched, unflattering shoes.

"Thanks," Marko replied. He remained standing.

"Suit yourself." She shrugged.

Silence descended on the small room as he waited. At one point, it became so quiet he could hear Delilah's pencil scratching against paper and the constant tick, tick, tick, of the second hand moving on the government-issue wall clock.

"What's going on with McJames?" Marko finally asked.

Delilah glanced to her left. "You'll have to ask him," she replied as McJames emerged from the hallway.

"All right," McJames said, again clapping his hands. "Woodford. What are we doing if he doesn't want the deal? Trial? Bench or jury?"

A bench trial was a trial before a judge only.

"Well, neither right now."

McJames placed his hands on his hips. "He can't have his cake and eat it too, Marko. He either takes my offer or we go to trial."

"Well, he was hoping you would agree to proffer."

"Proffer?" McJames narrowed his eyes. "With what infor—" His phone rang again. He took it out of his pocket and held it up. "I'll be right back." Without waiting for Marko's approval, he again disappeared down the hallway.

Marko issued a heavy sigh.

"Getting a little taste of your own medicine, eh?" Delilah asked. She pressed her lips together in what looked like an attempt to keep from smiling.

She was right, and he hated it. *I'm going to make McJames wait twice as long next time,* he promised himself. Two could play at this game, and he was far more practiced than McJames.

Again the silence descended. Again Marko paced, the clock ticked, and

Bodies of Proof 109

Delilah scratched at her paper—this time with such ferocity that Marko became convinced she was doing it simply to irritate him.

Finally, McJames reemerged from the hallway. "Proffer," he said as though they hadn't missed a beat. "With what information?"

"He says he has information regarding Rebecca Calloway."

McJames lifted his eyebrows, then narrowed his eyes, studying Marko closely.

It made Marko uncomfortable. "Why are you looking at me like that?"

"Why now?" McJames asked. "Where's he been? How long has he known—"

"I don't know." Marko shrugged. He looked away, avoiding McJames's stare. It was like he was trying to look into Marko's soul, which was creeping him out. "You'll have to ask him."

"What does he know?" McJames said.

"I'm not entirely sure," Marko replied truthfully. "It's something about notes left for her."

"What notes? When?"

"I don't know, exactly. I just found out today. This is all I've seen." Marko pulled out his phone and showed McJames the photograph Woodford had sent him.

McJames stared at it, then reached for the phone.

Marko pulled it away; he was not about to let a prosecutor go through his phone. "You can look, but you can't touch."

McJames crossed his arms. "What the hell? Your client wants to proffer and you're trying to keep secrets?"

"I'm not."

"Bullshit. The timing stinks, too."

"What do you mean? This is exactly what we should be discussing at a pretrial conference." Between the phone call interruptions and now this, McJames seemed to be talking in riddles. It had Marko feeling off-balance.

"I'm not talking about the proffer itself; I'm talking about the timing," McJames clarified. "That girl's been gone a year."

"Okay, but—"

"And all of a sudden, right after Rebecca's body is found in the woods, a day when you just happen to be in town, you wander in here and come to me with a proffer from your client about a dead chick."

Marko had to fight to keep his jaw from dropping. Negotiations generally required a poker face, and he prided himself in his ability to keep from reacting. "I—I didn't know that Rebecca's body had been found. I don't know where, either. And today is the date of our pretrial conference."

"Yeah, well, not many people know," McJames allowed. He paused for a long moment, keeping his eyes affixed to his phone and rubbing his thumb against it. At last, his eyes met Marko's. "Except her killer."

22

ALLEE

What the hell am I doing? Allee asked herself. It wasn't a habit of hers to stop and help men walking along the street—she didn't make helping others outside of work a habit to begin with, and she certainly didn't go out of her way to help cops.

"Out for a walk, Agent Jenkins?"

They debated back and forth before she finally offered him the ride. "Get in. I'll take you where you need to go," she forced herself to say. She was committed at this point, and it would only raise suspicion if she changed her mind.

The cop accepted her offer and climbed in the truck. He was in shape and nimble for his age. She wasn't good at guessing ages, but she'd estimate the guy was old for a cop—maybe late fifties, early sixties? Whatever. She waited while he closed the door and buckled his seatbelt.

"Thanks for stopping," he said, wiping his brow. "It's hotter than a Playboy Bunny double-page centerfold spread out there."

"I wouldn't know," Allee said, putting the car in gear.

"I'm Special Agent Adam Jenkins, by the way. I don't think we formally met when you were telling me to leave your business earlier today."

If he thought she was going to apologize, he was sorely mistaken. "Allee Smith."

"Nice to meet you."

The jury is still out on that one. "Where are you going?" she said.

"Back to the trailhead. I left my car there."

"Why?"

"Because I rode with someone else into town to do a death notification."

Yikes. "And they left you?" She spun the truck around and headed back toward the trailhead.

"Yeah," he said. "Something like that."

"Trouble in paradise?"

"Not hardly," he grunted. "This place is a long way from paradise," he added. "And I'm counting down the days."

"I've heard that's the most dangerous time as a cop," she said. "When you are on the way out, I mean."

"Thanks," Jenkins said. "And for the record, I'm not a *cop*. I'm an agent."

"Same thing," Allee replied. "You gotta know you still reek of cop and people like me can smell it a mile away."

They rode in silence. In moments like these, she wished she could switch on her stereo and fill the emptiness, but it had broken a long time ago and she'd never prioritized fixing it. Money was tight and it always went elsewhere.

"What do you know about Dennis Shaffer?" Jenkins finally asked.

"He's a dick," she replied without hesitation.

"Why do you say that?" he asked.

She could see him withholding a smirk. "Because it's true." She was suddenly defensive, regretting her decision to pick him up. He was prying, of course. That's what cops did. She'd talk shit about Shaffer and no doubt it would get back to him. Cops were all alike.

"I'm just asking," he said, putting his hands up in surrender. "He's the reason I'm in this mess. We were at a call, and he left me there."

Allee barked a dark, humorless laugh. "That's par for the course."

"I've known the guy for decades. Between you and me, I don't like him," he explained. "What can you tell me about him?" Jenkins cleared his throat. "You know, from your perspective?"

Should I buy this? "You mean, what are criminals saying about him?"

Bodies of Proof

"Yeah."

She kept her eyes on the road, feeling her grip tightening on the steering wheel. "Number one, don't be caught alone with him. He's handsy with women and aggressive with men, and his body camera rarely seems to work."

"Huh."

"Number two—" As Allee turned into the trailhead's parking lot, a wall of flashing lights filled her vision. Dozens of first responder vehicles were parked. The sight of so many cruisers sent Allee's heart galloping. She would never be comfortable around police. Never.

"What is going on?" she said, coming to a stop ten feet away from the closest vehicle.

"We—I—found what I think is Rebecca Calloway's body."

"Her body? She's been here the *whole time*?"

"I don't think so," Jenkins said carefully. He was clearly trying to be circumspect.

"Why not?"

"The condition of her body."

"What does that mean?" It had to do with the decomposition of the body, right? That had to be the case. Otherwise, they wouldn't be able to easily identify her. If the remains were skeletal, they'd have to send her off to a forensics laboratory to examine her teeth. It would take weeks to get a positive identification.

"I've probably said too much already, but you're on the right track," Jenkins said as he exited her truck.

"You're welcome," Allee said irritably.

His face reddened in embarrassment—just as she'd hoped it would. "Thanks for the ride."

"You owe me one."

He smiled quickly, then sobered. "We'll talk about that later."

What the hell is going on in this town? As Jenkins walked toward the mass of cops, Allee put her truck in reverse and turned around. While she was interested in whatever had happened to Rebecca, right now she needed to get over to Olde Bulldogs. Marko had asked her to interview witnesses and find out if anyone had either seen Leslie Martin arguing with Jack Daniels or overheard his alleged threat to kill her.

And hey, if she was lucky, she might find out some information about Rebecca as well.

23

MARKO

Marko rocked back on his heels, creating space between himself and McJames. Neither was inclined to lessen the tension by speaking.

"What, exactly, are you insinuating?" Marko finally asked.

"You heard me," McJames said.

"Say it again," Marko said through clenched teeth.

"Why?"

When Marko didn't reply, McJames leaned closer and dropped his voice to a growl. "Nobody outside of law enforcement knows about Rebecca's body."

"I didn't know, either."

"Seems like your client did."

Marko straightened and took a step back, forcing himself to calm down. When he could think clearly, he realized just how ludicrous the accusation was. McJames had nothing unless Marko slipped up and said something dumb.

"You're grasping at straws," Marko said.

"Am I?"

"You are accusing my client, and me"—he pressed a hand to his chest—"of having something to do with a murder I didn't even know about based on *what*? Supposition and coincidence! I don't know if—or how—my client knew anything, but I do know how news travels in a small town."

McJames opened his mouth, then closed it again. He had to know that Marko was right. If McJames approached a judge with a request for something as routine as a search warrant based on the information he had, he'd be tossed out of chambers on his ass. There wasn't a chance in hell he could get an indictment. His accusation was based solely on emotion. Law enforcement had gotten nowhere with Rebecca's disappearance; led by Shaffer, it was apparent they hadn't even tried to figure it out until Leslie disappeared from the same location. Now—probably as a result of public outcry—McJames was trying to play catch-up on what should have been a year-long murder investigation.

"You know I'm right." Marko crossed his arms. "You don't know who to blame so you are targeting my client. And me."

"I didn't—"

"Sounds like you owe Marko an apology." Delilah sounded almost bored as she spoke from behind her desk.

Marko had forgotten she was even there. Judging by McJames's expression, he had as well.

"You heard me," Delilah said. She was keyboarding and didn't pause as she spoke. "You know the judges are going to hear about this."

"How would they—" McJames began, but Delilah cut him off.

"You know they are going to find out." She looked away from her computer screen to level McJames with a hard look. "An apology would go a long way in making you look like less of a horse's ass."

McJames stared at her for a long moment, his mouth open in shock. She paid him no heed, and instead went back to typing as though she didn't have a care in the world.

"You heard her," Marko said, leaning forward. "Apologize."

"I—"

"Actually, you can do something better."

"What's that?"

"Accept my client's proffer and dismiss his charges."

McJames narrowed his eyes. "You still want your client to proffer?"

"I warned him of the risks, and he wants to do it. I'm not the decision maker here," Marko said with a shrug. "I'm just the attorney."

"Fine. Do you want to go inform the judge?" McJames said.

"One-month continuance for a proffer?" Marko said.

"One day."

"One day?" Marko asked. *There's no way.*

"Yes. Or would you rather set it for trial?"

"No trial." Woodford had been clear; he was insisting on a proffer. Marko would just have to work around it. He could move a few things in his schedule.

"You're sure?" McJames pressed.

"Yes."

A brief smile flashed at the corners of McJames's mouth. "It's your funeral," he said as he gestured toward the judge's chambers.

"That's the second time I've heard that today."

24

JENKINS

Jenkins turned and looked back toward Allee's truck as he approached the gaggle of law enforcement and first responders. She didn't wave or smile as she backed out and then left the parking lot. Instinct was a critical characteristic for investigators. It wasn't something to be presented in court and couldn't be considered evidence—more than one prosecutor had reminded him of that—but without instinct, an investigator or agent was unlikely to put the pieces of the puzzle comprising serious crimes together. Right now, Jenkins's instincts were telling him to trust Allee. She was a felon, of course, but he'd had dispatch run her criminal history and he'd discovered it was all drug-related—no violence, no serious crimes of moral turpitude. She was an addict. Fair enough. People didn't change for the worse as they aged; more often, they settled down and either began to live a law-abiding life or they died young from hard living and organ failure.

Allee wasn't involved in Rebecca's murder or Leslie's disappearance—he was certain of that. Certainly, as a long-time criminal, she might unknowingly have some connection to the murderer, but these were crimes committed by a man. Or men. The victims may have been nearby when they disappeared—Leslie certainly was—but he deemed it unlikely that anyone associated with Justice Bites had anything to do with either woman's disappearance or his discovery of Rebecca's body earlier today.

Today, he thought, shaking his head.

He could hardly believe how much had happened since he arrived early that morning. He'd come to investigate Leslie's disappearance and instead found Rebecca's body. He was now elbow deep in two investigations that *had* to be connected. Certainly, it was *possible* they were two separate offenses committed by an original offender and a copycat, but it was far more likely he was dealing with a serial killer. It was implausible that two women could disappear in the same place under similar circumstances and have those circumstances not be intrinsically intertwined. The cases were so similar that he could not separate them in his brain no matter how hard he tried. Of course, he wouldn't know until they found Leslie. Or her body. Either way, unless he got to work and figured something out, the future did not bode well for Leslie.

A member of his forensics team reached the trailhead just in front of Jenkins. She was carrying a large evidence box.

"Mia," he called out.

She turned to look at him. Mia Costanza was a stocky woman in her late thirties, with olive skin and the kind of sharp, observant eyes one would expect of a criminalist and the lead of the on-site forensics team. She'd been promoted from within the organization to the position two years ago and proven to be fantastic at the job. There was nothing she missed at a crime scene. She made sure every hair was collected and examined, every broken twig observed and reported.

"Just the person I wanted to talk to," Jenkins added when he had her attention.

"Let me put this in the car first," Mia said.

Jenkins did not offer to assist—not because he didn't want to, but because she would refuse and chastise him for trying to insert himself and thereby potentially compromise her chain of custody. Limiting the number of people who handled evidence was paramount in maintaining its sanctity. A single, minor interruption in the chain could taint the evidence, resulting in it being deemed inadmissible at trial. While his assistance was unlikely to result in the evidence's inadmissibility, Mia was not one to take any chances—just one of the many reasons she was so good at her job.

He watched while she placed the evidence box in the trunk of her vehicle, shut it, and turned to face him. "Now, what do you need?"

She looked ridiculous in her hair net, gloves, and booties, but he didn't comment on it. These items protected the crime scene. Some forensics departments would consider this overkill because they had previously obtained and recorded fingerprints and DNA evidence from all members of the team, but Mia wasn't interested in wasting time testing evidence and finding it belonged to her own team.

"Do you have a minute to talk about the crime scene?"

Mia looked down at her watch. "You can have one minute."

Jenkins sighed. She'd hold him to that, too. "Anything of interest?"

"A little of this and a little of that."

"That's not helpful," Jenkins said quickly, knowing the clock was running.

"We're still gathering evidence, Jenks. You know that." She was the only person he allowed to call him by a nickname. "We're taking soil samples and photographing disturbances in the plant life. We won't have much until we can start examining the items."

"Have you found any usable fingerprints?"

"Not so far," she said, shaking her head regretfully. "This guy was pretty careful."

"Not even from the rope?" Someone had tied it around her wrists and then secured it to a tree.

"It's a rough, round object," she snapped. "What do you think?"

"Damn," Jenkins said, issuing a heavy breath through his teeth. It was difficult to lift fingerprints from rough, porous objects like rope, he knew. Most likely, even if they lifted something, it would only be a partial print.

Mia looked down at her watch. "Anything else you need? You've got about ten seconds left."

"Yeah. Do me a favor and keep Shaffer and his guys out of the crime scene."

"We're trying. Those bumpkins are worse than a herd of bulls in a china shop. It's like they've never been to a major crime scene before. I've got a member of my staff who should be collecting evidence trying full-time to monitor Shaffer and his morons, but it ain't easy."

Bodies of Proof

"Tell 'em to try harder," Jenkins replied. "I have concerns. It's important."

She placed her hands on her hips and gave him a withering glare. "No shit. We are doing our best. Trust me on that."

"At the very least, make sure Shaffer stays out."

"Why?"

"I have my reasons."

She lifted an eyebrow. "Anything you care to share?"

"Not yet. Call it instinct."

"Well, well," she said skeptically. "That sounds scientific."

"You do the science; I'll do the investigating."

She looked down at her watch. "On that note, Jenks, your time is up. I'll just add that if you really think Shaffer might have something to do with this, you'd better get going. He has the power to sabotage your investigation. And if he is somehow involved in stuff like this—" She gestured toward the trail. "He will."

25

MARKO

"We're all set," Marko said, closing the door to the attorney-client room behind him.

"What took so long?" Woodford asked, standing.

Marko motioned for him to sit back down, and he did.

"McJames had some business to do . . . Interruptions."

"What kind of interruptions?"

Marko shrugged. "Phone calls—and before you ask, I don't know. I can guess the topic of discussion, but I can't be sure."

"Okay," Clint said, sitting back in his chair. "What's your guess?"

"Rebecca Calloway."

Woodford was again on his feet. "So he's going to accept my proffer? I'm not going to prison?"

"You weren't going to prison anyway," Marko said irritably. "His offer was for probation. Nobody goes to prison for drugs—at least to start."

"Yeah, but for me probation is only an interrupted prison sentence. You know I can't make it. I always get jammed up somehow and end up eating the elephant one bite at a time."

True enough, Marko thought.

"I'm proffering then, right?" Woodford leaned forward with both of his

Bodies of Proof 123

large, thick-fingered hands on the table. Marko was very aware of his client's size and the physical threat he posed.

"Sit," he ordered.

Woodford's eyes showed his irritation, but he complied.

"You can proffer, but I'm gonna tell you, I've got a case of the ass."

Woodford's eyes widened. "Why?"

"Because you neglected to tell me that Rebecca's body was found this morning, so when I showed McJames the note, he assumed I had something to do with it and—"

Woodford was shaking his head vigorously before Marko could finish the thought. "Marko, I swear I didn't know about that!" he said, making the sign of the cross in front of himself.

"Bullshit," was all Marko said in response. He didn't believe him. He'd been in business long enough that he rarely took a client's words at face value. They almost always lied, even to him. In this case, it didn't mean Woodford had anything to do with Rebecca's death—McJames was no doubt jumping to conclusions there—but it looked bad and meant word was traveling around the criminal world. At best.

"I didn't know," Woodford insisted. "You gotta believe me, man!"

"Well, you know now—does that change anything?"

"Not really."

"Even if you're a person of interest, or even a suspect?"

"Me?" Clint pressed a large hand against his chest, offended. "Why me?"

Marko cracked a smile. "Well, I'll be honest with you. He accused both of us, but since you're the one who is gonna be doing the talking, well . . ."

Woodford grunted and rubbed his face with a big hand.

"And you're the one who's gonna face any potential consequences because your words cannot be used against me, they can only be used against you."

"Why are you telling me this? Are you trying to talk me out of it?"

"I already tried that. Remember?"

Clint nodded.

"But if you are insisting on proffering, if you really think you want to do it, you better understand what you are walking into."

"Okay. I understand," Woodford said quickly. "I do."

"Right," Marko replied doubtfully. No way he could; he hadn't spent five seconds thinking it through.

Woodford shrugged. "I didn't kill her, man. So what do I gotta be worried about?"

"Lots."

"Why?"

Marko sighed heavily. "Come on, Clint. You know the deal." He didn't understand why he had to explain it all the time. "It doesn't matter if you *actually* did it. What matters is whether a jury *believes* that you did."

"Yeah, well, I'm not going to confess to something I didn't do."

"You'd be surprised how many people confess to things they didn't do."

"Not murder."

"Yes, murder," Marko said. He was being harsh, but his job was not to baby his clients. They had to understand that there were consequences to their decisions. "And you could go in there trying to work off a five-year prison sentence and end up spending life in prison."

"I won't confess to murder," Clint said.

"Good. Because you proffer tomorrow."

26

ALLEE

The hostess stand was empty when Allee entered Olde Bulldogs. She'd intentionally shown up between the lunch and dinner rushes; she'd spent years working in restaurants and understood the schedule. If she wanted anyone to speak to her, she couldn't do it during a rush. If the employees were forced to choose between tips and talking, there was no question what they would pick.

The restaurant was empty aside from a table of local politicians. Allee glanced their way and saw the mayor and members of the county board of supervisors. They were all day-drinking here at mid-afternoon.

What a life, she thought. When regular people drank midday, people gave them the side-eye and assumed they were alcoholics. But give a guy a title and a little status and his day-drinking was deemed "business."

Allee walked quickly to the bar, intent on not bringing attention to herself. She didn't belong here, and she'd learned to mind her business long ago—especially with powerful men like those at the nearby table. The bartender—Oliver, wasn't it?—was serving drinks to one of the two men seated on barstools at one end of the bar, so she pulled up a stool at the opposite end, far enough away to provide some privacy.

The bartender finished with the men, typed something into the cash register, and then came over to her. "What can I do you for?" he said as he slid a coaster in front of her. She was right; his nametag read "Oliver."

"I'm on parole," Allee said.

"That sucks."

"It's not bad."

A lot of things in Allee's life sucked, but an absence of booze and drugs were not among them. She'd done far too much of both, and ultimately that's what had landed her in prison. While she would always have the desire to partake, she had learned that one step down that slippery slope would have her sliding all the way back to a pair of handcuffs and a jumpsuit.

"What brings you in?" There was no negativity hanging around the word, which was how Allee knew he was different than most. He probably hadn't been in the joint himself, but he'd known enough who had so he wasn't going to judge her for it.

"I'm working for Marko Bauer."

"Oh, Marko." Oliver's face lit up. "How's he doing? I don't see him much these days."

You shouldn't see him at all. "He's back on the wagon," Allee said.

Marko had experienced a very public arrest a year earlier when Shaffer picked him up for operating while intoxicated, probably after he'd left this very bar, and likely after he'd been overserved by Oliver himself. But Oliver hadn't judged her, so she would return the favor and give him the benefit of the doubt. Besides, that was Marko's business, not hers.

"I miss him," Oliver said.

"His phone still works."

Oliver smiled wryly. "I miss his tips more."

"Bet that." She paused for a long moment, then switched topics to the actual reason for her visit. "I've got a couple of things I want to ask you."

"Cool," Oliver said with a chuckle. "I'll decide if I want to answer when I hear the questions." He reached over and grabbed a glass, then ran a rag around it, clearing off smudge marks.

Fair enough. "You know Jack Daniels, right?"

Oliver shrugged. "Kinda. About as well as I know Marko."

"He's a client of ours."

Bodies of Proof 127

"I wish I could say I was surprised."

"The charge is harassment first based on something that allegedly occurred a few days ago in here."

"You'll have to be more specific." Oliver set the glass aside, grabbed another, and ran the cloth around it. "This is a bar. People are always harassing each other. Part of the deal."

She nodded her understanding. "It allegedly happened on May 29. The reporting party was Leslie Martin."

Oliver's eyes shifted from the glass to meet Allee's. "Leslie." Tension filled the space between them. After a few seconds, he looked down and went back to cleaning the glass. "Okay, yeah. You got my attention," he said. "I think I know what you are talking about."

"Were you here?"

"I'm almost always here."

"So that's a yes?"

"Yes."

"Did you hear him threaten her?"

"No."

"Did anyone else?"

"Not that I know of."

Allee frowned. "If nobody heard it, then how do you know what I'm talking about?"

"Because Leslie told me." He paused, set the glass aside, and started on a new glass. "And then the cops showed up. I don't have much to say to them—you know what I mean?"

"I do."

"Anyway, she tells me she got threatened and the next thing I know the cop showed up. I was just minding my business, you know?"

"What cop?"

"Shaffer."

Why? The man is the captain of police. Why respond to an argument in a bar? "Did you hear what she told him?"

"A little."

"What did you hear?"

"She told him what happened."

"And?"

"And he was a dick."

"What do you mean? Was she upset?"

"Well, yeah, but not about what Daniels had said to her; she was calm about all that. I mean, you know the deal—it ain't something she should have to tolerate, but it's something women have to deal with in this industry. It was Shaffer who got her all worked up."

"Huh," Allee said. "I'm not surprised—he sucks. Always has."

Shaffer's nastiness was legendary, but in this case it sounded like good news. Apparently, nobody had heard Jack threatening Leslie, and she hadn't been upset, so whatever he said was probably not admissible in a court under the excited utterance hearsay exception, meaning that if there was no recording or anything—and unless Leslie turned back up—the State was going to have to dismiss their case against Marko's client.

The men at the other end of the bar started waving their hands and motioning to their drinks. Oliver glanced over at them and then back to Allee. "Duty calls."

"Got it."

"Real quick, what's the other thing you wanted to talk to me about?"

"It's not a real quick kind of question," she said. She motioned toward the men who were growing rowdier by the second. "Get them settled and we can finish up."

Oliver nodded and walked to the other end of the bar.

Allee was pleased with herself. He'd initially been a bit standoffish, but he'd opened up and answered her questions. Hopefully, he'd keep talking when she asked about the information Marko had passed to her from their other client, Clint Woodford. If she could get some good information that would lead to a proffer with Clint, she could chalk the day off as a success. She would've preferred to spend the day working in the food truck, but if she had to be gone, at least she could return with some positive information.

27

WHITNEY

The day was finally starting to wind down. Justice Bites was almost out of food; they'd sold all their favorites, and the line of customers had dwindled to a trickle. People were mostly stopping by to see if they would be there the next day (yes) and when (by nine o'clock).

The lull in business gave Whitney time to catch up on her law firm work. Each day she reviewed Marko's electronic filings to organize his calendar and prepare basic motions. In Iowa, prosecutors did not provide discovery unless and until the defense attorney filed a motion seeking it, which required the prosecutor to turn over any statements or recordings of the defendant and his or her criminal history. Once he had that evidence, Marko would decide whether to file a motion to view any additional evidence. Filing that motion would in turn trigger reciprocal discovery, meaning Marko would have to turn over any evidence in his possession tending to show his client was not guilty—which he did not always want to do.

She pulled her laptop from her bag, positioned it on the ledge used for ordering, and got to work. The first order of business when representing a new client was to establish a client file, then draft and electronically file Marko's entry of appearance. Because Innis had signed the fee agreement and paid double the retainer that morning, they were officially representing him. She created a file under his name, then found the case in the electronic filing system, downloaded the criminal complaint, and dropped it in the case file. In the client organization software, she had stored several templates for commonly used documents. She found the Appearance and the Mandatory Discovery documents and opened them both, filled in the required information, added Marko's electronic signature, and filed them with the court electronically.

With that complete, she returned to the electronic file and downloaded the Initial Appearance Order, dropping it in Innis's file. Then she opened it and read through it. She was looking for specific words. Bond was set at OR, which meant that Innis had been released on his *own recognizance*; he would not be required to post a cash or commercial bond or meet with a pretrial release officer. She noted that in the file where Marko would see it and searched for the date of the preliminary hearing. The court had set the hearing for Wednesday, June 9.

That's weird, Whitney thought as she put the date into Marko's calendar. *They are usually set that quickly when the person is in jail.* Whitney wasn't an attorney and hadn't received any formal legal training, but she had learned a lot about legal procedure over the past year by listening to Marko and reading through court orders. The preliminary hearing date was usually more of a date for the prosecutor to get the formal Trial Information, or indictment, on file. It had to be set within fifteen days of the initial appearance if the person was in jail; on the other hand, if the person had been released, the hearing was supposed to be held within forty-five days of the defendant's arrest.

Someone is either gunning for him or cutting him a break, Whitney thought. With his money, it could be either. Regardless, he was getting favorable treatment. That was going to irritate Allee.

Bang.

Whitney's work was interrupted by the sound of something hitting the side of the food truck. She paused and looked around her, trying to determine the direction of the sound. The Justice Bites truck faced south, she knew. She decided the sound came from her right (the west), which was on the side opposite the awning and seating areas.

Bang! Bang! Bang! The sound came in rapid succession.

Bodies of Proof   131

"Is someone . . . ?" She shook her head. *No.* They couldn't be. Why would anyone hit the truck?

Bang! Bang! Bang!

She closed her laptop and headed for the door, intent on seeing what was happening outside. Marko and Allee were both a good deal larger and probably tougher than she, but she was a mother and had spent years as a high school teacher. She could hold her own when necessary.

Once outside, she found Cameron hanging something on the side of their truck.

"Dale!" she cried. "What are you doing?"

Cameron didn't look up and continued hitting the side of the truck.

"What are you doing? Stop it!"

He'd been parked across from them since the start of that morning, and she had only seen one person approach his truck for a purchase: the detective who had come by earlier that morning.

"People need to know who you lot are," Cameron said. He stepped back and admired his handiwork.

Whitney moved closer so she could read the sign he had hammered into their truck. "Powered by Felony Convictions?" Whitney read aloud. "You can't say that!"

"If people knew how corrupt you folks are, they'd come and buy from me," Cameron snarled. "But instead, they keep coming here. Well, they need to know they are supporting criminals."

"I am not a criminal," Whitney said, placing her hands on her hips. "Dale, everyone makes mistakes. Marko and Allee have paid for theirs. Allee, especially, has totally turned her life around. She's productive, works hard—I trust her to care for my child. You'd understand that if you spent any time getting to know us."

"I don't want to get to know you. And you were arrested for raping a kid."

She felt her ears getting hot. "I was," she admitted. "But as you know, the charges were dropped after he admitted he made it all up. I was and am innocent. Would you want people going around calling you a criminal if I alleged you raped me and then later rescinded it?"

"You would never do that," Cameron said, his face reddening.

"And why wouldn't I?" Whitney cocked an eyebrow. When he didn't respond, she answered her own question. "Because I'm a good person and you know it. So take that nonsense down." She pointed at the sign. "If you don't, you're going to end up dealing with Allee and Marko, and you don't want that."

"I can hold my own." He lifted his sleeve and patted his Marines tattoo.

Whitney shook her head and sighed heavily. "Dale, take it down before I have to report you for harassment and destruction of property," she pleaded. "I don't want to get you in trouble, but you can't leave that there."

"Fine," he grumbled. He pulled the sign down. "But you are ruining my life."

She put her hands on her hips and measured him. "I think we could be friends if you would give it a chance."

"*Umm, hello! Is anyone here?*"

Someone was calling from the front of the truck.

"Yeah, give us a second!" Whitney shouted back.

She recognized the young man's voice. He could wait.

"Go on," she said to Cameron. "Come back when you are ready to play nice." She flashed him her sweetest first-day-of-school smile.

"I don't want to play nice," Dale grumbled as he walked away.

"*Yet,*" Whitney said under her breath. "You don't want to play nice *yet.*"

She watched as Cameron departed, then stopped and gestured to the unseen customer and gave him the universal *I'm watching you* gesture.

Well, at least he's good for something, Whitney thought as she headed back into the truck. A nosy neighbor was not always a negative. Once inside, she forced a smile when she saw the all-too-familiar face.

"Mr. Innis. You're back."

"I want to talk to Marko."

"He's not back from court yet."

"When will he be back?"

Innis was staring at her with his penetrating, unblinking eyes. She glanced at her watch as much to break his stare as to feign checking the time. "In the next thirty minutes or so." When Innis didn't respond, she pointed at the table under the awning. "Feel free to wait over there. If you care to wait, that is."

Innis nodded. He started to move in that direction, then paused. He turned and looked back over his shoulder. "Is your hair always that curly?"

"Yes," Whitney said.

She had naturally curly hair. With everything going on these days, she usually didn't fight it, and instead put gel in it and left for the day. When she was younger, she'd spent a lot of time straightening it or teasing it into gentle waves.

"You can't, like, flat-iron it or something?"

What the hell? "I *can*. I just choose not to. Why do you ask?"

Innis shrugged. "I think it would look nice that way."

Whitney seethed quietly. *Who the hell does this punk think he is?* That was completely inappropriate, but on par with what she'd seen from him to this point.

28

ALLEE

Allee watched as Oliver poured three shots and two large draft beers, then carried both beers and two of the shots to the men at the other end of the bar.

That shot better be for Oliver, she thought.

She wasn't surprised when Oliver placed the shot in front of her. "It's rumple mint," he said.

"I don't care what it is. Get it away from me," she said with a shooing gesture.

"On them," Oliver explained, nodding toward the pair of men.

Allee looked at the men, who were middle-aged and balding with beer bellies large enough to look six months pregnant. One of them made a kissing motion and ran his tongue along his chapped lips.

"Still a no?" Oliver quirked an eyebrow. "I mean, how can you resist?" he deadpanned.

"It's now a hard no."

He obediently retrieved the shot and set it between the men.

The man who had made the kissing gesture looked at the glass and then at her. "Too good for us, eh?"

"Well, there's that," she agreed. "And I'm sober."

"What the hell are you doing in a bar, then?"

Bodies of Proof

"That's none of your damn business."

"Feisty one, ain't she?" he said to the other man. "I think I'll be taking her home—whether she likes it or not."

"Touch me and you will regret it," Allee said quickly.

"See? I told you—she's feisty!" He licked his lips again, this time slower. Surprisingly, it was even grosser the second time.

"I'd take her word for it," Oliver said, smacking the table. "You see those tats?" He gestured toward Allee. "Courtesy of Mitchellville."

"Mitchellville, eh?" the man said. "Do you all become a bunch of dyk—"

Allee slammed the countertop and grabbed a nearby cocktail knife. "Finish that sentence and I'll turn you into a eunuch."

"What the hell is a eunuch?" the man asked with a laugh.

Oliver leaned over and said something in a low tone. The man stopped laughing.

"Jesus. Calm down, lady. We were just havin' a little fun."

My ass. Allee brandished the knife. "You have your fun, I'll have mine."

"Psycho," the man grumbled as he turned his back on Allee.

Allee looked at the knife in her hand, then dropped it when she came to her senses. This place. These people. They brought out the worst in her. Familiar playgrounds and familiar playmates. She needed to finish her conversation with Oliver and get out of there before she did something she really regretted.

Oliver made his way back to her. "That was one way to shut them up," he said, the hint of a smile forming at the corners of his lips. "Now that you are weaponless, I think I'm ready to resume our conversation."

"Do you know Clint Woodford?"

"Maybe," Oliver said, again picking up a nearby glass and a rag. It was a tell.

"I work for Marko Bauer, remember? He's a client of ours. I'm not trying to jam him up."

"Judging by your little display a few minutes ago, you might be more worried about getting yourself jammed up."

"Mind your business, and I'll mind mine."

"I am minding my business." He ran the rag around the outside of the wine glass, polishing it. "You're the one asking questions."

Why does everything have to be hard? "Look, I'm just trying to help get Clint out of trouble. Can you help me out?"

"That depends."

"On what?"

"On what you need from me. Ask your questions. I can't promise I'll answer them, but then again, maybe I will."

"Clint said that Rebecca and Leslie both worked here before they disappeared."

"Everyone in town knows that," Oliver replied dismissively.

"He also said that Rebecca was receiving creepy notes before she disappeared." Oliver froze, the rag still against the glass. When he didn't reply, she pressed on. "He said someone had been coming in regularly and leaving the notes behind."

Oliver slowly lowered the glass, setting it to the side. She had his full attention now, so she continued. "He also said that *you* have copies of those letters."

"Me?" Oliver placed a hand on his chest, but his reaction seemed far too exaggerated to be honest.

"According to Clint, after Rebecca disappeared, the person stopped coming in and the notes stopped, as well."

Oliver was watching her closely. He knew something. "Okay," he said uncertainly. "I guess that would make sense."

"Oliver, tell me what's going on. Please."

He shot a quick glance in both directions, then leaned across the bar and whispered, "Both girls worked here—that's true. Guy coming in is true. Someone leaving notes is true. Guy stopped showing is kinda true."

Hope surged in Allee's chest. "Do you have the notes?"

"Not anymore."

Shit. "Where are they?"

"Can't say."

Can't, or won't? "Who was the guy? The one leaving the letters?"

"I never said it was a dude."

"Well, was it a guy?"

"Yes."

What the hell? "Who was he?"

"Can't say." Oliver's gaze skittered away.

Liar! "Can't? Or won't?"

Oliver shrugged. He knew, but he wouldn't tell her. He probably wouldn't tell anyone. She wasn't about to let it go—she was too close. "Did the same person start showing up when Leslie was working?"

"The same guy showed up off and on."

"Did the notes start up again with Leslie?"

"Yes."

"What did they say?"

Oliver shrugged. "I never read them." He couldn't hold her gaze.

Another lie. "So it was the same guy leaving them?"

"I never said the guy was connected to the letters." Oliver picked up a new glass and began polishing it furiously. "All I said was that the letters started when the guy was coming and stopped when he stopped. Then started again."

Allee was about to unload on him when someone entered the bar, causing the place to go quiet. Allee's back was to the entrance, but by the expression on Oliver's face, and the faces of the drunks at the end of the bar, whoever it was didn't make them happy. She swung around in her chair to see Jenkins walking up to the bar. He wore street clothes, but he wasn't fooling anyone.

Shit, Allee thought irritably. *Interview over.* There was no way Oliver would answer questions with a cop at the bar. And who could blame him?

29

MARKO

The final few hours of the workday were usually his least busy—clients usually didn't call after four o'clock, and appointments were always scheduled in the mornings. It was his wind-down time, affording him an hour or so to catch up on paperwork and take a breath. He was looking forward to getting back to Justice Bites and calling it a day.

"Hi," Marko greeted Whitney as he entered the truck.

"Hello," she said stiffly.

She's pissed about having to staff the truck. I get it; she signed on as a legal assistant. "Allee should be back soon," he offered.

"Yeah?" Whitney lifted an eyebrow. "For what? The last few minutes we are open? How very helpful of her," she said sarcastically.

It wasn't that Marko wasn't sympathetic, but there was nothing he could do about it. He needed Allee to investigate. Whitney had offered to help with investigations, but she didn't have the same presence as Allee, who could go into any environment without hesitation and ask the hard questions. Whitney was far too polite.

"By the way, you have a client waiting," Whitney added.

"A client? Who?"

She nodded toward the black limo idling in the parking lot.

Bodies of Proof 139

James Innis. "Again? I've met with him once, he called Allee once, and now he wants to talk again?"

"This is the second time he's come while you were out," Whitney said. "High maintenance."

"What did he want the first time?"

Whitney shrugged. "He said he wanted food."

Marko shook his head. Innis was apparently going to be one of those clients who sucked all the energy out of him. But the fee was worth it—for now. He would bill the man for every second he took of their time, and it would not be cheap.

"All right." Marko tapped the ledge outside the ordering window with his hand. "I'll go talk to him. Allee will be back soon, I promise," he said again.

Whitney rolled her eyes. "Right, boss. I'm not going to bet on it."

"You're onto me," Marko replied, flashing his best smile as he made his way toward the awning where Innis was seated at the table.

"You're here. *Again*," Marko said, lowering himself into the seat across from Innis.

The younger man appraised Marko. "We didn't finish our conversation this morning," he explained.

"Yeah," Marko acknowledged. "And as I recall, I said I'd call you tomorrow."

"I couldn't wait."

"Okay." Marko made a show of removing his laptop, a pen, and a legal pad from his bag. "What's up?" he asked as he entered his password.

Innis didn't answer the question. "Do you always have an audience?" he asked instead, gesturing over his shoulder toward the Freedom Burgers food truck.

Marko followed Innis's hand and saw Cameron at his serving window with binoculars held up to his eyes. He lacked even the decency to look away when caught. Marko had often wondered whether Cameron could be the worst private investigator ever operating undercover, or if he was just a terrible businessman, stubbornly willing to burn every dollar he had just to aggravate Marko and his team.

"Guy's harmless." Marko shrugged.

"He's a Marine," Innis said.

"He has a Marine tattoo; that doesn't mean shit. Lots of posers out there," Marko corrected.

"People can just get that tattoo?"

"Why not?"

Innis shrugged and seemed to relax a little.

"All right. So," Marko said, rubbing his hands together and focusing his attention on the laptop screen. "You've been charged with operating while intoxicated."

"I know."

Marko ignored the sarcasm. "The complaint is signed by Shaffer," he observed, his tone dripping with disgust. "Is that who arrested you?"

Innis shrugged. "Dunno."

"It says here that he stopped you on May 29 on Main Street."

"Yeah."

"Will there be any video footage that shows you were inside one of the downtown bars?" There were quite a few hole-in-the-wall bars downtown, but there was only one place where Innis might fit in, and it seemed to be coming up all too often today.

"I was at Olde Bulldogs."

Marko sighed. "Of course you were."

Innis shrugged.

"It also says here that you refused field sobriety testing, the preliminary breath test, and the breath test at the station. Is that true?"

Innis nodded his agreement.

Marko noticed his client watching him carefully. "Good." Innis's refusals to cooperate with law enforcement gave him something to work with. "That means the only evidence they have is that you smelled of alcohol, which Shaffer would undoubtedly say whether you did or not, and anything dumb you might have said or done on the body camera footage."

"I didn't say anything dumb."

"So you say," Marko replied. "Trust me, what you remember might be different from reality. It's the, er, stress of the moment." *Or the haze of the alcohol.* Expecting a retort, Marko looked to Innis. Instead of replying angrily, his client was staring off to the west, not appearing to pay attention. "You understand what I'm saying?" Marko asked.

Innis kept his eyes fixed on the horizon. After a moment, he spoke quietly. "Question: is it true that if I confess something to you that you can't tell anyone?"

Marko felt the hair on the back of his neck stand up. "Not necessarily. As a general rule, you don't want to confess anything," he advised Innis in even, clipped words. "While it is the rule that I can't tell anyone what I hear about a lot of subjects, it is also true that a confession can limit your defense if you take the stand because I cannot present evidence that I know isn't true. In other words, if you tell me something and if I believe it to be true, I can't go back later and present testimony to the contrary. Does that make sense?" he concluded, holding his breath.

"It does," Innis replied, nodding his understanding. "But I'm not talking about this case. I mean about something else."

Marko slowly released the breath he was holding. *Something isn't right.* "What are we talking about?" he asked.

"Like, if I were to confess to a different crime," Innis replied. "To you. To, you know, like, to get it off my chest. Could you tell anyone else?"

"That depends," Marko answered carefully, fully assessing his client for perhaps the first time. He was young, but there was something in his eyes— a shrewdness, perhaps—that gave Marko pause.

"On what?"

"I guess the way to explain it is that it has to do with the level of completion."

"What does that mean?" Innis asked, quirking an eyebrow.

Marko took another deep breath, then released it. "I guess the best way to explain it is this," he began. "If a crime has already occurred, and I have been retained in connection with that crime, I am bound by the standard attorney-client privilege, and I am prohibited from telling anyone. But if the crime is only in progress, or if me telling someone could save a life or prevent severe property damage or something like that, I could report it. But I don't have to."

"Would you?"

"Would I what?"

"Report it? If I told you about a crime in progress?" Innis was leaning forward now, seemingly enthralled by their conversation. There was a glint in his eyes that Marko hadn't seen earlier that day.

"It would depend."

"On what?"

"On what I just told you. The crime itself, what the status was—like that." Marko was getting irritated with the line of questioning. "But I'm obviously not law enforcement's biggest cheerleader, so unless it's murder or kidnapping or something like that, I'd probably keep it to myself."

"I see," Innis said thoughtfully. He was silent for a long moment, then added, "What about the rest of your team?"

"You mean Whitney and Allee?"

"Yeah."

"They work for me, so they are bound by the same privilege."

"Oh, good," Innis said.

"What's good about that?"

Innis shrugged but didn't answer. "You know, you're probably right. We've talked enough for one day." He stood. "We can talk tomorrow."

"Maybe not tom—"

"I'll call or stop by. Will you be here?"

"Yeah," Marko said. Clearly, his client was going to show up whether he liked it or not. He sighed heavily, remembering this client was paying full price—double, really. "We're almost always in Franklin these days."

Marko had enough business in the area now. He didn't have to drive to the surrounding counties as much anymore. If business kept up like this—especially if he could land a few more like Innis here—he could look into opening a brick-and-mortar office on the square. He watched as Innis turned and walked to the long black car still idling at the curb and got inside without looking back.

Oddballs weren't unusual in his line of business, of course. He clicked a couple buttons and pulled up the electronic file for Jack Daniels. He opened the police report, ready to start taking notes. He felt around his pockets, then lifted the laptop, then looked under the table in an effort to find his pen. He'd had it a few minutes before. *What the hell happened to it?* It was a cheap ballpoint with chew marks on the end—a habit Marko had developed after getting sober. It was a small price to pay for sobriety, so he hadn't tried too hard to quit the habit.

Oh well. It's not the end of the world.

He'd just have to get a new one.

30

JENKINS

Jenkins got in his car and started the engine, but didn't go anywhere. Instead, he sat and considered his next move. Too much to do in a short time, with conflicting priorities. He still needed to get to the veterinarian's office; someone there had the small ballerina found in Shep's collar, and he'd really like to discuss the dog's wounds. But he also needed to get over to Olde Bulldogs and interview the employees since Leslie and Rebecca had both worked there.

What he really needed was an investigator to assist him, but there was no way in hell he could trust anyone at the Franklin Police Department—not with it being led by Shaffer (who was corrupt) and Chief Brown (who was weak). Given that, he couldn't turn any part of the investigation over to anyone trained or overseen by them.

He made his decision and called the veterinary office. It was the only one in town.

"Vet hospital," a young, energetic woman said after two rings.

"Hello, my name is Special Agent Jenkins. I'm with the Iowa Division of Criminal Investigation. I am hoping I can speak with a veterinarian."

"I'm sorry. Dr. Minsk went home for the day. She'll be back tomorrow morning at eight o'clock sharp—you can set your watch by her."

"Will she be available to see me that early?"

Bodies of Proof　　145

"She sees her first patient at nine o'clock."

"I'll drop by tomorrow, then," Jenkins said. He ended the call and put the car in gear. The dilemma had resolved itself. He still had more than enough to do, but it was no use wishing for something he wouldn't or couldn't have.

Moments later he was making his way down Main Street, looking for Olde Bulldogs. From what he understood, it was the town's only upscale dining place. It was easily located; the exterior decor reminded him of a chain family restaurant in a Des Moines suburb.

The parking along Main Street, including the spots in front of the restaurant, were all metered. He didn't have any change and didn't want to pay, so he drove around the block to the side of the building, pulling in behind an old truck he thought he recognized. As he entered the restaurant, he checked his watch. It was nearly five o'clock—dinnertime in many small towns, especially with the older clientele—so a hostess was already posted at the stand. She was young—too young, really—but then again, his daughters were now in their mid-twenties, and they still felt like babies to him.

"Table for one?" she asked, picking up a menu.

"No, thank you. I'll just sit at the bar."

"Sure." She gestured to her right, around a wall he couldn't see over. "It's just that way."

He hesitated. "If you don't mind me asking, how long have you worked here?"

"Maybe like a couple of months?"

"Do you know Leslie Martin?"

She smiled shyly. "Yeah, a little. I don't talk with her much, you know? I mean, she wasn't my trainer. But I, like, know who she is. Is she okay?"

Jenkins ignored the question. "You seem like a young woman who notices things," he lied. "Did you notice anything strange going on around here the last couple of days?"

The girl shrugged. "No, not really. I mean, I'm still the new girl, you know? I'm still kinda trying to figure out how to do my job without screwing up." She shrugged and flashed another shy smile before sobering. "Are you, like, her dad or something?"

"I'm a cop. Thanks for your help."

He made his way around the wall toward the bar. En route, he passed through a large seating area that was mostly empty. Even so, he could hear the volume of conversation lessen as soon as the patrons saw him. It wasn't surprising; he was a stranger in a small-town tavern on a Monday night. The bar was long and rectangular, with a mirror behind it and liquor bottles lined along the wall. Two very drunk men sat at the far end. Allee was seated at the near end, talking with the bartender. Her back was to him, but he would recognize her bright blonde pixie cut and prison tattoos anywhere.

The bartender looked up as he approached. He hadn't been smiling before, but whatever mirth was in his expression disappeared the moment he spotted Jenkins.

He'd been made.

Allee spun in her chair, clearly annoyed.

"Hello there," Jenkins said, dropping into the seat next to her.

She ignored him, and moved one seat over.

"What can I get you?" the bartender said.

Jenkins quickly read the name tag. "Oliver, is it?"

"What can I get you?" Oliver repeated.

"A ginger ale would be great."

Oliver made a point of rolling his eyes before sauntering off to get the drink.

"What are you doing here?" Allee growled. "I was talking to him."

"Can't we both talk to him?" Jenkins said.

"No. And you're making my job difficult—as you know."

Jenkins looked around. "Why does it seem like everyone hates me in here?"

"Because they *do*," Allee hissed. "You're a cop."

"They don't know that."

She gave him a sideways glance. "Yeah. They do."

"And here I thought I fit right in."

Allee shook her head and turned away from him, focusing her gaze on Oliver. "Trust me, you don't."

"Really? Why?"

Bodies of Proof   147

"Because you look, smell, and act like a cop. You might as well be wearing a sign around your neck," she snapped. "Now I'd appreciate it if you left me alone, so Oliver doesn't think I'm working with you."

Jenkins was watching Allee closely, trying to make her uncomfortable. She was smart, resourceful, poised, and—oddly enough—seemed more trustworthy than any of the Franklin PD officers. In another life, he'd gladly throw in with her, but because her boss was a defense attorney it would be a major conflict of interest.

"Here's your pop." Oliver placed the glass firmly on the bar in front of Jenkins. "Can I get you anything else?" he asked, clearly expecting Jenkins to decline the offer.

Jenkins forced a tight smile. "I don't think so. Not right now, anyway. I was wondering if you'd answer a few questions."

"No." Oliver crossed his arms.

Allee issued a resigned sigh. "I'm out of here," she said, waving to Oliver.

Jenkins watched Allee in the mirror as she rushed off. "Was it something I said?" He was trying to sound casual, like the men Oliver usually served. "What scared her off?"

"*You* did."

"Me?" Jenkins feigned a lack of understanding. "Why?"

"Because you're a cop. In here, uninvited, asking questions. They don't like it." He jerked his head to indicate the two men at the end of the bar. "And she certainly didn't like it."

Jenkins side-eyed the pair of men, who had stopped talking and were watching him closely. "I see," he said. He took a sip of flat ginger ale. "I take it you aren't too thrilled with me being here, either."

"Gee, what gave you that idea?" Oliver asked.

"I just want to ask about Rebecca and Leslie. Seems to me that if you care about them at all, you'd be willing to answer a few simple questions. I'm just trying to find out what happened to them."

"And I just want to do my job, which is to serve customers," Oliver countered. "And right now, the two I have are about to leave because you are making them uncomfortable. Nobody wants to drink around a cop."

"Okay," Jenkins said, tossing a five-dollar bill and a business card on the bartop. He knew when something was a lost cause. "I'll get out of your hair. You change your mind, let me know."

"Sure thing."

On his way out, Jenkins didn't encounter any employees. Outside, the heat was starting to break, which was a relief. Iowa's summer had arrived, and with it, humidity like a wet blanket. When he reached his car, the truck —which he now knew had been Allee's—was gone. She'd disappeared faster than a cricket in a snake tank.

He checked his watch and decided to return to the law enforcement center to see what the uniformed officers were thinking. He couldn't trust anyone on Shaffer's staff, of course, but office gossip often carried grains of truth. If he could get someone talking, and setting aside the usual cop gripes and bullshitting, he might learn something.

He parked in the same spot as he had earlier that day. It had been a long one, and his initial arrival felt like a lifetime ago. The food trucks were gone, and the courthouse had closed at four-thirty. He stepped out of his car, took a deep breath of the thick, warm air, and decided the word to describe the now-empty courthouse square was *tranquil*. The old court-house was beautiful, of course; they didn't build them like this anymore. They couldn't. It was way too expensive and far too controversial to build something to symbolize and memorialize law and order.

As he turned in a circle to take it all in, his gaze traveled from the large pillars to the stone steps, then to the expansive front lawn. A small, colorful object in the grass caught his attention.

Probably nothing, but then again.

His instincts kicked in. He approached slowly, scanning the grass between himself and the small object carefully. When he was within several feet of the object, he stopped, crouched, and studied it. He retrieved his phone and snapped several pictures of the small item from several angles, then placed his keys nearby and took a photo to give perspective on the item's size. At last, he donned a pair of gloves and picked it up.

He turned the item in his hands, wound the tiny little gear, then watched and listened intently. The lid opened slowly, and a tiny ballerina arose, spinning in circles to a tune he couldn't quite place. It was a music box.

Bodies of Proof

He suddenly felt as if someone was watching. He turned in a circle while the music played, looking for an unknown observer. Seeing none, he tried to identify the tune coming from the little box. It was familiar, but he couldn't quite place it.

Then he remembered: "Ding-Dong, The Witch Is Dead."

What a bizarre musical accompaniment to a dancing ballerina.

He dropped the box into an evidence bag. It could be nothing; it might not mean anything. It could be a coincidence.

But cops didn't believe in coincidences.

31

WHITNEY

"Is he gone?" Whitney asked.

She poked her head out of the ordering window and observed Marko under the table on his hands and knees. "What are you looking for?"

"He's gone," Marko answered. "But I can't find my damn pen. I swear I set it on the table, but I'll be damned if I can find it. I thought maybe it rolled off."

"Who cares?" Whitney said. "They are cheap pens. Get a new one."

Typical man, she thought. Always losing things. If she had a dime for every minute she'd spent helping her ex-husband look for stuff, she'd be a rich woman. This had to be the tenth pen Marko had lost in the last five days, which was why as office manager she'd been buying the cheapest ones the office supply place carried. When she had placed the order and asked Marko to sign the invoice, he had complained, telling her to buy the more expensive ones. She'd refused and told him that he'd have to keep track of the ones she got before she bothered purchasing anything of more value. Once again, he was proving her right.

"It's got to be about quitting time, right?" Marko asked as he crawled out from under the table.

Whitney looked at the clock. It was after five o'clock, and the drive back to Ostlund was a full hour. They needed to leave. Arlo had been at

Bodies of Proof

Adaline's house since the bus dropped him off after school. He'd want to see her, and she wanted to see him.

"It's past time," she replied. "We need to go. Where's Allee?" She tried to keep the panic from her voice.

"She's got to be back soon, right?" Marko said.

Whitney didn't answer—there wasn't time. Instead, she closed the ordering window and got out of the truck. She made her way over to Marko's setup and began to break it down, folding chairs and the table, then rolling up the awning. Marko, of course, didn't bother to help her. Occasionally, she glanced over to Freedom Burgers. The truck was still sitting there, and Cameron was still watching them. Despite a lack of business, he never left before they did.

She'd spent the last year trying to ignore him. He had every right to watch them in a public setting, of course, but it was disconcerting. Despite the passage of time, his surveillance still sent a sense of dread running up and down her spine. His hatred of them was clear, and although she had tried to make peace, he had rebuffed her attempts at a truce. Of course, neither Marko nor Allee had backed her or bothered trying.

"Do you think she's all right?" Whitney asked while she worked.

"She's Allee," Marko replied absentmindedly. She watched while he smoothed the grass with a scuffed shoe, then bent to part blades of grass, still focused on finding a fifty-cent pen. "She's always fine."

She pursed her lips. Marko didn't know Allee like she did. For one thing, he was a man—he couldn't. For another, she and Allee lived together. And while Allee portrayed unwavering strength around others, Whitney had seen the softer side of her roommate—especially when she was with Arlo. She wasn't all sharp edges and stinging remarks. That was just a defense mechanism.

"Look," Marko said, pointing to the west. "There she is. Just in time to help you."

Whitney turned to see Allee jogging toward them.

"Sorry," Allee said between breaths after she had joined them. "I had to take my truck back to the storage facility."

Whitney nodded, trying to keep her expression neutral. Now that she knew Allee was safe, her resentment was increasing.

When their eyes met, Allee apologized. "I was interviewing witnesses and lost track of time," she said. "I'm sorry. I know you want to get back to Arlo."

"I *need* to," Whitney corrected her. "It's not a matter of *want*." She tossed the last piece of awning into the back of the truck and closed the door. "Let's go. We don't need to waste any more time talking about it."

"Right," Allee said.

Allee hopped in the driver's seat, as always, while Whitney and Marko slid in beside her. On the way back, Allee back-briefed them on the progress she'd made. She started with promising news about Jack Daniels's case. To Whitney, it sounded like the State was going to have to dismiss the case against him due to lack of evidence.

Allee was reviewing her discussion with the bartender at Olde Bulldogs when Whitney's phone started buzzing. Reaching for it, she saw a message from her ex-husband.

Where are you? Leo had typed.

None of your business.

Leo wasn't dissuaded. *I'm at your house and you aren't here.*

Whitney took a deep breath and held it as she messaged him. *You have no right to be at my house.*

Where is Arlo?

At Adaline's house, like always.

Are you on your way home?

Yes.

I want to see you.

Not this. *You can see Arlo. Take him to the park if you want. I'll let Adaline know you are on your way.*

He didn't respond. She held the phone tightly for a few minutes while she continued holding and releasing deep breaths. In the background, she could hear Allee talking, updating Marko, but she was unable to focus on their discussion—she had bigger issues. If Leo wanted, he could see Arlo. Arlo wanted to spend time with Leo, and that was good. Fathers were important. But she had no desire to see or spend time with her ex—not after what he'd done to her, and what he'd *not* done for her. She searched for Adaline's number.

Bodies of Proof

"Is everything okay?" Allee asked.

Whitney shook her head. "Leo is at the house."

Leo's unannounced visits were problematic. They were an extreme and conscious invasion of her privacy, of course, but they made Arlo so happy—just as Leo knew they would. Arlo was a child, too young to understand what had happened between his parents. All he knew was that he didn't get to see his father as much as he used to.

"That's creepy," Allee said. "I'm sorry, Whitney, but your ex creeps me out. I seriously can't decide whether he still loves you or wants to skin you and wear you like a sweater."

"Allee, come on! You can't say that," Whitney heard Marko scold as she clicked on Adaline's number and brought the phone to her ear. It rang a couple of times before Adaline answered.

"Yes, dearie," came Adaline's sweet voice. "Arlo is doing just fine, if that's the reason you are calling."

"I'm on my way home," Whitney said. "But Leo is in town and—"

"That's odd," Adaline said.

Ostlund wasn't a place where people just dropped by. The interstate had long ago bypassed it, and the town had died to the point where the only points of interest—if you could call them that—were a gas station and a little-used park. To end up in Ostlund, you had to be heading for Ostlund. Leo was not there by chance.

"I know," Whitney continued. "But if he comes over, I told him he could take Arlo to the park."

"Okay," Adaline said uncertainly.

"But don't tell Arlo his father is coming. I don't want to get his hopes up in case his dad doesn't show."

"Understood," Adaline said. "He's in good hands. Do you want to talk to him for a few minutes?"

"Yes."

Whitney listened while Adaline handed Arlo the phone. He was a bubbly, happy little boy, and every second talking with him made her heart leap. While she listened to Arlo, she occasionally checked her watch. They talked long enough that Whitney knew Leo wasn't going to retrieve Arlo. It had been a ploy. The thought made her blood boil. Leo had broken her heart—that was bad enough. She wasn't going to allow him to hurt Arlo. If he thought he could manipulate her into getting back together with him, then he was barking up the wrong tree.

She was about to tell Arlo to hang up and that she'd be there soon when a text came in from Leo. She put Arlo on speaker and allowed him to talk to everyone in the truck while she navigated to the text. Arlo loved Allee and was becoming more comfortable with Marko. Allee and Arlo were debating the differences between ninjas and warriors when Whitney read the message.

You'll see me whether you like it or not, Princess.

She closed out of the messaging application, her heart racing. *What the hell was that? Was that a threat? He was just upset. He'll calm down.* She would hate to report him to law enforcement. Arlo was dealing with enough already. He didn't need to worry about his mom putting his dad in jail.

"What's going on?" Allee asked.

"What? Sorry." Whitney shook her head. "Nothing. Everything is fine. Just fine."

32

JENKINS

Jenkins manipulated his phone, turning off the camera function so he could make a call. "Mia," he began. "Are you still in Franklin?"

"Just getting ready to leave. Why?"

"So you're done processing the scene?"

"Yeah. We've got a shit-ton of stuff to take back to the lab." There was only one criminalistics laboratory in the State of Iowa, and that was in Ankeny.

"I've got one more piece of evidence I'd like you to examine," he said, glancing down at the evidence bag with the music box. "I'd like to hand it off to you so that we don't have any issues with chain of custody."

"What is it?"

"A music box."

"With a ballerina?"

"Yeah."

"Where are you?"

"Standing on the lawn in front of the courthouse in Franklin."

"I'll be right there. Don't mess with it."

Jenkins smiled wryly and bit his tongue. "See you soon."

While he waited, Jenkins studied the route he'd taken so he could inform Mia and enable her to examine the scene without spending unnecessary time at it. He had already decided his next step was to go to the law enforcement center, but it could wait. Six o'clock was shift change for most agencies, and because they generally worked twelve-hour shifts, they would be well into their changeover briefs and not interested in answering his questions. Better to wait right here.

True to her word, Mia arrived within minutes. When he handed her the bag, she studied the ballerina for a long moment.

"What do you think?" he asked.

"It looks a lot like the pieces you found along the trail where we believe both women were abducted." She paused a moment. "But visual inspection doesn't do us a whole lot of good. We won't know for sure until we get it to a lab."

"Then get it to the lab."

A nearby church bell started chiming. Six o'clock. *Shift change.* "You'd better get going," Jenkins said. "It's going to get dark soon, and I don't need you hitting a deer or a cow on your way back and destroying my evidence."

"You don't have to tell me twice." She looked around the town square. "I'm ready to leave Hicksville here and get back to the city."

He watched as she walked to her state car, opened the trunk, filled out some paperwork, and then placed the little box in the trunk before closing it. As she drove away, he felt a twinge of jealousy but quickly dismissed those thoughts. He had a job to do, and the sooner he got it done, the sooner he too could get back to Des Moines.

The gatekeeper at the law enforcement center was new, but that was to be expected. The civilian staff didn't follow the same twelve-hour shift rule as uniformed officers. The woman now manning the station looked tired and bored. She buzzed him through without asking for identification (which was beneficial to him, but posed an obvious security risk).

He passed several officers, noting that none made eye contact or said a word. They kept a wide berth, crossing to the opposite side of the hall as Jenkins passed. *What has Shaffer been telling them? Probably nothing good.*

Shaffer and the chief were gone for the day, of course. As the leadership, they were the only two men in the department who perpetually worked the day shift only. Jenkins began looking for the lieutenant on duty. He walked

Bodies of Proof 157

unmolested down the hallway and found a harried-looking man in his late thirties seated in an office—a sure sign of rank.

Jenkins knocked on the door.

The man looked up. There were dark circles under his eyes. "Come in," he said, rising to his feet. "You must be Special Agent Jenkins."

"I am."

"I'm Lieutenant Dan Davis."

"Lieutenant Dan? As in *Run, Forrest*—"

"Yeah. I get that a lot," Davis replied, cutting him off. "I almost wish I didn't get the promotion."

Jenkins shrugged. "At least it's easy to remember."

"There's that," Davis said as he began making his way around the desk. "You're probably looking for a place to work."

"Yeah."

"We've got two interview rooms," Davis said. "I'll set you up in room two."

"I appreciate that, but are you sure you won't need it?"

"Nah. Monday nights are usually pretty quiet."

Judging by the exhaustion in Davis's eyes, it appeared to Jenkins to have been one hell of a weekend.

"I've got small children," Davis explained. "My youngest is six months. We don't get much sleep these days. Come on, I'll show you around."

Davis led the way down the hallway. Again, they passed several officers who gave them a wide berth. Most failed to even acknowledge Davis, let alone Jenkins.

"I did put on antiperspirant this morning," Jenkins joked.

"Yeah, well, you still smell like Des Moines."

"Why is that such a bad thing?"

Davis gave him a sidelong look. "Agent Jenkins, you aren't the first special agent sent here to *assist* us." He made air quotes with his fingers as he explained his staff's reluctance to acknowledge Jenkins. "Historically, ya'll come in here, tell us what to do, don't explain anything, and treat us like we don't matter. Then you declare victory and leave, and we're left here to clean up the mess."

"I'm not that guy."

158   JAMES CHANDLER & LAURA SNIDER

"Tell me what you've done differently," Davis challenged.

Jenkins reflected on his actions that day. Certainly, he'd been businesslike, but in his defense, his welcoming party had been Shaffer. Franklin PD had been minimally cooperative since his arrival. DCI agents were highly trained. If others had been to the town, and if they'd gotten the same kind of reception as he had, then it was little wonder agents kept their distance and their mouths shut. He gave some thought to explaining all this, but didn't trust Davis enough to waste his breath.

"I got my answer," Davis observed after waiting while Jenkins mulled. "Is there some kind of license they issue you guys in Des Moines?"

"Nah." Jenkins shook his head. "We're dicks all on our own. I think maybe we were born that way."

"Thought so." Davis stopped outside a door labeled *Room 2*. "You can set up in here," he said, unlocking the door and flipping on the lights. There was a table at the center of the room and two chairs, but nothing more.

"I like how you decorated the place. I hope you didn't go to all this trouble just for me."

"Thanks," Davis replied stoically.

Jenkins stepped into the room. He turned to thank Davis, but the lieutenant was already gone. Which was fine; if Davis thought special agents were the source of his department's problems, he was no better than Shaffer or Brown. Anyone who didn't see Franklin PD's leadership for what it was wouldn't be a lot of help, anyway.

He pulled up a chair and sat with his back to the wall, facing a small mirror. He made sure that he was positioned to block the view of the camera in the room before he opened his laptop. He had little doubt he was assigned this room with malice aforethought.

He had received a lot of emails over the course of the day, but he was interested in one message only. He found it, buried with several he'd been sent just within the last hour. The subject line read, *Preliminary Autopsy Report, RE: Rebecca Calloway*.

"Bingo," Jenkins said aloud. After a cursory look around the room, he opened the attachment.

Special Agent Jenkins,

Bodies of Proof 159

I have completed my preliminary examination of Rebecca Calloway's body. Preliminarily, I am ruling her death a homicide. The official cause will likely be asphyxia. I believe she was suffocated rather than strangled. I see no evidence of that. At this point, I believe her air supply was cut off somehow.

The condition of her body is not what one would expect. She has no visible or latent pre-mortem scratches, bruises, or contusions. There are no defensive wounds. In fact, there are no wounds on her body at all. From the information I've received, Ms. Calloway has been missing for more than a year. My preliminary examination indicates that the victim was killed some time ago, and then kept in a freezer for an undetermined period of time. My examination reveals ruptured cell membranes consistent with her having been frozen, resulting in cell structural failure. However, my examination also indicates that the victim had been taken out of the freezer and thawed out for no more than forty-eight hours at most. That, of course, leads to additional questions.

I would note that her body not only shows no wounds, but also no physical signs of suffering. Her skin pallor indicates that she had access to sunlight. The body weight is normal for a female of her age. The hair and nails were healthy at the time of her death. If, as I was led to believe, this woman was held against her will for more than a year, she was in remarkably good condition. Whoever held her took good care of her.

My full preliminary report is attached.

Sincerely,

Dr. Jacob S. Smith, MD

Franklin County Medical Examiner

Jenkins sat back in the chair and looked toward the ceiling. He didn't know Dr. Smith, and the report raised more questions than it answered. From what he had been made to understand, Rebecca was young and fit. She was a jogger, and presumably would not easily be overpowered. If someone attacked her, there should have been *some* residual wounds on her body. But there were none. In his experience, a lack of defensive wounds usually meant the victim had known the killer and had been cooperative up to a point, but it could also mean she had been taken under duress or following the administration of some sort of drug or chemical. He would generally lean toward the former, but the posing of her body indicated otherwise. Hers wasn't a body posed as he'd seen when the killer was later determined to be an ex-boyfriend or husband or other family member; this was the work of a detached, methodical killer with a victim and an agenda.

As a beat cop and then as a detective, he'd always had someone to exchange ideas with, someone to point out the flaws in his reasoning. But working alone here in a small town with a suspect police department, he found himself volleying ideas around in his mind like a kid hitting tennis balls against a garage door.

As he pondered his next step, he considered enlisting the help of Allee Smith. Why? He couldn't really say. She was rough around the edges and not a person he should trust.

Standing, he shook his head and closed the laptop. He was tired. That had to be it. There was no other explanation. It had been a long day. He'd find a hotel room, get some sleep, and start fresh tomorrow. He'd just have to hope that whoever had kidnapped Leslie was treating her as well (relatively speaking, of course) as he had apparently treated Rebecca while she was held captive, and that he could figure this out before Leslie was similarly killed and displayed.

33

ALLEE

Tuesday, June 1

The day started just like every other, with Allee waking up early to make cinnamon rolls while everyone else slept. In some ways she despised this routine; on the other hand, early morning hours were her only hours of solitude. Later, when Arlo awakened, she'd get a little time alone with him, which was good, but it was out of character for her. She was not a morning person; it was not in her nature. In her old life, she often went to bed—if at all—at four a.m. and frequently slept well into the afternoon. For her, as with most addicts, part of the loss associated with sobriety was the loss of the wild life. Chaos was every bit as addictive as drugs or booze.

That's the false narrative of nostalgia, she reminded herself as she got to work. *Part of the disease.* Everything seemed better, more exciting when viewed through the 20/20 lens of hindsight. Of course she missed the absolute freedom of youth, of being devoid of any real responsibility and unencumbered by the complications of her eventual felony conviction. But for her, there was no way back—use of any sort would inevitably lead to incarceration. It was as simple as that. It would cause her to miss work and screw up investigations. The lives of the people she cared about would be negatively impacted. She owed them more than that, she knew—and that was the big difference between the Allee of old and the Allee in recovery. She had learned to put others first. She cared about others now. People depended on her—if only in small ways—so it mattered if she destroyed herself now.

Arlo is sleeping in late this morning, she thought as she began her third batch of cinnamon rolls. The smell of baking cinnamon usually had him up while the first set was still baking. *Maybe he's growing tired of our routine.* That made her a little sad, but she reminded herself that she'd just been nostalgic about living without a schedule. Arlo was a kid, and kids needed some flexibility.

She closed the oven on the third batch, set the second batch aside to cool, then delicately touched the tops of the first batch. Satisfied they had cooled sufficiently so that she could ice them without it all melting and sliding off the top, she began methodically spreading the icing. Finished, she carried the first tray out to the truck. They had purchased a warming oven for Justice Bites a few months back. It took up most of one wall and featured a glass window that allowed her to see inside. It had been a significant expense, but her cinnamon rolls were their top-selling item and the warming oven ensured they would be delivered hot to the customers.

She popped the tray inside and then went around the back of the truck to start the generator. It was another expensive purchase, but it was necessary to run their equipment. Returning to the front of the truck, she noticed something affixed to the windshield. It was some kind of paper, but it had to be cardstock or posterboard or something thicker than normal paper because the morning breeze was not catching its edges and causing it to flutter. She moved the wiper to retrieve a note, and a strange one at that.

Like something out of an old television show, the note's message was crafted from words and letters that had been clipped from newspapers and magazines, each a different size, color, and font. It was unsigned and unaddressed, but Allee's quick reading convinced her it had to be meant for Whitney—especially given her weirdo ex texting her the day prior.

"I will have you. It's my *Rite of Spring*."

What the hell? Allee wondered. The italicizing had to be intentional. It would have been a lot of work for the person to find that many italicized letters in a magazine and put them together like that. It had to be from Leo.

Bodies of Proof   163

Whitney had mentioned his appearance out of nowhere just yesterday. The breakup of their marriage had been hard on them both, but of late he'd become obsessed with getting her back.

Their divorce wasn't even final yet, Allee knew—mostly because of Leo arguing over small things just to drag it out. He'd forced Whitney into counseling for ninety days. That was bad enough, but when she got that done, he'd refused to agree to any property or custody settlement even though they didn't have a lot, and even though he didn't seem all that interested in having custody of Arlo. After that, he'd forced Whitney to participate in a day-long mediation, which had nearly pushed her attorney—Marko—over the edge. He'd agreed to handle Whitney's case pro bono even though he really couldn't afford it and he hated family law. He probably wouldn't have helped her at all, except she'd convinced him it should be pretty straightforward. Thankfully, as Allee understood it, all that was left was the scheduling conference and a trial.

It has to be Leo. Nothing else has worked for him, and now he's getting desperate.

She looked down at the note and studied the words again. It was creepy, for sure, but it didn't appear threatening—at least not like stuff she'd seen in her prior life and in the short time she'd served as Marko's investigator. Nothing about heads being cut off, lives being ruined, or the like. She wasn't a lawyer, but she'd become familiar with aspects of the law while working for Marko, and it seemed to her that the only possible crime under Iowa law was harassment. The note was unsigned, directed to no one in particular, and there was no handwriting to analyze, of course—Whitney would easily recognize Leo's handwriting. As far as Allee knew, Whitney had never received anything like this in the past. To prove harassment, the cops would need to pinpoint who made the note and who left it, and without a fingerprint or an in-depth investigation, there was probably no way of figuring that out.

And that wasn't going to happen.

Absent a clear threat, cops were unlikely to take the note and its vague threat seriously, and they wouldn't waste resources on it—especially since Whitney worked for Marko, and everyone on the force hated his guts.

She couldn't take it to law enforcement; they wouldn't do anything. She debated momentarily, and decided not to let Whitney know; it would only increase her anxiety about Leo and the upcoming custody battle. And she couldn't investigate it herself; she didn't have the money, the resources, or the time. All she could really do was trash the note and keep an eye out in case things got weird.

She climbed into the back of the truck and opened the cabinet that held their little trash bin, intending to drop the note in the trash and be done with it. Not surprisingly, the little container was almost empty—no one liked to take out the trash, so they generally used the garbage bins outside the courthouses where they parked.

She was looking at her watch and thinking about the tray of rolls still in the oven when the single slip of paper caught her eye. She reached in and plucked it carefully from the trash. It was another note.

"You are a modern-day *Cinderella Story*, but this isn't any *Midsummer Night's Dream*."

This one was handwritten, but some of the words were intentionally italicized. *What the hell?* Maybe Whitney had seen it and decided it wasn't worth keeping. It couldn't have been Marko—he went out of his way to avoid working in the back of Justice Bites.

Had Whitney recognized the handwriting as Leo's and thrown it away? Was this why she'd been so edgy yesterday? On the other hand, she hadn't brought it up on the drive back, so maybe it hadn't bothered her too much. While Allee pondered the meaning of the notes and her next move, the alarm on her phone sounded—the rolls were done. She made her decision and tossed the notes back into the trash can, but not before snapping a photo of each, front and back.

She was an investigator, after all.

34

JENKINS

Jenkins awoke with a start and looked to the ceiling, trying to recall where he was. Remembering he was in Franklin, he relaxed, knowing he was lying in an uncomfortable bed in a cheap motel in an unfamiliar town. He rubbed at his eyes, thinking that after thirty years of hotel after hotel he should be used to it by now. Such was the plight of the DCI agent: always on the road, always on the run, always investigating the worst of the worst.

He rolled to his side, stretched, then carefully slid his legs off the side of the bed, anticipating the pain. On cue, his lower back screamed in protest. He tried to focus on the case to distract himself. He remembered Rebecca hanging in that tree, dressed and posed as a ballerina. He pushed himself into a sitting position, trying to ignore the back pain that was becoming a regular part of his morning routine.

He'd investigated countless crimes during his ten years as a police officer and twenty-five years as a DCI field agent. He'd investigated murders of all kinds involving victims of all ages. It was the cases at the far end of the spectrum of senselessness that stuck with him—the shaken babies and the murders of the elderly were especially gruesome because the victims were helpless. Those victims were dependent on others for their care, and it was often those responsible for their care who victimized them.

But the murder of Rebecca was different; this one was bothering him for an entirely different reason. She hadn't been attacked by a loved one, he was sure of that. There was nothing intimate or even hateful about the staging of the crime scene. Not infrequently, that thin line between love and hate led to him finding the perpetrator.

But not here, not with Rebecca. Her body's position was a taunt directed to law enforcement.

Her killer is telling us he did it and he will do it again.

More than likely, Rebecca's killer had put the wheels of another murder into motion with Leslie's abduction. But how long would he hold her? A week? A month? Six months?

Gritting his teeth, he stood at last and went about setting up the small coffee maker in his room, but not before examining it carefully—tweakers used hotels like this one to manufacture methamphetamine. A lone packet of coffee was provided by his hosts—enough for a single cup.

That'll give me a reason to stop by Justice Bites, he thought as he flipped the switch. One cup was not going to do it today. Not after the way he'd slept.

He showered and dressed quickly while sipping unenthusiastically at the bitter, tepid coffee. He checked his watch: seven a.m. The veterinarian's office wouldn't be open for another hour, so he started by calling the forensics laboratory.

"Mia here."

"It's Jenkins."

"A little impatient, aren't you?" Mia said. "I just saw you last night."

"Yeah, well, we've got one dead girl and another missing," he replied sourly. "I'd like to see Leslie's story end in a different way than Rebecca's, so I'm willing to risk you biting me in the ass."

"Fair enough," Mia said. "And I figured that, so we started testing the evidence last night just as soon as we got it back to the lab."

Jenkins opened his mouth to respond, but Mia cut him off.

"Before you go telling me how thankful you are or how awesome I am, just know that I know, and you don't need to waste your time telling me something that I already know."

Jenkins smiled wryly. She was a peach. "Okay, well, great."

"So, what do you want to know?"

"Everything."

"That narrows it down," Mia deadpanned. When he didn't respond to her jibe, she took a deep breath and then began a recitation. "First, we performed a preliminary comparison of the pieces of plastic found near Rebecca's body with those found near where you think Leslie was abducted. Now, we won't know with absolute certainty until we get an expert to compare them, but—and I'm sorry to tell you this—they are similar enough for me to say they were likely made by the same person or persons."

Jenkins raised an eyebrow. "Made?"

"Well, I'm no expert, but it looks to me like pieces of plastic were cut and then glued together to make a little music box. This isn't something that was made in China or wherever."

"How do you know?"

"Well, it would say," she explained. "We recovered enough pieces to know that. Besides, the craftsmanship is such that . . . well, you can tell someone made this. These boxes were handmade."

"Great," Jenkins said sourly. Finding the maker would be like finding a needle in a haystack. A very, very large worldwide haystack. Impossible. "What about the third box? The one I found lying in the courthouse square."

"Now that was a find," Mia replied quickly.

Jenkins's hope surged.

"It was handmade, too. The box is intact, operational, and the music still plays. The song was identified as a tune from the original *Wizard of Oz* movie."

"I know," Jenkins said. "I played it."

"You said you wanted everything," Mia chastised. "I'm telling you everything."

"Okay, sorry."

"Now, this isn't absolutely conclusive—it won't be until we get an expert —but I can say the pieces found where you discovered Rebecca's body and the pieces found where you believe Leslie was abducted are consistent with the plastic of the music box you found in the courthouse square. In fact, if I was a betting woman, I'd bet—"

"They were made by the same person," Jenkins said.

"It *might be* the same person. We'll know soon enough. Of course, even if the same person made the boxes, I can't say they had anything to do with the abduction of these women," she cautioned. "That's your lane, as you know."

"Right. Yeah." He knew it would be impossible for Mia to say anything more than she had to this point. But it was something. A start.

"Don't sound so glum," Mia continued. "It's better than nothing. I think in your business they call this a *clue*."

"True."

"By the way, we were also able to pull a fingerprint from the music box found in the courthouse square."

Once again, Jenkins's hope surged. "What? You did? Why didn't you tell me?"

"I'm telling you now."

"Right. Well, have you run the print through CODIS?" CODIS was a law enforcement database containing fingerprints of all known criminal offenders.

"Yes."

"And?"

"No match."

Damn, Jenkins thought. But that would have been too easy. Investigations were never that easy.

"Have you asked for the courthouse video?" Mia asked. "I'm no expert, but it seems to me with all the cameras in that area you might be able to get the footage and see who dropped it."

Jenkins looked at his watch; it was still way before eight o'clock when the courthouse opened. He'd get to that later. He retrieved his phone and opened it to the series of photos he had taken, studying the location. He was moving between photos when he fat-fingered the screen and accidentally moved on to a different picture. He was preparing to swipe back to the picture of the box in the grass when something caught his eye.

Bodies of Proof 169

"Wait a minute," Jenkins said, using his fingers to zoom in on the image on the phone.

"What?" Mia asked.

"I took a picture of a defense attorney and his client while they were sitting outside the courthouse."

"Why would you do that?"

"Well, this attorney—Marko Bauer—works out of a food truck. He sees clients under an awning outside the truck."

"Lame."

"I know, right? Anyway, he and his client were being dicks so I snapped a couple of pictures just to bug them—"

"Sounds like you," Mia said sarcastically.

"But I think I've got something!"

"What's that?"

"The client's back is to me in the picture, but I recognize him now. Guy's name is Jack Daniels."

"Thanks, Mom," Mia deadpanned. "Meaning what?"

"Meaning I know who he is because he's the guy who supposedly threatened to kill Leslie the night before she disappeared." McJames had given him that and not much else. He'd said he was likely going to have to dismiss the case because he couldn't get the information corroborated. But that didn't mean anything in this case.

"And?" Mia asked impatiently.

"And in my picture, the music box is sitting on the table between Marko and Daniels."

"Maybe you don't need the video after all, Sherlock."

Jenkins was silent, thinking. "Except Daniels has a long criminal history, so—"

"His fingerprints would have popped up on CODIS," she finished for him. They fell silent for a long moment, Jenkins wondering how he could get a hold of an attorney's fingerprints.

"Don't attorneys have to submit their fingerprints before they sit for the bar exam?" Mia asked. "I thought all professionals in Iowa did before they sit for their licensing exams."

"They do," Jenkins said quickly, remembering something he had read. "Do you have access to that database?"

"Sure do."

"Can you check?" Jenkins asked, looking anew at the image on his phone. "We might have caught a break."

35

MARKO

The television in Marko's bedroom was on and the volume was up while he shaved in front of the sink in the tiny space a realtor would refer to as a "master bath."

"In a tragic turn of events, the body of twenty-two-year-old Rebecca Calloway was discovered yesterday in Franklin, Iowa," the impossibly perky news anchor read. "While a Franklin Police Department spokesman, speaking off the record, has confirmed that the death is being investigated as a possible murder, they are releasing few details at this time."

"Of course they aren't," Marko said aloud.

"Ms. Calloway was reported missing a year and a day ago by her parents, who have stated on numerous occasions in various public forums that law enforcement refused to take their concerns seriously," the reporter continued. "Her mother, Patricia Calloway, has publicly criticized Captain Shaffer of the Franklin Police Department, who assured the public shortly after her disappearance that—and I'm quoting here: 'We are rather certain Rebecca is a runaway who will eventually return.' It seems as though Rebecca has returned," the reporter added. "But according to our sources, she was no runaway."

Marko finished shaving and grinned at the reporter's characterization of Shaffer. When Shaffer—then a patrol officer—had arrested Marko for operating while intoxicated almost a year prior, his treatment of him had been rude and unprofessional—just as he would have expected. They'd been at odds for years, and Marko never missed an opportunity to listen to Shaffer's public shaming, and when Marko had beaten the conviction by refusing all testing, Shaffer's dislike for him had only increased.

"This reporter reached out to Captain Shaffer for comment. He refused an interview, but has submitted the following statement: 'This is an active investigation. I cannot comment at this time.'"

Active investigation, my ass, Marko thought as he made his way back into his bedroom to dress. The investigation no doubt was active, but there was no way Shaffer was handling it. It had to be the reason that DCI agent was snooping around, asking questions yesterday.

But, then again, those questions were about Leslie Martin, not Rebecca Calloway. Who knew?

He was putting on his socks when his thoughts were interrupted by the sound of a familiar horn blaring. *They're here.* Allee and Whitney, no doubt waiting impatiently. He didn't pick up the pace; he was the law firm. They couldn't operate without him.

The horn blared a second time, this time longer, like Allee was laying on it.

"I'm coming, I'm coming!" Marko grumbled as he shut off the television and headed out the door.

"It's about time," Allee growled when he opened the passenger door and hopped on the bench seat beside Whitney, who sat quietly. "You need to set your alarm five minutes ahead," she added, side-eyeing him. "It's not like you're doing a lot of prep work there."

From a business standpoint, Marko needed Allee. But he was starting to prefer Whitney's company—at least she didn't ride his ass about doing one thing or another.

They rode in silence, arriving in Franklin at the usual time despite his tardiness. He sat in the truck, making calls, while Allee and Whitney set up his "office." His first call was to McJames's office. He exchanged pleasantries with a newly hired, moderately attractive female staffer until she trans-ferred his call.

"McJames here."

Bodies of Proof 173

"It's Marko."

McJames scoffed. "I don't believe it. Can't be. It's only five minutes past eight."

"Well, good morning to you as well," Marko replied. "Did someone wake up on the wrong side of the bed?"

"You're calling to gloat about something, aren't you?" McJames said. "Whatever it is, go ahead and get to it. Lemme guess: you're filing a motion to suppress because I forgot to list a witness and can't get evidence in at next week's trial—that it? Or you just found out that my star witness has left the state and can't testify? Whatever it is, spit it out because I'll tell you up front it can't be worse than the shit I'm dealing with this morning. So if your goal is to get a rise out of me, sorry not sorry. I'm fresh out of shits to give."

"Yikes!" Marko said with mock exasperation. "Do you kiss your mother with that mouth?"

"Get to it or I'm hanging up," McJames snapped. "I don't have time for you this morning."

"Well, you're no fun." He *was* calling to gloat; he *did* want to get a rise out of McJames. And McJames was ruining it with his sour mood. "What has your panties in a bunch?"

"Goodbye, Bauer."

"Okay, fine," Marko said. "I'm calling about Jack Daniels."

"I don't give jack shit about Jack Daniels right now."

"Hey, just wondering: does your bad mood have something to do with Rebecca Calloway?" Of course, they'd argued the day prior when McJames had snidely insinuated that Marko or his client might have had something to do with the woman's death. McJames had apologized, but Marko knew he was still raw.

"Okay, fine," McJames seethed. "You got me. What about Jack?"

"Your Honor, the answer is unresponsive," Marko teased. He couldn't help himself; when he'd been struggling, McJames had been of no assistance whatsoever.

"What about Jack?" McJames repeated.

"Well," Marko said, "Jack's accuser, as you know, is Leslie Martin. My investigator, Allee Smith, has gone over to Olde Bulldogs and interviewed the staff. Nobody heard the alleged 'threat' to Leslie. And now she's gone, so—"

"So, what?"

"So I'm making a speedy demand and your witness-slash-victim is gone."

Marko habitually had his clients demand speedy trials, whether they were in custody or not. It was a tactic designed to gum up the court system and was especially helpful when a witness took off, refused to testify, or disappeared. McJames was up against a deadline, and he knew it.

"Fine," McJames said. "I'll dismiss it."

Is he really giving up that easily? Marko wondered. He'd expected— wanted, really—some argument. "Okay. Well, great." He didn't know what else to say.

"Is that it?"

"I guess?"

"Well, is it or not?"

"It is. I'll look for your motion and order," Marko said. "Pleasure doing business with you."

"I wish I could say the same."

The line went dead, and Marko pocketed his phone. He grabbed his laptop bag and got out of the truck. He should have been pleased, but McJames's surrender was unexpected, anticlimactic, and put a real damper on his morning. He'd been planning to bust McJames's balls after a vicious argument; instead, the prosecutor had mumbled feebly and given in. It was a terrible way to start the day. He was thinking things couldn't get much worse until he came around the truck and saw who was seated at his table waiting for him.

James Innis. *Again.*

36

ALLEE

As always, while Marko sat in the truck on the phone, she and Whitney were left to set up the awning and seating area.

"So much for chivalry," Whitney observed as they worked to pull up the large shade tent.

"Marko's not been chivalrous a day in his life," Allee responded. Not that she really wanted his help. They'd never needed him before, and he'd probably just get in the way. At this point, if Marko offered to help, Allee would probably run him off.

"Can I help?"

Allee froze. She'd heard and seen too much of Innis in the past twenty-four hours. She turned slowly and saw him seated at a picnic table about twenty yards away. When they made eye contact, he hopped to his feet and began making his way toward them. Allee side-eyed Whitney to see her reaction, and was not surprised to see a similar level of obvious . . . what? Disgust? Disdain? Something about the young man was not right. She was sure now that he was following them.

"What do you want?" she asked when he was close enough for her to ask without shouting.

"I'm your client." He shrugged, then shoved his hands in his pockets. "Or have you forgotten?"

Allee ignored his answer, focusing instead on erecting the awning while Whitney unfolded two chairs.

"Marko will be a minute. You're here for him, I assume," she said.

Innis winked lasciviously. "And you, I think," he said.

It was a ridiculous gesture coming from this twerp. "What do you want?" She made a show of looking at her watch. "You might find this surprising, but we do have other clients. Our lives do not revolve around you."

"Yet." He smirked.

"Ever."

"Just give me ten minutes and I'll be gone."

Allee shook her head. "I don't make the rules around here. Sit down," she said, nodding to the seating area, "and Marko will see you if and when he has time."

"Great." Innis's smile was wider now, but it was still bereft of humor or kindness.

Allee followed Whitney to the back of the truck, where they stopped just outside the door.

"Does he have an appointment?" she asked Whitney. When Whitney shook her head vacantly, Allee whispered, "Look, I hate to do this to you, but can you cover the truck while I deal with whatever he needs?" She nodded in Innis's direction.

"Sure," Whitney said vacantly.

Marko joined them. "What's he doing here?" he asked, indicating Innis.

"I was going to ask you that," Allee replied. "There's nothing on your calendar—are you making your own appointments now?"

"Of course not."

"All I know is he said he wants to talk with you, er, us," Allee said.

"Again?"

"Hey, you wanted to represent him. I told you rich people are a pain in the ass—remember? I gave you my best advice; this is on *you*."

Allee was watching an increasingly uncomfortable Whitney while she spoke to Marko. As she watched, Whitney disappeared into the truck, apparently intent on staying out of the argument. "You see that?" Allee asked Marko, nodding in Whitney's direction.

Bodies of Proof 177

"Yeah. Not sure what's up with her. We can argue about this later," Marko said. "For now, let's get on with it. Did he say what he wanted?"

"Ten minutes."

"That's not bad," Marko said, straightening his tie. "You're coming with me, though."

"Great," Allee replied sourly. She had hoped her scolding would piss him off enough that he would see Innis alone so she could work in the truck. But no, the little rich boy was going to get his way. Money might not buy love, but it bought and paid for other people's time.

She followed Marko to the table. Marko didn't look back to ensure she was following—he didn't need to. He knew she would support him. She didn't always like her assignments, and she was more than willing to give him a piece of her mind when the time was right, but she knew who was boss.

"James," Marko began. He adopted a false smile.

"Hi," Innis said. He didn't stand. He'd been sitting at the table doing nothing. He wasn't looking at his phone or reading a book. He was just sitting there, which was odd for his generation. Hell, it was even odd for Allee's generation now that everyone had grown accustomed to constant engagement.

Marko pulled a chair out and sat across from Innis while Allee lowered herself into the seat next to him, never taking her eyes off Innis. Once again, he was in a plain black shirt.

Marko waited for a beat. When it was clear Innis expected him to inquire, he did so. "What brings you here so early in the morning?"

"The cinnamon rolls, of course."

As Allee watched, the two men locked eyes.

Marko shrugged. "You obviously don't need me for that."

"You're right. It was a joke," Innis said, forcing a smile that dropped as quickly as it had formed.

"Oh, right, yeah," Marko replied uncertainly.

There was a long silence that Allee had no intention of filling. In a weird way, she was enjoying the sight of Marko squirming. Clearly, this wealthy young man had a way about him that was outside Marko's experience, as well as her own. She'd known he would be high maintenance. He had a driver, for Christ's sake.

"So, why did you need to see me?"

"And Allee." Innis's cool gaze flicked to Allee, then back to Marko.

"Why did you want to see me and Allee?" Marko amended.

"I wanted to talk to you about something."

"Your case?"

"Not directly, but I need some legal advice."

"We only represent you on the OWI case," Marko said. Allee could hear the regret in his voice.

Thank God, Allee thought. She watched that awkward encounter, thinking there was going to be a hefty round of "I told you so's" when Innis's case was finally closed.

"I thought you said that all of our conversations were covered by attorney-client privilege," Innis said.

"They are," Marko said. "If I'm your attorney."

"Even if it doesn't have to do *directly* with my OWI?"

"Yes," Marko said, but this time through slightly clenched teeth. "We're charging you our hourly fee."

"Of course. That's to be expected." Innis waved a well-manicured hand. "That's part of the reason I doubled your fee. Just in case, you know."

This guy is looking for a therapist, not an attorney, Allee thought.

"I've got to get into the courthouse," she heard Marko lie.

"Okay, well," Innis began. "I assume you saw the news this morning."

"I did. Something specific you're referring to?" Marko looked pointedly at his watch.

"Rebecca Calloway."

Allee felt her eyes narrow. She side-eyed Marko and saw that he was sitting very still. "What about her?" he asked.

"I killed her."

Innis's expression did not change. His forced smile didn't falter. His gaze didn't skitter away. He didn't lower his voice. It was as though he'd said something as nominal as *I lost my keys*, not *I murdered a woman.*

"I'm sorry," Allee heard Marko say through the buzzing in her ears.

Bodies of Proof   179

Beside her, he shook his head as if to clear it. As if he hadn't heard either. "What?"

"I killed her," Innis repeated softly. This time, his posture changed. He leaned forward in the small chair. "That's why I need you. Both of you."

Allee looked away quickly when Innis turned his attention to her, hoping Marko would find the ability to speak.

"You believe me, don't you?" Innis asked.

Allee was staring at the ground in front of her. She felt, rather than saw, Marko stand. "Jesus Christ, James! I don't know!" She watched as her boss ran a hand through his hair. "What the hell? Why are you telling us this?"

Innis smiled mirthlessly. "I was watching her for a while. I knew where she'd be. She really should have been more careful. I followed her into the woods, then waited until she was on her way back. I jumped her and took a rag I had soaked in chloroform and then I—"

"Don't!" Allee barked. Now she was on her feet.

This little weasel could not possibly have done what he was claiming. "Liar!" she finally bit out. "You are a liar. We represent you, but our relationship cannot—and will not—be built on a foundation of lies."

"Allee—" Marko began.

She quieted him with a quick look. "This little shit is not capable—"

"Oh, I'm capable," Innis interrupted quickly. "I did it. I killed her," he insisted.

"How? Where? What did you do with her? Where's she been for the past year? And why was she found yesterday? And why there?"

"I kept her in a storage unit," Innis replied quietly. He'd ignored the other questions.

Allee remembered his phone call from the day prior. "At Kum and Leave." It was a statement, not a question.

The buzzing in her ears was now so loud that she could scarcely hear a word of the ensuing discussion between the two men. She felt a tightness in her chest—was she having a heart attack? She was too young, right? She put a hand on her chest and took a deep breath as if to disprove her suspicions. Then she had an idea, a way to disprove his story.

"Can't be," she said when she could breathe. "No way. People have been looking. They'da found her. The word on the street is she was . . . fresh.

Someone woulda seen you keeping her alive. You couldn't have kept that secret. Someone would have noticed. People would have complained."

"Allee—" Marko began.

Innis had been watching her closely while she struggled to understand. "I kept her for a while, Allee. Then I put her in a freezer. A big one," he explained matter-of-factly.

"But someone would have noticed!" Allee insisted.

Innis smiled again. "What can I say? People mind their own. One guy asked and I told him I was keeping some elk meat from a hunting trip I took to Wyoming."

"And he believed that?"

"People believe what they want to believe. When I was, uh, done with her, I kept her there until I figured out my next move."

He paused as though enabling that to sink in.

"But why now? Why reveal her at all?" Marko asked.

Innis shrugged. "I needed the room."

37

JENKINS

That looks intense, Jenkins thought.

He'd parked outside the law enforcement center and was making his way toward the Justice Bites food truck when he noticed Allee, Marko, and a young man seated at the table outside their food truck. As Jenkins approached, Marko leapt to his feet, then ran his fingers through his hair, clearly upset. From what he could tell, Allee was agitated as well. He couldn't hear her words, but the look on her face and her body language made him think that she was barely holding herself back from doing something that would land her back in handcuffs.

I don't want to be anywhere near that.

From time to time throughout his career, there had been defendants with whom he'd formed a guarded mutual respect. He watched her place a hand against her breasts as if to check her own breathing, then lean across the table in an apparent effort to confront the younger man. Seeing her that worked up, he instinctively felt it best to leave the situation alone, veering away from Justice Bites and making his way to Freedom Burgers instead. Predictably, he found Cameron at the window watching the conversation across the street through binoculars. He had his elbows propped up on the ordering window in front of him, like he'd been in this position for a long time.

"They're talking about murder, Agent Jenkins," Dale said without lowering his binoculars or looking away.

"How'd you know it was me?"

"I'm a Marine. I'm aware of my surroundings."

Jenkins turned to watch the conversation. As he watched, Allee stormed toward the rear of the Justice Bites truck, having apparently heard enough.

"She's mad about the murder."

"What murder?"

"Rebecca."

"How do you know?"

"I know. I've got a vibe," Cameron replied. "She's a career criminal, and I thought she'd be game for anything, but I guess even she has her limits."

Jenkins bristled. Allee was indeed a felon with a long history, but all indications were that she had paid her debts and turned her life around, which was exactly what the public said it wanted. Despite that, people like Cameron continued to judge people like Allee for past behaviors. That didn't incentivize change.

"What makes you think they are talking about murder?" Jenkins asked.

"I can read lips."

Sure you can. "Really?" Jenkins asked. "How so?" Lip reading, he knew, was possible—but it required education and talent. Without one or the other, lip reading was about as reliable as fortune telling.

"I'm just good at it."

"Right." Jenkins shook his head. This wasn't helpful, and he needed to get back to the real investigation. While he'd been watching with Cameron, things across the street had settled down. Allee had departed, and the two men were much less animated. He turned again to Cameron. "Can I get a coffee?"

Cameron continued to watch the competition. "In a minute."

"I'm no expert, but I'd venture a guess that your customer skills might be one reason why there's no one else in line," Jenkins offered.

Cameron lowered the binoculars and fixed his stare on Jenkins. "What makes you think I don't have customers?"

"Well," Jenkins began. He blinked several times. How to say it? "I guess

Bodies of Proof 183

because I'm always the only one ordering anything?" This guy couldn't be serious.

"One black coffee, coming up," Cameron replied. "You want something else more substantial?"

"No," Jenkins said too quickly, trying not to remember the soggy breakfast pizza he'd choked down the day before.

"Fine." Cameron disappeared inside the truck and returned seconds later with a steaming cup of coffee. "That'll be three dollars."

Jenkins placed a five on the counter. "Keep the change."

Cameron nodded. "I'll keep an eye on them folks, too," he said. "Something funky going on over there."

Jenkins was torn. On the one hand, he was always inclined to listen to members of the public—he'd solved a lot of cases that way. On the other, he didn't really want to have anything to do with Cameron. He took a sip of the weak, bitter brew and made a face. "Keep me posted," he said at last.

38

MARKO

"No." Marko could barely hear his own voice over the buzzing in his head. "This is bullshit. You didn't kill anyone," he said as Allee stomped off.

Innis cocked his head in a way that might be cute if he were a dog, creepy if he were a reptile, but unnerving when coming from a human being. "Why not?"

"Because . . .well . . . look at you," Marko replied carefully. Rebecca, as he understood it, hadn't been a large woman, but she was fit and athletic.

Innis was leering now—daring Marko to finish his thought. "What?"

"You're like one hundred and fifty pounds soaking wet." Marko's gaze flicked to Innis's skinny arms. "I mean, no offense, but you're scrawny."

"Do you want me to show you?"

"Yeah," Marko said, then corrected himself. "Well . . . no."

"Well, that's . . . confusing," Innis replied. "Do you want to know or not?"

Marko had made up his mind. "No," he said. "One, because I don't know what I'm dealing with. I don't know what you're trying to tell me about Rebecca. You've already told me you got rid of her body, and I know that law enforcement found her. If what you're telling me is true, I'm stuck with information I'd rather not have, and I cannot act upon."

"But isn't it delicious?"

Bodies of Proof 185

"What is wrong with you?" Marko asked quietly, then corrected himself. "Don't answer that. The bigger question—the one I'm not certain I want to know the answer to—is why you needed that space."

"It's because—"

Marko hadn't heard Allee approaching from behind him. She must have changed her mind about assisting Whitney. "No!" Allee cut Innis off, her words harsh and biting. "Don't answer that! I am about two seconds away from marching around this table and kicking the shit out of your smug little face. This is screwed up—this entire conversation—regardless of whether you are telling the truth or not!"

Marko's stomach was turning inside-out. "Allee," he began in what he hoped was a soothing tone. "Don't."

He needed to get her under control. He didn't want to be alone with Innis, for fear he might say more. But he could see that if she remained here, she might well follow through on her threat. Sometimes—when she was acting professionally and had herself together—he forgot that hers had been a life filled with disappointment, abuse, and addiction. Then her temper would flare and he would see the fire in her eyes and know that Allee was a battler by nature and training.

"Don't *Allee* me!" The full heat of her glare swung to Marko. "I told you. I warned you that this little weasel was trouble," she added, jabbing the index finger of a tattooed hand in Innis's direction.

"I'm not a—" Innis began.

"Shut up," Allee said to him dismissively, before turning her attention back to Marko. "But you just had to represent him, didn't you? You just had to break into the private pay client world. It's always about money with you, Marko—and now we're dealing with a sociopath at best, a psychopath at worst."

"You know, I am right here," Innis said. There was almost humor in his tone.

"Don't remind me," she snapped. "And I thought I told you to shut your trap?"

Marko was afraid she was going to carry out her threats. "Allee," Marko began. "How about helping Whitney get ready? I'll handle this."

"Whatever." She turned and marched toward Justice Bites.

Innis and Marko watched in silence as Allee reached the truck in four long strides, yanked the back door open, and slammed it shut behind her.

"Well, that was . . . different," Innis said.

Marko was watching Innis closely. He might as well have been talking about the weather. His tone was normal, unruffled, as though nothing had happened. It was alarming. Marko was rarely at a loss for words with clients; this was one of those times.

They sat quietly for a moment.

"She can't tell anyone, right?" Innis asked at last.

"About what?" Marko asked.

"About me and Rebecca. She can't report what I just said, right? Like, attorney-client stuff, right?" For the first time since they'd met, Marko could sense a note of concern in his client's voice.

"We are prohibited by the Iowa Rules of Professional Conduct from reporting or revealing past crimes committed by clients we represent."

"So I'm good?"

"No, you're a scumbag."

"But you can't tell anyone, and she can't either—right?"

"Not about anything occurring in the past." Marko nodded. "But it's permissible to report an ongoing crime if reporting it will or could result in preventing future harm." He was speaking in a monotone, as if he were lecturing in a law school ethics course, not answering a question being posed by an admitted killer.

Innis leaned forward. "I assure you, the harm has already been done. Twice."

Marko shut his eyes tightly, as if doing so could make it all go away. "That sounds more like an assurance for you, not for me." He blinked hard. "Or Allee."

Innis laughed. It was a cold, mirthless chuckle that made Marko cringe.

"Do you believe me yet?"

"I don't know," Marko answered honestly.

"Well, let me tell you how I did it," Innis said.

"Did what?" Marko didn't want to know, but he couldn't shut it down.

"Rebecca," Innis replied quickly. His eyes appeared to light up as he remembered. "See, I was hiding along the trail, in the woods. She was

Bodies of Proof 187

running. I was somewhere near the middle of the trail because I wanted her to be tired when I got her."

Marko pinched the bridge of his nose.

"When she passed, I jumped out, grabbed her, and put a chloroform-soaked rag over her face. She went limp almost immediately."

"Then what?" Marko crossed his arms.

"We got her back to the storage unit, I placed a bag around her head, and watched the air disappear."

"You . . . watched?" Marko asked, swallowing hard. "You're a monster!"

"Of course," Innis said matter-of-factly. "Watching her face through the plastic as she tried to breathe air that wasn't there," he added wistfully. "I've never felt more . . . powerful."

"Jesus Christ!" Marko exclaimed.

"Was nowhere to be found." Innis shrugged. "She didn't struggle. She wasn't awake for it. I'm not *that* bad."

"You're a freak," Marko said. He felt his pulse in his neck.

"Your calling me names means nothing," Innis said quickly. "Then I put her in the freezer and the rest is history."

Marko was dismayed. He was face-to-face with a murderer unlike any he'd ever represented. Most murderers were family members or acquaintances of the victims who acted in the heat of passion. He felt a sudden, intense urge to get stinking drunk and to forget—if only for a few hours—what his client was, and what he'd told him. He needed to forget, but the only thing that would accomplish was the thing that would end his career as a lawyer. Because if he started drinking, he wouldn't stop. He quickly recited the Serenity Prayer, and as he finished, he had a thought. *Maybe, just maybe, this guy is full of shit.*

"I can see how you overpowered her," Marko began, a glimmer of hope in his voice. "But how did you get her out of the forest without anyone seeing you? I mean, that's a ways."

Innis nodded, as if he'd been expecting the question. "I had . . ." He paused for a long moment, looking down at his hands. Then his gaze lifted and met Marko's. Marko saw the glimmer in Innis's eyes and felt his hopes dashed even before the younger man finished his thought. "Help."

"Oh, Jesus!" Marko repeated. "Who? Your driver?"

"I think that's enough talking for today," Innis said. For the first time, he seemed gleeful.

"Wait, what?" Marko asked.

"I'll be back later," Innis said, slowly rising to his feet.

"Later? Later, as in later this week? Later this month? Later when?"

"Just . . . later." Innis turned and began walking toward the street. The black limo pulled up, stopped, and Innis got in without looking back.

Marko stood rigidly, watching as the vehicle pulled away. He'd never been more relieved to see a client go. He wiped a tear from his eye with a sleeve, knowing Innis would make good on his promise.

He would be back. And soon.

39

WHITNEY

I'm out of here, Whitney thought.

When she saw Innis approaching, then heard Marko call for Allee, she took it as her cue to get inside the truck. Someone had to ready Justice Bites to open and serve customers, and for once she was happy to oblige. She unlocked and slid open the ordering window. As she did so, she saw Cameron bring his truck to a stop across the street. After he parked, he turned and used both hands to flip Whitney off. She ignored him. If he wanted to get a rise out of someone, he would have to wait for Allee.

Cameron got out of his truck and started readying it for customers. When he opened his window, it was directly across from Whitney's.

"Good morning, Dale," Whitney called.

"It'll be good when you're gone," he shouted back.

"You're always such a pleasure to be around."

"It'll be a pleasure when I never see you bunch of crooks again!"

"But then how would I enjoy your company?" Whitney kept her tone sweet and even smiled.

"You won't!"

She chuckled and turned to power up the register. Her exchanges with Cameron were part of an unspoken, ongoing routine. He was consistent, and there was something oddly comforting about it. She was looking for a hot pad when the back door flew open. Allee marched inside and slammed the door behind her so viciously it caused the entire truck to shake. Whitney stumbled with the sudden movement but steadied herself with a gloved hand on the counter.

"Sorry," Allee apologized. Her breaths were quick and shallow, and her hands were shaking. "I had to leave."

"What's going on?" Whitney asked. "If you're upset about Dale, you really shouldn't let him get you so—"

"Screw him! It's not him. It's . . . nothing," Allee replied tersely.

Whitney watched as Allee trudged to the ordering window, placed both hands on the counter, and lowered her head, leaning her full weight against it.

"It doesn't look like nothing," Whitney offered.

"It's just . . ." Allee shook her head, then looked up. "That Innis kid, he's . . . a creep."

"You can say that again," Whitney agreed. She walked to the coffee maker and flipped it on. Once the first pot was brewed, she would pour it into a carafe and start brewing a second. When customers showed up, they almost all wanted coffee to complement the sweetness of Allee's cinnamon rolls.

"Stay away from him," Allee warned, her tone low and intense. "Promise me."

Whitney looked up to see Allee's ice-blue eyes locked onto her own, pleading. "Why?"

"Just promise me," Allee repeated.

Whitney crossed her arms. "What happened out there?"

"It's nothing," Allee answered far too quickly.

Whitney pressed her lips together, forming a thin line.

"You don't need to worry about it. I promise."

Whitney gave Allee her best disappointed-mother look. The *Come out with it already* look that she used on Arlo for only the most serious of occasions, like the time he put gorilla glue in his hair and wouldn't admit it.

"I really think it's better if you didn't know," Allee said.

"Fine. Don't tell me." Whitney went back to her business. Allee would

Bodies of Proof 191

either trust her, or she wouldn't. There was nothing Whitney could do about it either way, apparently.

"It's for your own good."

"If you don't want to tell me, then don't," Whitney said, swinging around and giving her friend a hard look. "But I'm an adult. You don't get to decide what is 'good for me.'"

"Don't be angry."

"Allee, I really don't have the time or patience for any of this," Whitney said. "I have my own stuff going on right now," she added, thinking about the text messages she continued to get from Leo. He'd already sent ten that morning. They alternated between begging and menacing, but whatever the tone, they were gaining in frequency and growing increasingly demanding. She watched silently as Allee considered her response.

"I'm only trying to protect you," she said at last.

Whitney had had enough. "If you're going to be here today," she began, "I've got law firm work to catch up on."

This was a golden opportunity to get started reviewing Marko's electronic filing cue and organizing his case files and calendar. It might be her only opportunity. She had no idea where the day would lead, but judging by the weirdness of the morning, it would be in her best interest to get to work.

She turned toward the computer, and as she did so, she saw Allee open her mouth as if to respond before apparently thinking better of it and snapping her jaws shut.

40

JENKINS

This coffee just flat sucks, Jenkins thought as he took another sip of the bitter liquid and forced himself to swallow it.

Minutes earlier, he'd parked in front of the Franklin veterinary hospital and was immediately overcome by a wave of exhaustion. He needed to retire. But not today. Not until he closed these cases. Not until he had justice for Rebecca and Leslie, who were roughly the same age as his two daughters. Until then, he'd have to depend on caffeine to keep him up and at it.

He took another sip, winced as he swallowed the now-tepid coffee, and glanced at the clock on his dashboard. When it showed eight o'clock, he walked to the clinic and pulled on the door. A bell above the door jingled as he entered. A young woman sat at the front desk wearing purple scrubs decorated with whimsical depictions of different dog breeds.

"Are you here to pick up or drop off?" she asked when he reached the counter.

"Neither. I'm a Special Agent with the Iowa Division of Criminal Investigation." He retrieved his badge and displayed it. "I'm here to see Dr. Minsk. I need to talk to her about an ongoing investigation."

"Of course!" The woman's brown eyes widened in understanding. "This is about Shep, am I right?"

Bodies of Proof 193

"Yes," Jenkins replied in a tone he hoped would discourage further questions. "Is the doctor available?"

"One moment." She picked up a nearby phone, pressed a button, and began speaking into the receiver in a hushed tone. After a few seconds, she cradled the phone and looked up at Jenkins. "She says she'll be right out."

Less than a minute later, an attractive woman of about thirty-five emerged from the back area. She was wearing green scrubs and a white lab coat. Her long, straight hair was pulled back into a low ponytail. She didn't wear a stitch of makeup, revealing a light dusting of freckles across her high cheekbones.

"Dr. Minsk?" Jenkins said.

"Call me Julie." She extended her hand in greeting.

"I'm Special Agent Jenkins," he said, again flashing his badge. "But you can call me Adam."

"All right, Adam," she replied uncertainly. "Come on back."

He followed her through an exam room and down a hallway lined with portraits of different dog breeds, all shot from angles and using camera settings that made them look ridiculous. He followed her into an office.

"Have a seat," she said, motioning to one of the two padded chairs across from her desk. The office was both feminine and minimalist.

He sat in the chair closest to the door.

"You're here for this," she said as she walked to the corner of the room and opened a closet where a small safe sat on a row of shelves. She shielded the keypad and typed a code, then reached in and retrieved a small plastic bag containing a figurine. "This is what I found in Shep's collar. It's a ballerina."

"I see," he said quietly. "Why do you still have it?" He was wondering why she hadn't already handed it over to law enforcement.

She closed the safe, then the closet, and then handed the bag containing the figurine to him as she walked to her chair. "Nobody came to get it. But before you get all worked up about the chain of custody, I found it while examining Shep. He was mostly unharmed, but he did suffer a concussion. I bagged it and brought it straight in here. I didn't know at the time his owner had . . . disappeared. It's been locked in that safe ever since."

"Are you—?"

"Yes, I'm the only one with access to that safe. Your chain of custody is clear."

"For a vet, you seem to know an awful lot about handling evidence."

She flashed a smile. "My mother is an attorney. I knew enough to bag it, but she's the one who told me what to do with the safe."

"Smart lady."

"Runs in the family," she replied without a trace of false modesty.

"Clearly." He looked down at the tiny ballerina in the clear baggie. The music box he had discovered on the lawn in front of the courthouse featured a tiny ballerina wearing a leotard and a tutu, with her hands positioned above her head. Turning the bag in his hands, he confirmed the ballerina was similar—except for one detail. "Uh . . . Julie," he began. "Was the figurine's face like this when you found her?"

"Of course." Julie scrunched her nose like she'd just smelled something rotten. "I didn't know what it meant—I just kept it to return to the owner when she turned up. When I heard . . . well, I've watched my fair share of police procedurals. I know better than to alter evidence."

"Okay. Well, it's just . . ." He looked back down at the little figure. "Well, her face. It's gone." Her hair was tied up in a bun above her head, framing what had once been the face, but the markings that would be her features had been carved or cut away.

"I noticed," she said. "It's creepy."

Jenkins wouldn't tell her that Rebecca's features—like those of the little figurine—had been cut away. He was trying to think of a way to explain the significance without alarming or alerting her when she sighed and asked, "Is there anything else you need from me?"

He looked up and met her eyes, noticing that she suddenly appeared exhausted.

"Just a couple of things," he assured her. "I think I heard the dog was concussed. Do you have any idea what might have caused that?"

"No," she said. "He was definitely concussed. My guess would be a blunt object of some sort, since he had no cuts."

"You have no idea what possibly could have caused it?"

She shook her head vigorously. "Honestly, your guess is as good as mine. It could have been a shoe or a boot, a fist, a book—anything, really.

Bodies of Proof 195

All I can tell you is that someone hit the dog hard enough for him to lose consciousness. When he awoke, he wandered over to wherever he was found."

A boot? "He was found near the courthouse," Jenkins explained. "Do you have any idea why he would have gone to the courthouse?"

"Shep couldn't tell me what happened," Julie said after a pause. She folded her arms defensively, and Jenkins was afraid she was going to ask him to leave. "In some ways, that makes my job harder than a medical doctor's; in others, it makes it easier."

"I don't follow."

"Animals can't tell me what they are thinking or what happened, but that also means that they can't lie to me. A dog acts on instinct, so when a dog is injured, I would expect it to go somewhere that feels safe."

"Okay."

"I think that Shep most likely went to the courthouse to see Allee and Whitney because he felt safe around them."

"You know Allee and Whitney?" Jenkins asked.

"Everyone in the tri-county area knows Whitney and Allee. They make the best cinnamon rolls in at least this area, but I'd venture to guess the entire state. I'd bet that Leslie didn't go anywhere without Shep, and I know the trailhead isn't far from the courthouse square. So it's only a guess, but I think Shep got hurt and went somewhere he'd been before, somewhere he felt safe."

"What about Marko? Do you know him?"

"No." She checked her watch. "I really ought to get back to work."

Jenkins stood. Years of interviewing witnesses had taught him when to end an interview, especially if he was hoping for that person to be a sympathetic witness when trial eventually rolled around.

You're getting a little ahead of yourself, he thought. He'd have to find and charge someone first.

"Thanks, Doc. I'll be on my way."

Moments later, he opened the trunk of his car, then snapped a photo of the little ballerina and texted it to Mia before securing it in his trunk. She texted him back before he was settled in his seat.

Can you talk?

Jenkins called her.

"You're going to be excited about this," Mia said by way of greeting.

He was holding his breath. "Tell me."

"We got a match on the fingerprint lifted from the music box."

"And?"

"It belongs to Marko Bauer."

"Yes!" Jenkins pumped his fist in the air, nearly hitting the car's roof. "What about the ballerina picture I sent you?"

"I'm looking at that now," Mia said. Her voice sounded farther away and echoed a bit, like she'd switched him to speaker phone. "It looks consistent with the one in the intact music box, except for the face. That's different."

"Yeah. I noticed that."

"Well, this ballerina is the one you got from the vet—from Leslie's dog, right?"

"Yeah," he said. "It was on her dog's collar."

"Rebecca's face—"

"I remember," he said, trying not to.

"Maybe he carves or cuts the faces after he kills them," she offered. "Part of the ritual. A lot of these guys—"

"That's a theory," Jenkins said quietly. He'd been thinking the same thing, of course. "But we don't know that Leslie's dead."

She was silent for a long time. "Adam, you need to find that girl before you find another doll without a face."

41

ALLEE

The conversation with Innis had gnawed at Allee throughout the remainder of the morning, even while she attempted to distract herself by serving customers and making small talk with the regulars. Was Innis lying to get a rise out of them? Was he just a little shit playing mind games? He'd been so smug about it, smiling while taking credit for a heinous crime. She'd observed no regret, heard no remorse. He hadn't said it like it was something that he had to get off his chest or the weight of it would crush him. Instead, he'd copped to killing Rebecca with a degree of satisfaction, like he was proud of himself.

He's either lying or he's a psycho. Either way, I need to know more about him, Allee thought as she served her last cinnamon roll.

She affixed the "Sold Out" sign for the rolls, made her way around the side of the truck, and found Whitney in the front cabin, looking at her computer. Allee could see the electronic filing system filling the screen.

The window was down, so Allee spoke through it to Whitney. "I need your help," she said.

Whitney jumped and the laptop nearly fell off her lap. "Jesus, Allee! You nearly scared me to death!" She placed a hand on her chest as if to slow a beating heart.

"Sorry," Allee said. She paused and made a point of looking around before she spoke. "I need you to cover Justice Bites while I investigate something."

"What?"

"I just need a couple hours," Allee began. "Can you do it?" She watched as Whitney bit her bottom lip, clearly upset with Allee for keeping secrets from her. How to explain it was for her own good?

Whitney looked down at the small computer screen and then back up at Allee. "I'll do it," she said, resignedly.

"You know I wouldn't ask if this wasn't important."

She waited until Whitney closed her laptop and climbed out, seemingly intent on working the food side of their business. When she had closed the door of Justice Bites behind her, Allee began a fast walk toward the law enforcement center. It was a short walk, and she didn't need the truck for this portion of her investigation. She was intent on learning more about Innis, and the best source of information would be law enforcement's files. Minutes later, she approached the front counter. While Innis's OWI complaint had been signed by Shaffer, there was another officer listed in the complaint who Allee viewed as far more trustworthy.

"Is Lieutenant Davis here?" Allee asked the woman at the desk.

The woman looked up from a report she was completing just long enough to recognize Allee and sneer. "He's working night shifts right now," she said.

Allee's heart sank. She could ask for his personal cell phone number, but they wouldn't give it out. Not to her. She was about to turn away when the woman continued unexpectedly.

"But he happens to be here right now. I can see if he's available."

"Thank you," Allee said, and she had never meant it more.

A few minutes later, the secure door swung open and Davis stepped out. "Allee," he said, a smile stretching across his face. "It's so nice to see you clean." He'd arrested Allee more than a few times over the years.

She looked both ways to indicate she needed privacy. "I need to talk to you about something."

"Sure," he said, motioning to a seating area by the window.

"I work for Marko Bauer," Allee said when they were seated and comfortable. "You know that, right?"

Bodies of Proof

"Yes. I've heard. I'm honestly not sure I'm happy about it. Bauer is a dick. Is he treating you well? Do I need to rattle his cage?"

Allee smiled in gratitude, but her appreciation for his concern was tempered by a continued, healthy dose of suspicion regarding the motives of cops. The truth, of course, was that Marko had been good to her over the past year, and had listened to her counsel—at least until Innis had come along. She'd warned him about Innis. She hadn't known exactly what was wrong, but she'd been suspicious of the guy from the start. And nobody paid double for no reason. Yet Marko had brushed her off, refusing to give her concerns any real consideration.

Still, she couldn't help but be appalled that she was here, sitting and talking to a cop—a cop!—about her boss and about a client.

"We're fine," she assured him.

"Well, from my vantage point, things seem to be working out for you," Davis said. "Right?"

"Sure," she replied unenthusiastically.

"Look, you're clean," he began, sounding as if he was trying to convince himself. "And I hear you make the best cinnamon rolls in town."

"I do," she acknowledged, pleased to be reminded of the joy Justice Bites brought to her life. "You should come down and try one sometime."

"I will," Davis assured her. "But my guess is that you aren't here to talk about pastries." His brown eyes were soft yet inquisitive.

"You're listed in a complaint charging James Innis with OWI."

"I am," he acknowledged. "How'd you get mixed up with him?"

"He hired Marko yesterday," Allee replied. She appreciated that Davis had the insight to understand without being told that her relationship with Innis was professional. Too many cops would have jumped to the conclusion that they were acquainted on the outside. "I'm just trying to get some background on him."

"I see," Davis replied. He scratched his chin. "That was a weird one."

"Because he's rich?"

"No . . . Well," he amended, "that made it more complicated, but not weird."

"What made it weird?"

Davis looked at his hands and lowered his voice. "Look, I probably shouldn't be telling this to the defense team, but it's all coming out during depositions, anyway—right?"

Allee nodded and leaned forward, her interest piqued. She held her breath and waited, sitting as still as possible.

Davis had made his mind up. "This is going to sound strange, but I'm not even sure that guy was drunk, or had even been drinking, for that matter."

"What? Then why was he arrested?"

"It was weird," Davis said, shaking his head and then squeezing the bridge of his nose.

"You already said that."

"The kid refused all breath testing," he explained. "He wouldn't take the preliminary breath test and he wouldn't blow into the breath machine here at the station."

"So what was the evidence against him?"

Davis sighed heavily. "That's what was so weird. He willingly took the field sobriety tests and failed miserably. And I mean *miserably*. I've never seen anyone stumble around like that during the testing." She watched as he shook his head, as if he still couldn't believe what he'd observed. "How do I explain this? I see drunk people all the time, obviously, but they all at least pretend to be sober when they are around police officers—you know what I mean?"

"Unfortunately." Allee could remember several occasions over the years when she had done exactly that. She could remember practicing the tests in the ladies' room before going to her car.

Davis smiled quickly, then sobered. "But Innis wasn't like that; it was almost like he *wanted* to be arrested. I could swear he was intentionally slurring his words. It was all quite . . . bizarre."

"Why would someone want to be arrested?" Allee asked.

Davis shrugged. "Beats me. Most of the time when people are trying to get arrested, they are homeless and trying to get out of the cold," he said. "I'll tell you what else was weird about the entire thing, and that was this: we were taking him into custody and the captain shows up."

"Why?"

"Dunno." Davis shrugged. "He shows up out of nowhere and watches

Bodies of Proof

and tells Innis, 'I got you,' like he's exulting over an OWI arrest—you know what I mean?"

She ignored his question. "Did you draw blood?"

"No. He refused all testing, and he's not entitled to an independent blood test unless he takes a breath test," he said. "Allee, I want you to know I see the change in you. You are remarkable."

She shook her head. "I'm not okay."

He laughed. "You're going to be fine," he assured her. "Anyone can walk down the middle of the road; it takes a special person to get where she's going after spending half the time in the ditch."

"Thanks, I think. Did you find out where Innis was before he started driving?" Allee asked.

"We don't know that either. We pinched him just up the street from Olde Bulldogs, but naturally, nobody would fess up to serving an underage person."

That tracks.

"The bartender said he hadn't seen Innis in the restaurant at all."

"Do you believe him?"

Davis shrugged. "Oliver hates cops—always has. But we've got nothing to counter it."

"Couldn't you get a copy of the restaurant's surveillance footage?"

"If they were cooperative, sure—but they aren't, and we had nothing that would convince a judge to sign a search warrant when we've already got a confession and video evidence of him failing the tests. Innis never said he'd been there, so him being in Olde Bulldogs was just a hunch, and hunches aren't probable cause."

Allee was thinking, weighing possible motives for Innis to feign drunkenness. "That makes sense," she commented at last.

Deep lines appeared on Davis's forehead when he raised his eyebrows. "What's that?"

"Work stuff. I—I can't tell you. Yet."

"Privileged information?"

She nodded. "Exactly. All right, well, I think that's all the questions I have for now."

She stood. Davis had given her what she needed. She knew now that

Innis was a liar—probably habitual, possibly pathological. That didn't matter; what did matter was that it was looking like for reasons known only to him, he had gotten arrested for OWI when he was probably not even drunk. It was a strange set of facts. She had spent a lot of time around cops, and she'd never once heard one admit that a criminal defendant might be innocent. She was almost to the door when she heard Davis clear his throat.

"Hey, Allee?"

She paused and turned. "Yeah?"

"Be careful."

42

JENKINS

"All right, I'll bite," McJames said. "What do you have on him?"

After hearing from Mia, Jenkins had raced to the county attorney's office to discuss the evidence against Marko.

"Well, I've cross-checked Marko's court calendar, and he was in Franklin the days Rebecca and Leslie disappeared, and on the day I found Rebecca's body."

"So was I," McJames replied. Jenkins watched the attorney arch an eyebrow. They were in McJames's sparsely furnished office. It had an executive-style desk and two chairs across from it, and that was it. There were no bookshelves, knickknacks, or framed pictures. "What else do you have? Tell me you have something more than that."

"He knew both victims."

"How?" McJames leaned forward slightly. Jenkins could see he wasn't convinced, but he was listening.

"Leslie used to run daily and stop at Justice Bites on her way home. She must've known Marko. And I spoke with the vet, and she thinks that's why her dog went there after she was attacked."

"The vet's reading the dog's mind? How do you expect me to get that in front of a jury?" McJames asked. "And from what I've read, I don't think Marko was there when the dog showed up. I believe it was Whitney Moore who called. She and Allee Smith were the only two interviewed at the time. Granted, Bauer could have been out there killing her or whatever, but he just as easily could've been called into court. It happens."

"But you're the county attorney; you'da known, right?"

"Not necessarily. I've got assistants who can handle short-notice stuff or things that come up when I'm double-booked," McJames explained. "We need a little more info on what was going on in the courthouse at the time, where Marko was, details like that."

"I'll find out," Jenkins said, writing down the information so he wouldn't forget.

"And what do you have about him and Rebecca?"

"She worked at Olde Bulldogs."

"And?"

"Well, she disappeared a year ago," Jenkins replied. "I'm told Marko used to have a drinking problem."

"Among all his other problems, yeah. How did you find out?"

Jenkins shrugged. "Everyone seems to know."

He'd heard the information from virtually every officer he'd asked about Marko; that was how he knew he could trust it. As an out-of-towner, people seemed to steer clear of him unless he was asking about Marko, and then they were all too willing to tell stories of his drinking. To Jenkins it seemed every other story began with, "So, Bauer was at Olde Bulldogs drinking . . ." Bauer had to have known Rebecca—and probably very well.

"He's a drunk; she's a server. Interesting, but doesn't prove anything," McJames said.

Jenkins opened his phone and searched for a photograph he had taken. He could sense McJames's impatience as he scrolled quickly, searching for the picture where Marko was meeting with a client, and the small music box was on the table between them. At last, he found it and handed it across the desk to an openly skeptical McJames.

"What am I looking at here?" McJames asked. "It looks to me like Marko meeting with Jack Daniels." He looked up and pointedly met Jenkins's eyes with his own. "Who is also a drunk, by the way."

"On the table there. The object in front of Bauer is a music box," Jenkins said. "A handmade music box that is rare, just like the other two

Bodies of Proof 205

that were found broken at Rebecca and Leslie's abduction sites. I think that's the one I found yesterday in the courthouse grass."

"Okay, so that may be something," McJames allowed. "But how do you know that's Marko's box, and not something belonging to his client?"

"Well, I don't—for sure," Jenkins replied carefully. When McJames flashed a smug grin, he continued, "But it has his fingerprints on it."

McJames narrowed his eyes. "Tell me again how you came across the box?"

"I found it in the courtyard square," Jenkins replied, lifting his hands in a gesture of innocence. "I didn't take it without his permission, if that's what you're insinuating. He must have dropped it when they were preparing to leave. I'm not Shaffer."

McJames shook his head. "No, you're not. You got a good rep. If you were Shaffer, you wouldn't be in my office."

"We're going to have to talk about him at some point," Jenkins argued. "He severely handicapped my investigations when he refused to investigate Rebecca's initial abduction. A *runaway*," he scoffed. "Young women with everything to live for don't just up and leave."

"I know," McJames said, sighing and rubbing a hand over his face. "What else do you have on Marko?"

"Isn't that enough?"

"For a search warrant for an attorney's law practice? Not hardly." McJames issued a mirthless laugh. "Not a chance."

Jenkins wasn't laughing. "Not the practice; the food truck."

"The food truck *is* the law practice."

"Yeah, well." Jenkins crossed his arms. "I didn't say I had anything conclusive."

"No, you didn't."

Thinking McJames was done, Jenkins started to stand.

"*But* I'm proffering with one of Bauer's clients tomorrow. Guy named Clint Woodford."

"Okay." Jenkins lowered himself back into the chair. "What's that about?"

"Woodford wants to discuss Rebecca's case," McJames explained. "He seems to know something about notes left for Rebecca and Leslie before they were both abducted."

"Really?"

"And Marko brought it up yesterday—even before anyone knew that you'd found Rebecca's body."

"Really?" Jenkins said. "That's . . . convenient."

McJames nodded. "That's what I thought. I said something to that effect and the court attendant felt otherwise. She made me apologize after I accused Bauer of being involved."

"You *accused* him?" Jenkins asked. It was never a good idea to accuse a suspect before you were on the verge of an arrest. It almost always backfired. And by the sounds of it, McJames's accusation had fallen flat. "And if Bauer is somehow involved—"

McJames finished Jenkins's thought. "Why would he allow his client to proffer?" He shrugged. "Hell, I don't know. My point is that we will be discussing Rebecca tomorrow. You could come and pose a few questions of your own."

"To Clint or Marko?"

"You've done a proffer or two over your career, right?"

"More than I can count," Jenkins said.

"Then you know how these defense attorneys are—especially the arrogant ones, like Marko. They spend half their time answering for their clients."

"You think he might admit something?"

"All I know is, he's not half the wit he thinks he is." McJames shrugged. "It's worth a try; Woodford's got his balls in a vise—who knows? He might give up Marko."

43

MARKO

Despite everything, Marko rolled through the morning conducting business as usual. He met with clients, appeared for hearings, and argued with the prosecutor.

But everything was different.

He tried in vain to focus on a client's file and found his mind drifting back to the conversation from earlier that morning. Allee's reaction was immediate and predictable, of course. She'd stormed off, disappearing into the truck for a while before coming back and insulting Innis again. Finally, she'd taken off in the direction of the law enforcement center. She hadn't told him where she was going or why, and he hadn't asked. But now that she'd been gone a full hour, he was starting to wonder what she was doing. He was just about to call her and find out what was going on when she exited the front door of the law enforcement center, walking quickly toward him. There was a spring in her step that he hadn't seen all day. He studied her as she approached, wondering if he was misreading her. Perhaps she was marching over to hurl more accusations at him.

"Allee?" Marko asked when she was close enough to hear him. To his surprise, she was grinning from ear to ear. Had she lost her mind? He would guess that she was using again, but it didn't make sense that she'd willingly go into the building that housed every law enforcement agency in the county while actively high.

There was manic and then there was insane.

"Are you okay?" he asked cautiously.

"Fine." She folded her fingers together. "Actually, I think I'm better than fine."

"Why's that?"

She started to explain, but their attention was diverted as the black limousine pulled up and stopped on the street in front of Justice Bites. The back door flew open, and an enraged Innis emerged. He was dressed in his usual plain black T-shirt and jeans. He approached Marko and Allee with the arrogance of a successful man twice his age.

"We need to talk," he said.

"We just finished talking," Marko said.

"We need to talk *again*." He picked at a nail. "What does it matter anyway? I'm paying you. Isn't that what you want?"

Allee and Marko exchanged a look. "How do you know that I don't have a client coming to meet with me?" Marko asked.

"Because I know."

"How?" Marko asked, bristling.

"It's almost the lunch hour. You take a lunch break."

Well, he's got me there, Marko thought. He never scheduled client meetings over the noon hour. The clerk of court was closed for the hour, and judges didn't have hearings either. He was completely free right now, and unfortunately Innis knew it.

"This is the busiest time of day for me," Allee said, edging her way around the table and toward Justice Bites.

Marko stepped in her way. He didn't want her to leave him alone with Innis.

"That's what Whitney's for, isn't it?" Innis asked.

"No," Allee replied.

"Yes," Marko answered at the same time. They exchanged a look, and Marko could see she was about to blow up on the young man.

Innis looked from Marko to Allee, then back to Marko. "You run a strange operation."

Bodies of Proof 209

"Yeah, well, we could say the same about you," Allee shot back.

"What do you need, James?" Marko asked, trying to divert Innis's attention from Allee before she said something that might get him in trouble. "I've got nothing for you. I don't have discovery yet in your OWI case."

"I'm not here to talk about the OWI."

"Then why are you here?" Allee said, her tone challenging.

"To talk about the bodies."

Allee made a point of rolling her eyes. "Not this again," she said.

Marko barely registered Allee's reaction. His attention had been diverted by one word. "Bodies?" Marko asked quietly. "As in . . . plural?"

"I told you I needed the space in the freezer."

"This is nuts." Allee shook her head. "I'm out of here." She trudged off toward Justice Bites, continuing to shake her head.

"She can't just go, can she?" Innis asked.

"Watch me," Allee called over her shoulder.

"Can't you, like, make her stop?" Innis insisted. "I'm the client."

"If you don't like it, then fire us," she challenged. She was standing on the steps of the truck with her back to the door. "I'd prefer it, actually." Then she stepped inside and slammed the door closed behind her.

Innis turned to Marko. "But you're her boss," he said. "I would've thought you would have more control."

"Yeah, well," Marko huffed. "Allee doesn't do anything she doesn't want to do. And I'm not going to fire her, and she knows it."

"Well, all I know is that—"

"Is this a conversation we need to continue, or should I get Whitney out here to refund what's left of your retainer so you can go hire someone else?" The question was hard to ask but it was something that had to be done.

"No. We don't need Whitney. Not yet," Innis replied.

There was something in his voice that set Marko's teeth on edge. "If you are going to fire us, you might as well do it now. Bad news isn't like wine; it doesn't get better with age."

"I'm not delaying, and I don't want to fire you."

Marko sighed. Whether it was relief or frustration, he couldn't say. All he knew was that he was on uncertain ground with Innis, shaky ground with Allee, and unknown ground with Whitney—none of which was good for his nascent sobriety. Even worse, he was standing face-to-face with a man who claimed to have killed two women. Nonetheless, he was in the business of making money, and Innis had plenty of that. Now, if only he could limit his involvement with Innis to his defense on a charge of OWI, perhaps things could get better.

"Remember, I hired you for a reason," Innis concluded, a smile twisting the corners of his mouth.

44

ALLEE

Allee took several deep breaths. She'd been inside Justice Bites for fewer than five minutes and had just finished tying her apron around her waist to help Whitney fill orders when Marko opened the door and stepped inside.

"What do you need?" Allee asked impatiently. "We're trying to—"

"Innis wants to show us something," Marko said. "I can't go alone." He was pleading with her.

"Sure you can," Allee said, crossing her arms. "You're a big boy."

"I can't."

"You can."

"Would you two keep it down?" Whitney asked through clenched teeth. "You are going to upset the customers."

Allee and Marko exchanged a look. Whitney was right; they were arguing loudly while Whitney was up front filling orders. Sooner or later it would cost them business; the last thing a customer wanted—especially one who worked in the courthouse—was to listen to people arguing while they were getting coffee.

Allee forced herself to calm down. She took several additional breaths. When she felt composed enough to extend their conversation, she continued, "I'll remind you, *you're* the one who chose to represent him. *You're* the one that got us into this mess. Why do *I* have to have anything to do with him?"

"Step over here," Marko ordered, with a knowing look toward Whitney. When she had complied and they were face to face in the very back of the truck, he whispered fiercely, "You're my investigator!"

She shook her head vigorously. "Marko, you hired me to chauffeur you around and to investigate. I find witnesses and provide you evidence that can lead to a better result in your cases. Outside of his OWI, Innis's games don't fall within my job description. It is not a defense to anything, and it has absolutely nothing to do with his criminal charge, which, in case you forgot, is not murder."

"I didn't forget."

"Look, it's simple: you are placating this kid for money!" she said. "That's obviously something you're okay with, but I'm not."

"No, I'm not."

"Then ask yourself this: if this was Jack Daniels telling you he wanted to take you somewhere to prove some point or to 'show you something,' would you go?"

Marko didn't answer.

"That's what I thought. You are treating clients differently based on their finances, and I don't want to be part of that."

"Don't make me beg."

Whitney's voice, coming from the front of the truck, startled them both. "Maybe I can go."

Allee turned quickly. *How did Whitney hear us?*

"If Allee doesn't want to do it," Whitney said to Marko, "I can. After all, Justice Bites is more her project, and the law firm is mine."

Allee's response was immediate. "That's not a good idea."

"Why not?" Whitney challenged.

Allee knew this was at least the second time she'd been asked by Whitney to explain what was going on. "Because," was all she could manage.

She didn't trust Innis, and she trusted him even less around Whitney. He was young, but he was a liar and backed by a family name and stacks of cash—always a dangerous combination. Whitney had been taken advan-

Bodies of Proof 213

tage of a year ago by a young man with similar means; she should have learned her lesson when a student from a then-prominent family accused her of seducing him and trying to get him to murder her husband. It was the whole reason she'd left teaching, the whole reason they'd met, the whole reason she worked with them now.

"That's not an answer," Whitney persisted.

"Listen, Whitney, it's just not safe, okay?" Allee said. There was so much more that she could say, of course, but she wouldn't because she felt protective of Whitney. "He's dangerous; let's just leave it at that."

"I thought you didn't believe him," Marko asked.

"About what?" Whitney asked.

"He says he killed . . . someone," Marko explained. "Allee says she doesn't believe him, but now she's saying he's dangerous."

"Well?" Whitney asked. "Is that true?"

"I'm not sure," Marko replied, raising his hands in surrender. "But I need one of you to come with me. I've got to have a witness. Who is it going to be?" he asked, clearly hoping Allee would volunteer.

"Fine. I'll go," Allee said bitterly. He had her backed into a corner; they both knew that. If she didn't go, then he'd take Whitney. She'd never allow Whitney to mix with someone like Innis. Marko knew that, she knew that, and Marko knew that she knew that. Especially when they had no real idea what Innis was up to.

"Then let's go," Marko said, motioning for her to follow. "We have a client waiting."

Marko opened the back door; Allee was surprised to see Innis standing right outside, watching them. He must have been eavesdropping.

"Is everything okay?" Innis asked.

Marko stepped outside and Allee followed, slamming the door behind her.

"Fine, just fine," Allee said.

"Were you listening to us?" Marko asked.

Innis shrugged. "Would it be a problem if I was?"

"Hell yes!" Allee snapped.

"Why?"

"Because it's creepy, that's why," Allee shot back. "You've got no right—"

"I've got ten thousand rights, the way I look at it," Innis replied calmly.

"Let's not," Marko said. He made eye contact with Allee, and she felt herself shrinking under a withering glare. "James, if we're going to work with you, then we require your trust. If you are listening in on our private conversations, you are showing me you don't trust me or my team."

"Do you trust me?"

"No," Allee said.

"Yes," Marko said at the same time.

Innis looked from one to the other, his expression one of mild amusement. "You two really need to get your game together, you know that?"

"What do you want to show us?" Allee said. "I don't have all day." Her patience had grown thin long before they'd exited the food truck.

"Follow me," Innis said. His smile widened, but it wasn't one that showed any joy. Like a smile plastered on the face of a doll, it was merely an expression behind which anything might lie.

I hope I don't regret this, Allee thought.

45

MARKO

It's hot, Marko thought as he followed Innis and Allee across the street and down the alleyway toward the storage facility. They moved between buildings, which provided shade from the sun but also blocked the breeze, making the sticky Iowa air feel even thicker, heavier, and stickier.

"Do you really walk this every time you need the truck?" Marko asked Allee in a low murmur. He had increased his pace to catch up with her and was breathing hard and already breaking a sweat.

"I generally jog," she replied. She then picked up her pace and quickly put space between them.

She's still pissed. Could be a couple of things. He'd asked her to come with him, and she clearly didn't want to do that. But accompanying him was part of her job. Was that it? Maybe, but she'd also accused him of treating paid clients and court-appointed clients differently. Well, yeah, no shit. Paying clients were rare, highly-sought-after commodities; court appointments were almost a dime a dozen. One came with buckets of easy cash; the other required complicated fee claims and still paid barely enough to keep the lights on, or in their current situation, just enough to keep gas in the truck.

They moved in silence as they continued down an alleyway until they emerged behind Kum and Leave Storage. They followed Innis around the chain link fence that surrounded the property until they reached the front entrance. The sign was old and faded. Marko couldn't help chuckling at the sight of it. Some local joker had spraypainted a C over the K. It was childish, to be sure, but Marko had never been accused of being particularly mature. A vacant guard shack was positioned astride the gate.

"Not very secure," Marko observed.

"You get what you pay for," Innis replied over his shoulder. He had slowed so he was walking just in front of Marko.

Allee was beside Innis, but she kept her distance. "What's that supposed to mean?" she asked, her voice both tense and challenging. Marko thought briefly that he wasn't the only one on her shit list.

"It means that this place is cheap, and that means no security. Just the way I like it." Innis turned toward Allee and bared his teeth in a mirthless smile. "I pay in cash each month and the name on the storage unit is not my own."

"Whose name is on it?" Marko asked.

Innis made a zipping motion across his lips.

"Lame," Allee said, placing her hands on her hips. "Now are you going to show us what you think we need to see or not? Like I said before, I don't have all—"

"It's Unit 31," Innis interrupted, his smile widening. "Follow me."

He led the way down the aisle and toward a back corner where it was darker and more secluded. He stopped in front of an end unit. It looked exactly like all the other end units, which were double stalls with a standard door, a rolling garage door, and a regular side door.

"This way," Innis said, indicating the side door. He produced a key and inserted it, then stepped back as the door opened with ease.

Allee scoffed. "This is exactly why rich people can buy happiness."

"Why?"

"Because I spend at least ten minutes trying to get the key to turn in the garage door on our center unit."

"Not gonna lie," Innis said, stepping inside and motioning for them to follow, "I would definitely recommend being rich."

"Yeah, well," Allee began. "We weren't all born with a silver spoon in our mouth. Some of us have had to actually work for what we've got."

Bodies of Proof 217

Innis didn't respond. Instead, he quickly shut the door. Because there were no windows, the three of them were instantly plunged into darkness. Marko froze, feeling his entire body tensing. For a moment, he was back in the basement of The Yellow Lark, holding two hands on his belly in an attempt to keep himself from bleeding to death after being stabbed by an assailant. He remembered Allee finding him alone on the cold concrete floor.

He shook his head, willing himself to leave the past and the associated panic behind him. He looked around, forcing his eyes to adjust. Just as he began to make out the barest of shapes in the dark, he heard a click. He shielded his eyes from the blinding light produced by a single bare bulb suspended in the middle of the unit. He removed his hand and felt his heart beating as his eyes settled on a large object located in the center of the unit.

"Is that a freezer?" Allee asked. There was a trepidation in her voice Marko had never heard before—not even in the basement of The Yellow Lark a year ago.

"Yes," Innis said.

Marko looked around. The unit was mostly empty aside from the chest freezer, a large designer suitcase, and a pile of round objects in the corner of the unit too shrouded in shadows for him to identify.

"I think you need to see that I'm serious." As Marko watched, his eyes still adjusting, Innis reached into a pocket and produced a shower cap, a face mask, and a pair of gloves.

"What's with all that?" Marko asked, his throat tightening. "Where's ours?"

Innis ignored Marko's questions. Instead, he walked quickly to the freezer and lifted the lid.

"Jesus Christ!" Allee exclaimed.

In the corner of his eye, Marko could see her step back and cover her mouth, probably to stifle a scream. She'd been closer than he was, but Marko could see the contents of the freezer.

"Is that . . .?" Marko felt his throat tighten as his voice trailed off. He tried, but couldn't finish the sentence. The words simply wouldn't come.

"Oh yes," Innis said excitedly. "It's Leslie Martin—or should I say it was

Leslie?" he asked. "Well, I could be more accurate, even, and tell you it's what's left of her." As he finished, he was looking into the freezer.

Allee shook her head vigorously. "No! No! Holy shit, no!" she screamed.

Marko's stare was fixed on Innis, who had a frozen smile plastered on his face and a glint in his eyes as he looked at Allee and then Marko. "I told you," he said simply.

Marko had never wanted a drink more than he did in that moment.

Innis turned his attention back to Allee. "She didn't suffer, if that's what you are worried about." His tone had softened, as though he were trying to calm a frightened horse. "I want them in pristine condition when displayed; that's why I keep them in the freezer. Well, that and the smell— spoiled meat is the worst."

"Meat?" Marko heard the words come from his mouth but had no control over them—it was as if someone else were speaking in his voice.

Innis ignored him. Still looking at the contents of the freezer, he spoke almost wistfully. "This one's my little ballerina," he began. "Isn't she perfect? I think so, and when the time is right I'll set her free and display her for all to see. It's not right that only I could enjoy her, is it? Oh, there'll be some preparation involved, to be sure, but nothing that could mar her. It's very important that she is displayed just as she was—a perfect specimen."

Marko turned to see Allee vomiting in one of the dark corners of the unit. She had her back to him, but he could see her wiping her mouth. "How—how did you get her in here?" he asked.

Innis nodded to the large brown suitcase in the corner. "She fit perfectly inside, because she was—is—perfect, you see."

"But surely, somebody saw you rolling a bag like that down the trail?"

Innis was shaking his head before Marko finished the question. "They did not. Perhaps a bit of luck, of course, but I know from my prior experience that nobody asks questions when you are pulling a designer bag."

Again, Marko was hung up on particular words. "Prior experience?"

"Nope." Allee had turned and was wiping her mouth with the back of her hand while her eyes remained fixed on the freezer. "I'm not—I'm out of here," she said.

Marko and Innis watched silently as she made her way to the door in

Bodies of Proof 219

four long strides. She stopped, wrapped the end of her T-shirt over her hand, and used it to open the door. She was distraught, Marko thought, but still composed enough to realize that leaving fingerprints in this garage would be a disaster.

When she was gone, Marko turned his attention back to Innis. "Do you want a closer look?" Innis asked.

Marko shook his head.

"The two of you are no help," Innis said. As Marko watched, horrified, Innis reached into the freezer and touched Leslie's face, then quickly closed the freezer.

Marko had yet to regain full control of his vocal cords. His chest was tight, and his heart was pounding. What now? "Yeah, well, we're not going to get involved in this," he managed to say.

"Oh, Marko." Innis shook his head as if in sorrow. "Don't you understand? You're already involved. I've shared my secrets with you, and there's nothing you can do about it. In fact, if you were to share, it would guarantee my freedom. Isn't that just perfect?"

Marko swallowed his revulsion. "Why us? Why me?" he heard himself ask.

"Because the two of you were just too perfect," Innis said. "She's a felon and you're an alcoholic. Each of you has undertaken efforts to try and change, but you were just right the way you were; the way your creators made you. Like Rebecca was. Like Leslie was." He took a quick look at the freezer. "It was just too perfect," he finished, repeating his favorite word. He'd explained it all matter-of-factly, as if their past behaviors were their entire genetic makeup.

"And you're a murderer," Marko snapped. "You're a—a psycho! A murdering psycho!"

Innis looked steadily at Marko in a manner reminiscent of Whitney dealing with an angry Arlo—tolerant but weary and a touch disappointed. "So I am," he admitted as he removed the hair net, gloves, and mask. He broke eye contact just long enough to stuff them into a pocket, and then met Marko's open-mouthed stare with a smile that stopped short of his eyes. "But I'm one who isn't going to get caught."

46

WHITNEY

They treat me like a child, Whitney thought as she watched Marko and Allee leave through the back door of Justice Bites. She caught a glimpse of Innis's face through the open door as well, his expression one of deadly calm. His eyes were fixed and staring, but he wasn't watching them.

He was watching her.

Their eyes met and Whitney froze. Her entire body grew rigid, like a rabbit stuck in a field with a predator and nothing between them except newly mown grass.

That's what he is, Whitney thought, *a predator.* He was on the hunt. For what, she wasn't sure, but she knew enough to know she wanted no part of it. She'd already had her life upended once by an immature younger man —the last thing she needed was to be victimized by another boy in a man's body. She'd almost lost her freedom once; she was damned sure not going to allow that to happen again.

When Marko, Allee, and Innis were out of sight, Whitney's chest expanded and she could breathe again. She hadn't realized she'd been holding her breath, and it took several minutes and several deep breaths to regain her composure. She disliked Marko's and Allee's lack of confidence in her. It was clear they believed she was weak and scared, easily breakable. But hadn't she shown them differently? She'd been through a lot in her life-

Bodies of Proof

time. Not as much as Allee, of course—but who had? And they seemed to have forgotten that Whitney was the one who had rescued them both a year ago. Could their memories really be that conveniently short? Maybe they needed a reminder. She'd be happy to give them that—but not until they were done representing Innis.

A steady flow of customers limited Whitney's ability to focus on her troubles and kept her hands busy for a while. But after twenty minutes or so, her attention began to wander and she checked her watch frequently. *Where did Innis take Allee and Marko? Shouldn't they be back by now?*

She was unaccustomed to Marko and Allee meeting with clients anywhere other than a courthouse or Justice Bites. This was unusual—reason enough for her to be concerned. Add to that the weirdo Innis and their secretive communications and why wouldn't she worry? *Are they okay?* she wondered. *Should I call?*

She didn't want to irritate them if they were busy, of course, but they had become more than merely co-workers to her. They were friends as well. She'd already lost Leo—first to bad choices, and now to controlling behavior; she couldn't handle losing the only other adults in her life.

After twenty-eight minutes of serving customers and worrying, she was startled when the back door swung open and Allee marched inside. Whitney issued a heavy sigh of relief. She was about to comment snidely on their extended absence, leaving her to face customers alone, when she saw Allee's red eyes and tear-stained cheeks and the words caught in her throat. Instead, she gave voice to her concerns.

"Allee! What's wrong?" she asked.

"Nothing." Allee marched across the truck and grabbed a spatula, palming it in her hand. "Everything." She paced, slapping the spatula into her open palm with a *thwack* with each turn. "Nothing," she repeated.

It wasn't much of an answer, but it was a start.

"Did something happen with Innis?"

Allee issued a mirthless laugh, one so obviously pained that Whitney winced. Whatever was going on was big.

"I told Marko that kid was bad news," Allee began. "I warned him. He should have listened to me. I've spent time in the can; I can see trouble coming a mile away."

"We've all been behind bars," Whitney interjected. When she'd been falsely accused, she'd been held on a bail that was far too high for a teacher with a small child to post. And Marko himself had been locked up in connection with his OWI.

Whitney watched as Allee's expression darkened. "Prison's just a little different than county jail. Trust me, I've done time in both. Besides, you were on your own."

"Which was worse in ways," Whitney said.

Because Whitney's student had accused her of sexual assault, she had been kept segregated from the rest of the jail population for her own safety. Like the rest of society, jails and prisons were hierarchical, and just as in society at large, sex offenders occupied the very bottom levels.

"That's not my point." Allee made another turn and again slapped the spatula against her hand. *Thwack.* "My point is that I've been around bad people—the kind of people society wants to lock up and then throw away the key. Hell, I was one of those people."

"Okay," Whitney said. She was annoyed that Allee was dismissing her experience behind bars, but she wanted her to keep talking, so she shut down. Perhaps if she showed an inclination to listen, Allee would explain what was really going on.

"Innis is a monster."

Whitney watched as Allee side-eyed her; she thought she might answer. Instead she turned on her heel and marched away from her.

"How so?"

Allee ignored the question. "Of course, Marko wouldn't listen to me. Oh, no. He thinks he is so damn smart." *Thwack*, the spatula hit Allee's palm again. "Dumb bastard has been stabbed once, so now he thinks he's some kind of expert on how to survive on the streets. Thinks he can read people and shit. He wouldn't make it a week," she added derisively.

Whitney recalled that Marko's wounds had almost killed him. In her book, that should have given him a little bit of credibility, but she wasn't going to raise the issue now. Not when Allee was like this.

The back door swung open, and Marko stepped inside. His expression was flat, his color ashen, but where Allee was obviously angry, Marko looked terrified.

Bodies of Proof 223

Whitney watched as they sized each other up. "I don't want to hear shit from you right now," Allee warned. She had stopped mid-step and was pointing the spatula at him like a drunk's wife with a rolling pin.

"I'm sorry," Marko said.

Whitney actually felt sorry for him. Allee did not.

"Yeah, well, you can take your apology and—"

Whitney had heard enough. "What's going on?" she asked sharply, looking from Allee to Marko. "I need some answers!"

"Nothing," they both said in unison.

As Whitney tried to make eye contact with one, then the other, neither would hold her gaze. They were like two guilty children who'd been caught with their hands in the cookie jar.

"Really?" Whitney said. "Nothing? Nothing for the third member of the team here?"

Allee and Marko again exchanged a quick glance, but neither spoke.

"Well." Whitney placed her hands on her hips. "I guess the two of you *can* agree on something—and that's to keep me in the dark on whatever the hell is going on around here."

Not surprisingly, Marko broke first. "Whitney, it's not like that—"

"Then what is it like, Marko? Tell me. *Tell* me. Because I'm getting damn tired of being treated like a child. It's pissing me off." She paused to allow one or both to respond, but Marko was looking at his feet and Allee had her back turned, rhythmically slapping the spatula against her palm. "For Christ's sake, the two of you rarely argue, let alone fight—and even when you get on each other's nerves, it's not like this. If you remember, we're supposed to be a team, but for reasons I cannot fathom, you two have decided to shut me out."

"It's in your best interest," Allee muttered at last. "To protect you."

"Oh, silly me," Whitney said, shaking her head. "And here I was thinking that I was a grown adult and member of this team, one who could decide for herself what is good or bad for me. But I was wrong, I guess. I'm just little Whitney, dependent on Mommy and Daddy to keep me safe."

"It's not like that," Allee snapped. But Whitney could see her anger was dissipating. She now looked forlorn, almost lost.

"Then tell me, Allee, what is it like?" Again, she waited. "That's what I thought," she said at last. "Whatever it is, I have a right to know. But since neither of you can respect that, I'll be catching up on my work after spending all day covering for *you*."

She glared at Allee, then turned. Before leaving she paused briefly, giving them one more opportunity to demonstrate a degree of trust in her. Neither spoke, so she stormed out of the truck. If they wanted to fight some secret fight, they could do it without her as an audience. She was done being the weak wallflower; done doing as she was told.

47

JENKINS

Wednesday, June 2

Jenkins was awakened long before it got light. He made himself a cup of coffee from the in-room coffee maker, then read the news on his phone until it was time to head to the courthouse. There was no point in stopping by the law enforcement center first; nobody there was expecting him, and no one would care to help him, either.

As he drove and reflected, he became increasingly frustrated. Despite his best efforts, he'd been unable to make real progress. He'd heard nothing more from the forensics laboratory, and he hadn't been able to dig up any more information. He'd stopped by Leslie Martin's house, but her family and friends weren't any help. Understandably, they were distraught and feeling guilty that their relationship was frayed at the time of her disappearance. "Political differences," was how they'd explained it.

Despite the absence of good news, he'd remained hopeful that Woodford's proffer might turn up information regarding the death of Rebecca and/or the whereabouts of Leslie. He looked at his watch; the proffer was scheduled to begin minutes from now. He parked and was walking to the courthouse when Justice Bites rolled to a stop in its usual location. He ignored his growling stomach, choosing instead to take the two flights of stairs to the third-floor jury room, where he found McJames. For a brief second, his optimism remained. Then he saw Dennis Shaffer seated next to McJames.

"This the place?" Jenkins asked McJames. He had yet to so much as look at Shaffer.

"There's no jury trial today," McJames replied. "So yeah. We'll do it here."

"What are you doing here?" Shaffer asked.

"Exercising the authority granted me by your boss," Jenkins responded tightly. He surveyed the room quickly. The room was rectangular, dominated by a large table stretching along its length, with twelve wooden chairs evenly spaced around it. The only other furniture was a side table with a coffee bar. As far as he could tell, there were no electronics in the room. Shaffer and McJames were seated on the side of the table opposite the door with their backs to the wall, a single chair between them. Jenkins made his decision and walked around the table, then selected the chair between McJames and Shaffer.

"Can you boys play nice?" McJames asked. "Just for today. Fake it if you need to; I need you both to help with the questioning."

"We get along just fine," Jenkins said. *When I ignore his lazy ass.*

They fell silent, reviewing notes and checking and rechecking watches, until Marko and Woodford arrived five minutes later.

"I'd say 'Good morning,'" Marko began as he and Woodford settled in. "Unfortunately, any morning around you fellas isn't good at all."

Shaffer scoffed, McJames shook his head, but Jenkins sat quietly, refusing to take the bait. Bauer's little gambit was pure theatrics; he was hoping to start them off wrong-footed. And by the look of the red-faced McJames and bug-eyed Shaffer, he was off to a pretty good start.

"Have a seat," Jenkins directed Woodford. *Two can play this game.* He pointed to a chair across from McJames.

Woodford sat as ordered, but Marko's head swiveled. "Any coffee?" he asked, indicating the pot on the coffee bar.

"You just came from Justice Bites," Jenkins observed.

"Yeah, well, drinking my stuff cuts into my profits."

"You'd rather suck up the taxpayers' money instead," Shaffer snapped.

Bodies of Proof

227

"Exactly," Marko replied calmly.

"We didn't make any coffee, Marko," McJames said. "This is not a social call. Now sit down and let's get started. We don't have all day."

Jenkins watched as Bauer placed his briefcase on the table and spent the next few minutes retrieving pens, legal pads, and notebooks from the bag. At last, he placed his briefcase under the table. After doing so, he remained bent at the waist, as if examining something under the table. Jenkins was about to look under the table when Marko straightened.

"Yo, Shaffer," he began. "Them's some pretty good chew marks on your boot. What happened? One of your girlfriends get hungry?"

Jenkins suppressed a laugh and watched as Shaffer's face turned beet red.

"Are you about ready?" McJames asked. Jenkins could see the prosecutor was growing more agitated by the second. He wished McJames would leave it alone; Bauer was obviously not going to follow a direct order from him. He was clearly refusing to sit simply because he'd been told by McJames to do it. He snuck a look and—as expected—saw that Shaffer was similarly irritated by Bauer's little game. Jenkins shook his head in disgust at himself. He'd expected McJames, Shaffer, and Bauer to be used to each other by now. *Apparently not.*

Jenkins had seen enough. "There are a number of documents you will need to sign before we proceed," he said, ignoring McJames and sliding a stack of papers across the table to Woodford, who looked to Marko for guidance. When Marko nodded his assent, Woodford signed without reading and then pushed them back.

"Good," Jenkins said. "Let's get started. I'll be recording this interaction," he added as he retrieved a small, handheld recording device from his pocket and placed it on the table in front of him.

"So am I," Shaffer said. "And for the record, I'll be leading this investigation. You can ignore *Special Agent* Jenkins over there," he said to Marko and Woodford, enunciating his title as a little boy might *cooties.*

Jenkins held his tongue. It would do no good arguing in front of a defense attorney. They'd already shown too much disdain for each other.

"You're here because you want to work off some charges," Shaffer began.

"Yeah," Clint said.

"So, tell me, what information do you have that you think is worthy of us wiping your slate clean?"

Shaffer's bottom-line-up-front questioning wasn't how Jenkins would have started the discussion; he would've spent a few minutes building rapport with Woodford. But then again, this was a small town, so Shaffer and Woodford were probably well acquainted. If Shaffer treated this man like he did everyone else—and there was no reason to suppose he would not—then any show of kindness would have aroused suspicion.

"I got stuff about Rebecca Calloway," Woodford said.

"Excellent," Shaffer replied quickly. "And I'm interested in finding out whatever I can about her, so how about you go ahead and impart your wisdom upon us all?"

Woodford, oblivious to the sarcasm, nodded. "Someone was coming to Olde Bulldogs and leaving her notes."

"What kind of notes?"

Woodford shrugged. "Weird ones. They didn't make no sense."

"Can you remember what they said?"

"Not really."

"Well, do you have a copy of these 'notes?'" Shaffer made air quotations with his fingers as he said the word.

"I took a picture of one of 'em."

Shaffer sat expectantly, until—seeing Woodford wasn't going to volunteer the information—he couldn't stand it any longer. "Well, what does it say?"

Woodford removed his phone from his pocket and pressed several buttons. "It says, 'The world is a *Carnival of Animals,* but I will free you soon.'" Woodford's reading was stilted and slow, Jenkins noted. Reading was not a strength.

Jenkins leaned forward eagerly. "Can I take a photograph of your phone with the image on the screen?" he asked.

"Yes," Woodford said.

"And will you text me a copy of it?" Jenkins asked. When Woodford nodded, he jotted down his cell phone number and slid it across the table to Woodford, then watched as Woodford typed the number into his phone.

Bodies of Proof

Jenkins's phone buzzed and he nodded in satisfaction. He now had a copy of the image as well as Woodford's phone number in case he needed to follow up with questions.

"I want a copy, too," Shaffer said, shooting Jenkins a look of irritation.

Jenkins ignored him and resumed his questioning. "Why do you think this letter has anything to do with Rebecca's disappearance?" He was watching Woodford closely for a tell. A lot of defendants looking at time in prison exaggerated the importance of information they had; even more held back what they could while trying to get a deal done.

"Because she got it the day she was taken."

"How do you know that?" Shaffer said.

"Because I was there when the person gave it to her."

"Who was the person?" Jenkins asked, leaning forward in his chair.

Woodford looked to his left and right—as if there was yet another person who might be listening. It was a ridiculous gesture, Jenkins thought, given the setting.

"Marko Bauer," Woodford said at last.

Jenkins watched as Marko, who had been alternately chewing on an ink pen and doodling on the notepad in front of him, now jumped to his feet and slammed the pen on the table. "What the hell are you talking about?"

"I'm just doing what you told me to do," Woodford replied, looking up at Marko, who was leaning over him, enraged. "You told me to tell the truth. That's what I'm doing," he added, looking to Shaffer as if asking for assistance.

"The hell you are!" Bauer shouted. "This is total bullshit!"

"Counsel, let him answer the questions," Shaffer said. Jenkins was eyeballing Shaffer carefully; he looked and sounded almost gleeful.

Marko wasn't having it. "I'm not going to sit here and let him lie about this."

"Who says I'm lying?" Woodford said.

"I do, you little rat-bastard!"

Shaffer was smiling broadly now. "You seem awfully defensive for an innocent person," he said. "I haven't seen you this angry since I busted you for driving shit-faced in front of Olde Bulldogs—or was it The Yellow Lark? I can't remember; I just remember you were drunker than—"

Bauer turned on Shaffer, who stood quickly. Each man was now leaning over the table and pointing at the other. The discussion devolved into an argument, with each red-faced belligerent attempting to shout threats over the voice of the other. While they focused exclusively on each other, McJames turned to Jenkins and spoke loudly.

"I think you ought to go ahead and apply for that warrant," he said. "I don't like it, but I think you've got enough now."

"Understood," Jenkins assured him. He was watching Bauer and Shaffer as they exchanged threats, personal and professional. "I'll get right on it."

He stood and stepped quickly out of the room, closing the door behind him. Once he was alone in the hallway, he took a deep breath, savoring the quiet, musty air of the ancient courthouse. He'd brought his laptop with him for the proffer; all he needed now was thirty minutes to draft the search warrant and find a magistrate to sign it. Then he'd be in business.

This might be the break he'd been looking for.

48

MARKO

"What the hell is wrong with you?" Marko shouted as he reached in his pocket and clicked the record button on his phone.

He'd dragged Woodford from the meeting room over the objections of Shaffer and McJames as soon as he'd realized that the DCI agent had taken his laptop and disappeared. They were now together in an attorney-client meeting room down the hall.

"What do you mean?" Woodford wore the blank expression of a true sociopath.

"What do you mean, what do I mean?" Marko gestured toward the room they'd just departed. "All of that, everything you said, was bullshit! Lies! All of it!"

Woodford's eyes narrowed. "Was it?" he asked. He dropped into one of the two plastic chairs in the room.

"You know damn well it was!"

Marko watched, astonished, as Woodford calmly picked at a cuticle. "I do?" he asked. "I'm not so sure. I think the really important question here is whether *you* remember what happened back then."

Woodford's nonchalance was infuriating. For as long as they'd known each other, Marko had assumed he was a nobody—a no-account criminal totally dependent on him. He'd busted his ass for the guy and his reward was this? Marko took a deep breath.

"What is that supposed to mean?"

"It means that you were drunk a lot back then. All day, every day." Woodford met Marko's stare.

Marko saw something in Woodford's eyes. Was it confidence? "So what? I drank a lot, but I remember what I did."

"No, you don't."

"Says who?" Marko asked.

"Oliver . . . he told me stories."

Fucking Oliver, Marko thought. The bartender who wouldn't talk to cops and barely spoke to Allee was apparently willing to flap his gums to anyone about him. He sighed heavily and ran a hand through his thick hair. He turned, ready to give Woodford another piece of his mind, when without warning the fight left him. This was getting him nowhere. The damage had already been done. Woodford couldn't take his words back even if he wanted to, and it didn't seem like he did.

"I'm done," Marko said. "I can't keep representing you. I'm going to file a motion to withdraw."

"Can you do that?" Woodford sat up, suddenly alert. "Why?"

"Why the hell do you think? Because you told lies about me," Marko snapped, again pointing down the hall. "Lies that the DCI agent is using right now to get a search warrant to investigate *me* for something *I* don't know jack-shit about!" Marko patted his chest firmly. "You've made yourself a witness against me in a murder investigation. Does it sound like I'm going to be in any position to help *you* out?" Marko began pacing in the small room.

"Look, uh, Marko . . ."

"And that's assuming I would want to help you." Marko stopped and turned to glare at Woodford. "Which I don't, by the way. I'd rather crawl over a hundred yards of broken glass naked."

"I didn't realize—"

"Bullshit! You've played this game before. You're gonna try and tell me you didn't realize that your words during a proffer would have ramifications? Please. If only there was someone who could have told you that lying

Bodies of Proof   233

your ass off would come back to bite you—a lawyer, perhaps? Oh, wait, I told you to tell the truth; you lied and screwed me over and so now here we are!"

Marko was putting materials into his briefcase in preparation to leave when Woodford spoke.

"But he told me that nothing would happen—"

Marko swung around quickly, his fists balled. "Excuse me?" His heart was beating rapidly against the walls of his chest, and his ears were buzzing. He took a step toward Woodford. "Who? Who told you what?"

Woodford, so confident just seconds prior, had now taken on a defensive position in the small chair. "Nobody! Nothing! I swear!"

"Who. Told. You. What?" Marko asked again. He was now standing directly in front of Woodford, staring down at him.

Woodford attempted one last act of bravado. "Don't worry about it," he said.

"Why me?" Marko persisted. "There are millions of people in this state alone. Why would you lie and say it was me?"

"He—he said because you were a lawyer, you'd have . . . I dunno, some kind of privilege or something. I didn't really understand but—"

"Who is advising you!" Marko barked, slamming his palms down on the table as he screamed the words into Woodford's face. "Tell me!"

Woodford crossed his arms in front of himself. Marko half-expected him to push out his bottom lip. He did not, but he didn't say anything, either.

"You know what?" Marko began. "That's fine; don't say anything, but I'm withdrawing as your attorney, effective right now. And you—you little shit —you can deal with whomever the court appoints for you. And guess what?" he asked as he reached into a pocket.

"What?"

"I gotcha on tape, you dumb bastard. I got your lies on tape, and now I got your admission that you lied."

"Marko—"

"And now I'm gonna get back to my truck so I can try and stop those cops before they get to digging through my drawers and examining my skivvies or—and worse for you—going through my case files. All my case files, including yours."

"Marko, I didn't realize—"

"Of course you didn't, you dipshit." Marko turned toward the door, still speaking over his shoulder. "But that's what happens when you start taking advice from someone other than *your attorney*."

"But who will help me?"

Marko opened the door and paused in the doorway. "Not my problem."

Then he slammed the door shut behind him.

49
WHITNEY

Whitney was pleased, because for the first time in a long time, Allee was inside Justice Bites, running the morning sales. While Whitney watched, Allee greeted customers, took orders for cinnamon rolls, and made change with a genuine smile. It had been a long time since she had watched Allee lose herself in the business, and it was a welcome sight.

"You really love this, don't you?" she asked when the line of customers finally broke.

"Yeah," Allee said, wiping her hands on her apron. "Honestly, if I had it my way, this is all I'd do." She paused, studying Whitney for a long moment. "You know that, don't you?"

"I mean, I guess," Whitney said. "You seem to do whatever Marko asks —and you do it well."

"Yeah, well, false enthusiasm is better than none at all." Allee was running water over a large baking pan while she spoke. "Investigating . . . well, it reminds me too much of my past."

"Why not allow me to do it, then?"

Whitney watched as Allee blinked several times, opened her mouth, closed it, and then blinked again. "I didn't know you wanted to," she said.

"Allee, I just want to be part of the team, and you and Marko seem hell-bent on keeping me out."

"Whitney, it's not that," Allee replied. She flipped the baking pan over and ran water over that side. "We're not trying to shut you out. We're trying to protect you."

"From what?"

"From—"

A heavy knock at the back door interrupted Allee's explanation. They exchanged a look and froze. If it was Marko, he would have simply walked in. Again they heard pounding, louder this time, more insistent.

"Police! We have a search warrant. Open the door!"

Whitney opened her mouth to respond but couldn't. Her mind went back to the last time she had heard those words, when law enforcement had knocked on the door of the home she had shared with her husband and Arlo. She remembered Leo opening the door and officers storming into their home, ripping Arlo from her hands, and dragging her off to jail. Those knocks and the subsequent events had changed her life forever.

Bang! Bang! Bang! The man at the door was hitting it hard enough to shake the entire food truck.

Whitney looked to Allee. Her expression had gone from startled to steadfast. This was why she and Marko had so much faith in her. Allee might be scared, but she was never deterred.

"You break it, you've bought it, asshole!" Allee shouted. She put the baking pan in a drying rack.

"Open the door! Now!"

"Stop pounding on it and I will," Allee said.

When the pounding stopped, Allee stepped to the door, then opened it to reveal half a dozen officers, some with guns drawn. Jenkins was front and center, holding a stack of documents in his hands.

"Well, good afternoon, Special Agent Jenkins," Allee said. "To what do we owe the pleasure?"

"I have a search warrant for your truck and the law practice."

"It's not my truck," Allee replied calmly.

"Whatever," Jenkins said dismissively. "The warrant was signed by a judge and allows us to search the truck no matter who is here."

Whitney's mind was awhirl. "You said *the practice*," she mumbled.

Bodies of Proof 237

"Yes. That too."

"What are you looking for?" Allee asked. "Maybe we can help so you don't scare the shit out of our customers."

Whitney marveled at Allee's apparent nonchalance; if she hadn't known her so well, Whitney might have believed she wasn't intimidated at all.

"Here you go." Jenkins handed Allee a copy of the warrant. "Read it and weep. Now if the two of you will step outside, we can get started."

"You want to get out of the way? We're not going to climb over you."

Jenkins moved to the side, seemingly unperturbed by Allee's attitude.

When they were outside, Jenkins and several low-level officers Whitney had never met swarmed the two businesses they had worked so hard to build, virtually devouring them by their very presence. Word would get out, no doubt. Whitney walked around the truck, keeping a wide berth, and looked across the parking lot to see Cameron snapping photographs and grinning maniacally.

Allee stood beside Whitney. She scanned the papers Jenkins had given her, then folded them and put them in a back pocket as she nodded in Cameron's direction. "He's loving this," she said. "I wonder if he's behind this somehow."

"He might be," Whitney replied tightly. "And you know what? I'm not surprised."

"Why would you say that?"

"Because you and Marko keep secrets, and secrets cause problems. You give every indication that you have information no one else does, act like something's going on, and keep people like Dale and me at arm's length. That makes people paranoid."

"That dumb bastard would be paranoid no matter what," Allee shot back.

"Yeah, well, *I* wouldn't be. Like right now, we've got a bunch of cops going through our stuff. I have no idea where Marko is, but I'm smart enough to know you probably do," Whitney said. "And I have no idea what the hell is going on with these cops, but I suspect you probably do. But instead of telling me what's up, you keep secrets from me."

Allee pulled the papers from her back pocket and handed them to Whitney. "You want to know what's going on? Here you go."

As Whitney eagerly scanned the three-page document, she felt her blood run cold. When she finished, she looked to Allee. "This—this can't be right. They can't think Marko had anything to do with those women disappearing!"

"Not only do they think it, but they've done enough thinking to put it on paper and convince a magistrate to find there's probable cause to believe a crime was committed and Marko—and by extension you and me—is involved."

"But that can't be! It's ridiculous to think—" Whitney began.

"Well, I'm going to give you two a choice," Jenkins said, coming up behind them. "Someone can tell me about the notes I found in the trash can inside the truck, or we'll go to the station and have a more in-depth discussion. Who wants to start?"

"Notes?" Whitney asked.

"What notes?" Allee echoed.

"Notes," Jenkins replied. Whitney watched him staring at Allee. When she snuck a look at Allee, she could see her calculating, trying to figure out what Jenkins was asking about.

"As in *plural*?" Allee asked.

Whitney's mind had stuck on the same word, but she hadn't told Allee about the note she'd thrown away—had Innis given one to Allee, too? Why else would she ask that question?

"Yes. Plural." Jenkins's eyes had narrowed. "Does that make a difference to you?"

Whitney watched Allee measuring Jenkins.

"Well?" he pressed.

"I don't want to talk to you," Allee said. "I don't have anything to say."

Jenkins turned his attention to Whitney.

Whitney's view of Jenkins was blocked when Allee stepped between them. "She doesn't want to talk to you either," she said.

"She's an adult; I'm pretty sure she can answer for herself," he said.

They were both eyeballing her, and Whitney felt herself tensing up. She knew of one note, of course—the one that Innis gave her, but she wasn't sure if she should say anything. Innis was a client—their first private pay client. All ethical considerations aside, Marko would never forgive her if she threw an accusation out that would cost them future clients like him.

"I don't have anything for you," Whitney lied. The words slid off her tongue like a fruit smoothie.

50

JENKINS

Jenkins snapped on a pair of plastic gloves, and while the other officers rooted through cabinets and poked around for loose floor tiles, he placed a trashcan on the counter and carefully went through it, removing each piece of refuse from the can, examining it, and then placing it on the countertop. He anticipated the search would come up empty. For one thing, he was a cop —a profession that attracted pessimists and eventually turned the few optimists in the ranks inside-out. For another, he harbored serious doubts about Marko being a killer. Despite the evidence, he just wasn't feeling it. And third, even if he was wrong and Marko was the guy he was looking for, would he really be stupid enough to leave evidence lying around? It was doubtful.

Unless he thought he had his bases covered.

A small piece of crumpled paper caught his eye, and he carefully photographed it and then removed it from the trash can before opening it with shaking hands. He scanned it and then returned his attention to the trash, carefully moving things around until he spied what he was looking for—another note. This one was different; whereas the first was handwritten, this one was made by the unknown author using letters cut from newspapers and magazines. He took pictures of this one as well, and then returned to digging carefully through the small trash bin.

"Anything?"

It was a sergeant with the Franklin police. Jenkins didn't know the man, and certainly wouldn't trust anyone Shaffer had appointed to a leadership position. On the other hand, should this case come to trial at a later time, cross-examination could prove tricky if he testified to a piece of evidence he had denied existed or minimized the importance of now.

"Agent Jenkins, isn't it true that you told another officer you hadn't found anything you deemed important at the conclusion of your search?" was how it would go. Such was the stuff of which acquittals were made.

"Maybe," he allowed, stuffing the notes into a pocket. "I'll know more later; I need to get back to the station to decide."

Back at the law enforcement center thirty minutes later, Jenkins examined the notes he had carefully placed on a table. Each was encased in a clear evidence bag. He retrieved his phone and thumbed to the image Woodford had sent him before the proffer hearing went south—the note Woodford had said Rebecca received shortly before her disappearance. He quickly located the image he was looking for and laid his phone next to the bagged, handwritten note.

I'm no expert, but they look the same to me, he thought. They were both written in the same careful, slightly sloped cursive writing. For one thing, the writer had added a slight wing to the first and last letters of each word of the handwritten notes. Then, examining the printed letter and comparing it to the pair of handwritten ones, he noted the cryptic italicizing of certain phrases in each: *Carnival of Animals, Cinderella Story, Midsummer Night's Dream,* and *Rite of Spring.*

Jenkins rubbed his chin. "Gotta mean something," he said. "But damned if I know."

"Talking to yourself is a sign that you are crazy."

Jenkins issued a heavy sigh and answered without looking up. "Yeah, well, we're all a little nuts."

"Sergeant Jones says you mighta found something," Shaffer began. "Notes, he said."

Jenkins reflected on his quick interaction with Jones. He thought he'd obscured Jones's view, but perhaps not. "Not sure yet," Jenkins replied carefully. "This isn't nothing, but I can't say for sure what it is." He gestured toward the table.

Shaffer gave the notes a cursory glance. "Looks like a whole lot of nothing to me," he said, slurping his coffee.

Jenkins pinched the bridge of his nose, sucked in a breath, and counted to five before he responded. How could a trained law enforcement officer be so wrong, so frequently? "What do you want?"

"To tell you that we've got another body."

"What?" Jenkins took his eyes off the notes for the first time. "Christ, Shaffer! Why the hell didn't you lead with that?"

"No rush." Shaffer shrugged. "She ain't goin' nowhere."

"Where is she?" Jenkins rounded the interview table.

"Same trail," Shaffer said, calmly slurping coffee. "Same general location."

"Let's go," Jenkins said as he passed Shaffer.

Jenkins ran to the car without waiting for Shaffer and drove to the scene. En route, he called Mia, who had somehow already heard and told him she was on her way with the forensics team. He ended the call just as he arrived at the trailhead, and pulled in among the law enforcement vehicles, ambulance, and firetruck already on scene. Shaffer arrived seconds later.

Without speaking, they made their way down the trail, following the sound of hushed voices.

"Should be right up here," Shaffer remarked as they approached a bend in the trail.

The voices grew louder, and they came to a line of police tape with a young deputy standing watch behind it. The deputy recognized Shaffer and lifted the tape. They ducked under it and headed for the cluster of people standing near the center of the trail. To Jenkins's surprise, Chief Brown stood at the center of the group.

"Where?" Jenkins asked. He was breathing heavily, his heart rate elevated and palms sweaty from the excitement and exertion of the rush to get to the scene.

Brown motioned for Jenkins to turn around. He did so, and his breath caught. It wasn't the same place he had found Rebecca, but it was very simi-

Bodies of Proof 243

lar. Thick foliage in the area had been thinned in this location, creating a small clearing. The clearing featured a single tree, from which a woman was suspended.

"Leslie," Jenkins whispered. Damn it! He'd been too slow!

Just as with Rebecca, the killer had not hung Leslie by the neck; rather, she was posed with one arm above her head and the other stretched out as if in receipt of a gift from above. One leg was straight down with the toe pointed, and the other was bent with the pointed toe resting against her upper thigh, forming a triangle. Her hair was in a bun, and she was dressed in a white costume.

"That's a piqué, right?" Shaffer asked.

Jenkins looked sharply at his old adversary. "Say what?"

"A piqué," Shaffer replied. "It's a ballet thing."

"I'm getting the feeling I don't know you as well as I thought I did," Jenkins commented. He didn't know anything about ballet; all he knew was that from where he stood Leslie looked a lot like the tiny ballerinas from the music boxes.

"Who found her?" Jenkins said.

"Another jogger," a nearby deputy answered.

"What'd they use to suspend her?"

"Fishing line. A lot of it," the deputy said.

Just like Rebecca. "We've got a serial killer on our hands," Jenkins concluded. He studied Leslie's lifeless form. "Too many similarities; this can't be a coincidence."

Shaffer scoffed. "What proof do you have of that?"

"Look at her!" Jenkins snapped. He was done trying to make peace with the man. "She's the second one, posed just about the same, in the same general location. Anyone who knows anything about homicide would recognize that this isn't a coincidence. Our killer is sending us a message. And the bodies are proof of it."

"Could be a copycat," Shaffer opined.

Jenkins was watching Shaffer for a tell. "But nobody knows what we—I —found, unless you or your men told—"

"Aw, shit!"

It was a familiar voice. Jenkins turned to see Mia and her team approaching. Forensics had arrived before Shaffer and his team could pollute the scene. He'd never been more relieved to see her. "Not another one," she lamented.

Soon after, the locals departed, enabling Mia and her team to get to work. Jenkins stood quietly to the side, awaiting preliminary results and watching Shaffer closely.

After about fifteen minutes, Mia came out from under a tentlike structure that had been erected around Leslie's body while brandishing a small plastic bag. "I think we've got something," she offered, excitement in her voice as she held it up for Jenkins to see.

Jenkins narrowed his eyes, studying the object in the bag. "Is that a pen?"

"Yes." Mia pointed to the cap. "And those are bite marks."

Jenkins's heart jumped. "That means DNA."

"It might," she agreed.

"Where did you find it?"

"Directly below the body."

It was a break, and a big one.

"You've got to get that to the lab. *Now*," Jenkins said.

"On it." Mia nodded. "My team can process the rest of the scene without me." She was already headed toward her car.

"Thank you!" Jenkins called after her.

She didn't break her pace but threw up a hand in acknowledgement.

If they could get a DNA match on the pen, Jenkins knew, they'd have some very solid, albeit circumstantial evidence. But most killers were caught via circumstantial evidence, and they had more than just the pen.

Five minutes earlier, he was half-convinced he needed to look into Shaffer's whereabouts on the days those women disappeared. But things had changed quickly—and he'd bet his bottom dollar he knew whose pen it was.

51

WHITNEY

While the cops were rummaging through Justice Bites, Whitney and Allee sat on the curb nearby, waiting in silence, each lost in her own thoughts. For her part, Whitney was still furious with Allee and Marko. She side-eyed Allee, whose mood had abruptly (and understandably) changed with the cops' arrival. Whitney knew any talk between them would quickly devolve into an argument, so she held her tongue.

She was thinking about Arlo in an attempt to change her own mood when she heard Marko yelling.

"What the hell is going on here?" he bellowed. "Who is in charge here?"

Whitney whipped around. There was something odd about his speech. Was it because he was yelling?

As she watched, Marko pounded on the door to Justice Bites. "I wanna know who is running this shit-show!" he yelled.

"Oh, no," she said. She wasn't afraid for Marko due to what he was saying—it was the sing-song, slurring manner of his words.

"Christ," Allee snapped. "He's drunk." As Whitney stood, she saw Allee push herself off the curb and march toward the truck.

Marko was standing in front of a young officer, pointing a finger at him, shoving it into his chest. Unknown to Marko, Jenkins and the more senior officers had all left the scene minutes before, presumably taking the items of importance with them, and leaving two young cops to finish the job.

"I demand to know. I demand—" Marko was saying.

Whitney watched in shock as Allee grabbed Marko by both shoulders and shoved him away from the young officer to avoid having him getting arrested for public intoxication, breach of peace, or both.

"I'll handle this," Allee told the cop. "It's been a long couple of days."

"Keep him away from us," the cop warned.

"Got it," she said as she guided Marko toward a bench outside the courthouse. He stumbled a couple times, but Allee caught him.

Whitney followed behind. Allee and Marko worked well together, and she could see from Marko's muted reaction toward her physically removing him that there was real trust there. When one stumbled, literally or figuratively, the other provided support. But for whatever reason, neither was compelled to include her in their little circle of trust. They stood in front of her rather than beside her. This couldn't continue; she wasn't a child and didn't need protection.

Whitney had slowed, keeping her distance and allowing Allee to handle the immediate danger. But as she watched from afar, a question popped into her mind.

Why is Marko drinking again?

Before he and Allee had left to speak with Innis, Marko seemed like his usual self. An hour later, Allee returned furious and unwilling to talk. Then there was the proffer and Marko had returned two hours later drunk as a skunk. Marko, she knew, was not a problem drinker. He was an alcoholic, meaning he couldn't drink at all. A heavy drinker—a problem drinker, even —could fall off the wagon, wake up with a hangover, and go on with his life. Not Marko. For him, a relapse was truly a life-threatening matter and caused a chain reaction that would take weeks or months of work to get through.

I'm not going to interrupt, she decided. Because Whitney wasn't a sufferer, Allee and Marko didn't believe she knew much about addiction. But she was not ignorant; her brother had been a drug addict before taking his own life. If she walked over to them now, they'd view it as an intrusion—just one more subject that was off limits between them and her. They were obvi-

Bodies of Proof 247

ously in emotional turmoil, but if they didn't want to talk about it, there was nothing she could do to make them.

She turned and walked purposefully. She didn't know where she was going, but she knew she didn't want to be where she was. She walked west, her mind blank, with no thought other than to get out of there. For thirty minutes, she focused on nothing but putting one foot in front of the other. As the distance between herself and Allee, Marko, and Justice Bites increased, she started to feel better, freer. She was no runner, but between the fresh air and distance she was putting between herself and her problems, she could see why so many runners laced up and hit the pavement day in and day out.

Suddenly, she found herself in a dirt parking lot facing a tree line. Something about the place was familiar to her despite never having been there.

This is the trail! The trail where Rebecca and Leslie had disappeared, and where Rebecca's body had been found! Curious, she walked the edge of the brush, searching for an opening in the foliage. At last, she found a small opening in the dense brush. She ducked and shimmied through the woods, covering her eyes as branches and twigs pulled at her, until she reached the crushed rock path. It was quiet and secluded, and she felt isolated despite the location in town. A sudden burst of paranoia overcame her and she looked around quickly. Was she safe? Hearing muffled voices to her right, she turned quickly in that direction and peered into the trees but saw nothing. Still, the voices gave her comfort. If someone attacked her and she called out, someone else would hear and come to her rescue.

Won't they?

She walked east, away from the cacophony of voices. Birds chirped, squirrels scurried above her in the trees, and rabbits hopped around in the long grass. Normally, she wasn't one to spend much time outdoors, but today she found it relaxing. Maybe she'd have to start. She walked at a quick pace until she came to a small wooden sign on the right side of the road. She read, *3.5 M.*

She was three and a half miles from the trailhead. She paused, again listening for the sounds of humanity, but this time she heard no one.

Maybe I ought to turn back.

She was debating her next move when it occurred to her that the woods had gone utterly silent. No birds, no squirrels, nothing.

She'd read long ago that woods fell silent when top-tier predators were nearby. But what kind of animal would hunt here? Coyotes? Dogs? She'd heard of a few mountain lion sightings in Kansas and Iowa, but never near Franklin.

Time to go.

She turned and—avoiding a terrifying temptation to break into a jog—began walking quickly back toward where she'd entered the trail. Again, she was no expert, but she thought she remembered hearing guidance from a park ranger somewhere that if a large predator was following, the best thing you could do was to avoid running.

She heard the man before she saw him. She tried to run, but he was on her too quickly. He wrapped an arm around her shoulders and neck and pressed something wet over her face. *A rag of some kind.* She panicked and tried to draw a breath, but in lieu of air she felt her mouth and nostrils draw only fumes she would later recall as pungent and sweet. She stomped on his foot, but he didn't react. She fought as best she could, but soon weakened. Darkness crowded the edges of her vision, obscuring her attempts to identify her attacker.

What is that smell? She tried again to fight, to struggle free, but her punches were slow and her kicks ineffectual because her arms and legs were sluggish now, as if she was underwater. Seconds later, the darkness was complete. He had won.

52

ALLEE

"Seriously, Marko?" Allee said as she guided him over to a bench outside the courthouse and forced him to sit. She sat down an arm's length away.

"Seriously, what?" he slurred.

"You stink, for one thing," she scolded. She leaned away from him. "You smell like a freaking bar rag."

"*You* shmell like a bar rag." He jabbed a finger at her and swayed. "I smell just . . . good," he added, then giggled. "'Sides, who're you to be tellin' me anything? I'm you're boss—you 'member that?"

Allee ignored him and looked again for the two officers who had remained behind. She was still worried about him catching a public intoxication charge. They were in deep shit already; the last thing she needed was him in jail. The warrant said Jenkins had probable cause to search for evidence of kidnapping and murder. Until and unless they found something, Allee knew, Marko would be a free man—unless he gave these cops reason to bust him.

"Why didn't you call me?" Marko asked.

She continued to ignore him, but instead looked over and around him, still searching for the pair of uniformed cops. They hadn't given her a property inventory yet, so they were probably still there somewhere, tearing stuff up.

Marko grabbed her chin and jerked her head so she was forced to look him in the eyes. "Why didn't you call me?" he drunkenly demanded.

Allee reacted instinctively. She placed both hands on his shoulders and shoved him hard. *Nobody touches me. Ever.* "Get your freaking hands off me!" she hissed.

"Whoa!" he protested as he attempted to maintain his balance and avoid falling off the bench. "Why'd you do that?"

"Don't touch me. Ever."

"Why didn't you call?" Marko repeated.

Allee stood and turned back to him, standing over him as she spoke in a firm but quiet voice. "Because you were supposed to be in the middle of a proffer. Because I was dealing with *your* employee, Whitney—who wants to know what the hell is going on, by the way. Because when she and I were talking, Jenkins and the cops showed up and gave me *this*." She shoved the warrant at him. "Because it never occurred to me that you'd leave the courthouse and get shit-faced. But most of all, because you are now a murder suspect and—even if I don't think you did anything—you being a suspect is about to ruin all our lives. How's that?"

"I'm not shit-faced," he slurred. "Jus' had a coupla beers. Can't a guy have a coupla beers?"

Allee threw up her hands in frustration. "I don't really care, Marko. Kill yourself—whatever. My point is that we are in deep shit and it's all because of your love of money and that idiot Innis."

"He confessed to murder," Marko said. "I—I wasn't ready for that to begin with, then Woodford said I gave Leslie a note before she disappeared. I needed to think, so I had a drink or—"

"Or fifteen."

He waved a dismissive hand. "That's not my point."

"What is your point, then, because I'm getting tired of waiting for you to get to it."

Marko took a deep breath and held it, then began to speak. "My point .. . my point is that *we* aren't in trouble; *he* is."

Allee pressed a hand to her forehead and forced herself to breathe deeply. "Marko, you're holding a warrant showing Jenkins has probable cause to search your business and Justice Bites for evidence."

Bodies of Proof 251

"But I—"

He started to stand but she shoved him down again. "Sit down!" she ordered. "You're not going anywhere. I'm going to tell you why they are here searching, since you're too drunk to read."

"O—Okay," he said.

"The application for a search warrant says Clint Woodford claimed you were stalking Rebecca before she disappeared, and that you left creepy notes for her."

Marko's eyes bulged with recognition. "It said that?"

"Not in those words exactly, but that was the gist of it. Did your proffer this morning go sideways?"

"Yeah. You can say that," he acknowledged with a sleepy nod. "Woodford said that Oliver said I gave Rebecca a note. But that ain't enough for a warrant!"

"It also says that your fingerprints were found on a music box that matches music boxes found at the scenes of Rebecca's and Leslie's abductions."

Marko shrugged. "I dunno what that's all about."

"Me neither, but it's a problem."

"That's nothing. They can't make a case out of that."

"They probably can't," Allee said. "But you have no idea what else they are going to find."

"They aren't going to find anything, 'cause I didn't do it."

"Ah, great," Allee said sarcastically. "The famous some-other-dude-did-it defense. Like I've never heard that one before. That's always so helpful with our clients, isn't it? What is it that you usually say to them?" She tapped a finger on her chin, pretending to think. "Oh yeah: 'Nobody gives a rat's ass if you did it or not. The only thing they care about is if they can prove it'—did I get that right?"

Marko nodded, a drunken grin forming on his face. "You listen."

"That's not my point!" Allee growled, taking a step closer to him. It was hard enough to confront any man—especially her boss—under normal circumstances, but it was much, much harder when Marko was drunk. She leaned down so she was eye level with him. "My point is that someone is setting you up, which means they are setting *us* up."

"Us?"

"Us! Me and Whitney!"

"Who is?"

"Jesus, Marko! Are you even listening to me?"

"Listening," he replied, and tapped his ear. "But I'm having a hard time following."

Allee sighed heavily and tried to think of a way to explain the situation to him in terms that would make sense to a man whose BAC was probably higher than his GPA.

"We know that Innis murdered Rebecca and Leslie, right?"

"He said he did," Marko agreed. "We saw Leslie's body."

"No shit."

"Why you mad at me? It isn't my fault that he killed her, and it isn't my fault that he showed—"

"Shut up and listen," Allee snapped. "He kidnapped Rebecca, killed her, and then kept her in the freezer," she explained.

"I know," Marko agreed.

"And at some point, he kidnapped Leslie."

"And he needed the freezer space," Marko interjected. "Or so he said. I dunno why he didn't buy—"

"It doesn't matter. He needed the freezer space, which means that he had to do something with Rebecca's body."

"Right."

"Meaning that he had to move Rebecca's body."

"So?"

He still wasn't getting it. "So he needed to create an alibi," she explained slowly. Seeing he wasn't following, she moved closer and looked in his eyes. "He purposely acted drunk so he could create at least the appearance of an alibi."

Marko's eyes widened in recognition. "But—but the cops might find out that—"

"Right! So what did he need, then?"

Marko snapped his fingers awkwardly. "A mark."

"Excellent," she said. "You. He needed someone to pin it on. He chose you."

"Why me?" Marko asked, slurring the last word.

"Because he needed someone he could be around regularly. Someone he could steal stuff from, maybe get some DNA. Someone with a less than stellar reputation." She was putting the pieces together as she spoke.

Marko sat quietly, thinking. Even in his drunken stupor, he could weigh defenses. "How do you know he pretended?" he asked. "There was no testing."

"I *don't* know," Allee said. "But Lieutenant Davis said something like that when I asked him about Innis."

"Well, that would have been good to know," Marko observed. "It could have helped with Innis's defense."

"Marko, it wasn't evidence! It was a guess posed by a cop. And we're defending *you* now—right?" she asked. "Innis somehow got your fingerprints on one of the music boxes. Do you remember him giving you one or touching one?"

"Umm . . . I found one on the table during the meeting with Jack Daniels." Marko chuckled at the memory. "He told me it wasn't his, so I chucked it over my shoulder. I guess he was right."

"You had a meeting with Innis before that, right?"

"I—I think so."

"Yeah, you did. "So was the box there when you started your meeting with Innis?"

"I don't remember."

"Well, it wasn't there when Whitney and I set up Justice Bites," Allee replied quickly. "Think, Marko!"

"I'm trying," he said blankly.

"I think it had to be. That's how the prints got on the box. Had to be," she concluded, before changing subjects. "Woodford. Do you think he's working with Innis?"

"Gotta be." Marko nodded sleepily.

"Why?"

"'Cause he said. . . he said . . ."

She was losing him. She reached out and shook his shoulder. "Marko, damn it! Wake up!"

"Huh? What?"

"Why do you think Woodford was working with Innis?"

"'Cause he said that he said that he wouldn't get in trouble if he helped him."

Allee shook her head in confusion. "Who said what?"

"Woodford. Woodford said *he* said—"

"He who?"

"I dunno." Marko shrugged.

"Marko! You didn't think to tell me that?"

"It's complicated," he said slowly. "We got attorney-client privilege with Woodford, and attorney-client privilege with Innis . . . I mean, it's complicated."

"Okay," Allee replied, considering. "But the conversations while you *were* representing both of them are still privileged, right?"

"Yes," Marko said, lowering his head. "That's how it works."

"Then there is the credibility issue."

Marko struggled to lift his head. "What's that?"

"It's your word, and my word, against Innis's. A felon," she said, indicating herself with a thumb, "and a drunk." She pointed at Marko. "So, us versus a rich kid golden boy who will no doubt have the best mouthpieces money can buy. So even if we break privilege, who do you think they will believe?"

"Can't," he said. "Won't work."

"What do you mean?"

"It's not just that it's unethical to break privilege." He shook his head. "It's inadmissible—can't come in." It came out *inadmisshable*.

"What about what Woodford said?"

"Hearshay," he slurred.

Allee rubbed her eyes and tried to figure out what to do. Christ! So even if they told someone—Jenkins, maybe?—he couldn't use it. Maybe it was time for them to tell Whitney what was going on. They'd tried to keep her out of it, but if Marko was going to be arrested, their business would suffer. There was no protecting Whitney from that. Besides, Whitney was smart; she might be able to look at the problem differently.

Marko was sitting on the bench, about ready to pass out. Allee stood and looked for Whitney. She wasn't sitting on the curb anymore, and she didn't seem to be anywhere nearby.

"Whitney?" Allee hollered.

"Whitney?" Marko repeated. "What about her?"

"She's gone."

53

ALLEE

Hours passed and there was still no sign of Whitney. Allee paced outside Justice Bites, trying to figure out what to do next.

For the first hour, she had maintained her cool. For sure, Whitney was pissed—and she had a right to be, honestly. They'd ignored her; they'd shut her out. But if she would've known why—if she had possessed the horrific information they had—she might have understood, or she at least wouldn't have been so angry. But she didn't, of course. There was no point dwelling on that.

She called Whitney's cell phone once in the first five minutes, twice in the next thirty minutes, and five times over the remaining part of the first hour. Each time it went to voicemail.

"This is Whitney," Whitney's sing-song voice said. "Leave me a message."

Allee did not leave a message.

Over time Allee's shock turned to aggravation, then to irritation, and now she was alternating between uncontrolled rage and debilitating fear. Something was wrong—Whitney wasn't like this. She didn't strike out on her own, and it was nearing time to leave; she wouldn't risk missing a ride back to Ostlund—and Arlo.

Allee needed to act. She walked to the front of the truck and peered in

Bodies of Proof 257

the window to find Marko passed out, lying across the entire bench seat. He was so drunk that he wouldn't be any help. The best thing she could do was leave him to sleep it off.

Of all days to fall off the wagon, Allee thought.

She was an addict; she understood. The stress had been too much. He'd gone back to his old ways—using booze to substitute for healthy coping skills, to give himself just a little relief, just a little time to gather his thoughts and put things in perspective. But as an alcoholic, the first drink turned into ten. She couldn't blame him; she wanted a fix right now, and seeing him like this wasn't doing her any favors.

She knew—felt, anyway—that Whitney needed her help. And Arlo certainly needed them to come home. What would he say if Allee came home without his mother? How would she explain the situation to him? She couldn't do that to him. She made her decision and did something she'd never done in her life—not when she was overdosing, nor when some man was beating her, stealing from her, or whatever. She called a cop.

He answered after one ring. "Jenkins."

"Hey," Allee said. "It's Allee Smith. I need to talk to you."

"If you're gonna piss and moan about that search warrant, I already explained—"

"Not about that."

There was a long pause. When he spoke, his tone was softer. "What's going on?"

"It's Whitney," Allee said. "She's missing."

"Whitney?" Jenkins repeated.

"She has a small child. He's six. She's never disappeared like this," Allee explained. "It's past time for us to head back, and she's always the first one ready to head home at the end of the day to get back to him. We usually leave by four forty-five." Allee lowered her phone so she could check the time, then brought it back to her ear. "It's five o'clock now."

"How long has she been missing?" Jenkins asked.

"An hour, maybe two? I think she walked off when I was dealing with Marko, and now, well, now I'm calling the cops for help." She sighed heavily. There. She'd done it.

"Where's Marko?"

"Passed out."

"I need to talk with him."

Allee felt the hair on her forearms stand up. "You're barking up the wrong tree," she snapped. "Marko didn't kill anybody."

"I just go where the evidence takes me," Jenkins replied calmly. "Besides, what makes you so sure?"

"Because he's a . . . not a strong man. He's not wired like that."

She waited while Jenkins thought. "Send me what you know about Whitney," he said at last. "Where did you last see her?"

"Sitting on the curb beside Justice Bites while your guys were rifling through our shit."

Allee ran a hand through her short hair. She couldn't believe she was doing this. Marko was going to have her head when he found out that she'd called the very person who had executed a search warrant on their place of business for help.

"I'll get someone on this. I'll start looking for her myself," he promised. "And Allee?"

"Yeah?"

"I'm gonna need to talk with Marko here real soon."

"He can't be a suspect. I just told you—"

"Let's go with *person of interest* for now."

She hung up, trying to decide what to do next. Should they stay? She could help look for Whitney, but someone had to pick up Arlo. Adaline was great for a few hours before and after school, but she was old and tired. She couldn't leave Arlo with her all night.

What would Whitney want?

The answer was simple: Whitney would want Allee to take care of Arlo. She had done what she could; one more person tromping around Franklin looking for Whitney wouldn't make a difference. She'd alerted law enforcement—that was what solid citizens did, right?

She packed up Justice Bites, opened the door to the truck, and—after shoving Marko into a semi-seated position—began the drive to Franklin. At some point she realized that for the first time in her life, she was praying for the cops to succeed.

54

JENKINS

Twenty-four to seventy-two hours—that was how long Mia said it would take to get the DNA back on the pen cap.

He had expected to spend that time pacing, looking at his watch, and trying not to encounter Shaffer. He'd been in his makeshift office at the law enforcement center when Allee had gotten ahold of him. Because Whitney hadn't been missing long enough to initiate a missing persons report, he'd started by sniffing around unofficially to see if anyone had heard or seen anything. Whitney was an adult woman and had every right to simply take off, of course, but given the fact that she had a child, and because two attractive women had already disappeared in this town, he was taking Allee's concerns seriously.

More importantly, all three women had contact with Marko Bauer.

He knows, Jenkins thought. They'd executed a search warrant on his business earlier that day. *He's gotta know his time is limited; maybe he wanted one last kill.*

Outside the courthouse, Jenkins found Cameron still parked in the lot, packing up for the day. When Jenkins approached, Cameron was inside with his back turned, transferring a box from one place to another.

"Dale!" Jenkins called.

Cameron looked up and turned around.

260   JAMES CHANDLER & LAURA SNIDER

"Do you have a minute?"

Cameron forced a smile. "Of course. Anything for my favorite customer," he said, setting the box down and coming to the window. Suddenly, his brow furrowed. "I'm, uh, closed for the day. I've put my food away, but if you come back tomorrow, I—"

"Right. Yeah. Maybe I will," Jenkins said, but he wouldn't. At least not if he could avoid it. "Right now I need some information. Word is that Whitney Moore has disappeared."

"Whitney, huh?" Cameron mused. "She was the only decent one out of that lot." He nodded to where Justice Bites usually parked.

"How about Allee?"

"She's got a hot temper and tattoos," Cameron replied dismissively.

Cameron had a hot temper and tattoos as well, but Jenkins let it pass.

"She's also a felon," Cameron pointed out.

"True, but from what I can tell, she paid her debt to society and is now holding a job, staying straight . . . Isn't that the idea?"

Cameron merely grunted. It was the closest thing to agreement Jenkins figured he would get on the issue.

"What do you want to know? You want to know the last time I saw her?" Cameron asked.

"That'd be a great start."

"Oh, I remember, all right. I've got pictures."

"Pictures?"

Cameron extended a tattooed arm through the window and handed his cell phone to Jenkins. A picture was displayed on the screen. "Swipe left."

The first image, the last taken, showed Justice Bites. It looked deserted. Nobody was in the picture. Not Whitney, Allee, or Marko.

"I took that one right after the officers left."

"Where is everyone?" Jenkins asked.

"Beats me."

Jenkins swiped left and observed another picture of the truck. In this one he could see Whitney walking out of the frame. He swiped left again. In the third image, Whitney was sitting on the curb with her elbows on her knees, her chin resting in her hands. Unlike the other two pictures, Whitney seemed to be the focus of this photograph.

Bodies of Proof 261

"Why did you take these pictures?" Jenkins asked.

He'd long felt uncomfortable around Cameron, but now he was feeling downright uneasy, and questioning everything he'd been thinking. Something about this guy wasn't right. Had he fallen victim to a cop's worst nightmare—tunnel vision? After all, Cameron had a connection with all three women, and if he wanted, he could probably pilfer pens and leave stuff around to frame Marko. Focusing on one suspect too closely too early could lead to confirmation bias and the easy dismissal of other potential suspects. It was something he had spent his career trying to avoid. Had he blown it this time?

"I wanted proof that they"—Cameron nodded toward where Justice Bites usually sat—"are still criminals. People need to stop going to them for business."

Jenkins nodded and looked back down at the phone. He swiped left again. The image showed Allee and Whitney sitting on the curb, side by side. Here, Cameron had clearly zoomed in on the women. Whitney's head was down, but Allee was sitting straight, her head turned as though she was looking or listening to something behind her. There were no officers in the photograph, nor was the truck included. It made Jenkins more uneasy.

Jenkins continued swiping left, seeing and swiping past multiple images of officers going in and out of Justice Bites. In one picture, Shaffer was bellied up to the ordering window—as if they could do business while a search was ongoing. He handed the phone back to Cameron.

"Will you text me those images?"

"Sure," Cameron promised.

"Was that the last time you saw Whitney?"

Cameron shifted his weight and pocketed the phone. "I mean, yeah, come to think of it. She walked off and never came back."

"Which way did she go?"

Cameron pointed. "That way."

Jenkins looked to the west. The trail was in that direction, of course, but it was a good distance. Would she have walked that far? And if so, why?

"I don't see Marko in any of these pictures," Jenkins said. "Do you know where he was?"

"Dunno." Cameron shrugged. "I never pay much attention to him."

Because he isn't involved with your competition, or because he isn't a woman? Jenkins wondered. "I won't take up any more of your time," he said, stepping away from the truck.

Back at the law enforcement center, he was gathering materials to begin his search when Lieutenant Davis approached him.

"I've been looking for you."

"What's up?" Jenkins asked.

"I got a call from Allee Smith. I just arrived for my shift. She asked me to help you search for Whitney."

"Good for her," Jenkins said. "Not in her nature to call cops. That makes twice in one day."

"I like Whitney. I knew her brother; poor girl was always in and out of the police station, trying to find ways to get him sober. Unfortunately, she never really succeeded. He committed suicide a little over a year ago."

Unfortunately, it was a tale each of them knew far too well.

"Well, I could damn sure use the help," Jenkins admitted.

"What do you know?"

"Only that Whitney was last seen by Dale Cameron, and that he says she just walked off, heading west."

"The only thing west of here is the trail."

"That's what I'm afraid of." Jenkins pocketed his keys and patted his holster to ensure the automatic was still there. "Wanna ride?"

55

JENKINS

Thursday, June 3

Jenkins awoke with a start. In his dream, he'd been walking down a hallway with his gun drawn, looking for a woman being held hostage. But instead of finding the woman—or even confronting the bad guy—all he'd done was open door after door. One door opened, then closed quietly behind him. Creep to the next door, open it, scan for threats, close it behind him, and repeat the process. The process had been repeated over and over until Jenkins awoke, screaming in frustration.

He and Lieutenant Davis had searched for hours to no avail. They'd left the station and had driven straight to the trail, entering through an opening in the brush the local cop knew about that was just about halfway along the trail. Parting the brush, they stepped into a clearing, revealing a portion of the trail Jenkins had never seen, as there'd been no need. From the evidence, Rebecca and Leslie appeared to have been abducted closer to the trailhead, and their bodies were found near that area. He and Davis had done their best, but after several hours they hadn't found anything—no disturbances in the grass, no crushed music boxes, no notes.

No pens.

Perhaps she had simply wandered off; perhaps she hadn't fallen victim to Marko—or, as the local media had christened him, the *Trailside Abductor*. It was corny as hell, of course, but he couldn't blame the press; in a town of this size, a story like this might come along once in a generation. After it got dark, he and Davis had returned to the station and interviewed all the courthouse's nightshift employees. Nobody admitted to having seen Whitney leave. They called the cops who had helped serve the warrant and conduct the search—the ones who had stayed on after Jenkins left with the notes. They'd all sleepily claimed they'd been focused on the execution of the search warrant. They were left with nothing and nowhere to go with the investigation. By midnight, Jenkins called it quits so he could return to his hotel and get some sleep.

Still shaking off the effects of the nightmare, he met Justice Bites as Allee and Marko pulled into the lot. Marko looked exhausted. Seeing Jenkins, Marko lifted a bottle of water, took a long pull from it, then rubbed his eyes. When he put his hand down, Jenkins noted the bags under his eyes. Was he tired? Hungover? Worried? All three?

Allee parked and jumped out, heading straight for Jenkins. Marko did not leave the truck.

"Did you find her?"

Jenkins shook his head. "No sign."

"This is bad." Allee's eyes filled with tears, then, seeing Jenkins watching her closely, she apologized. "I'm sorry." She pressed the heels of her hands into her eyes as though she was trying to force the sadness back inside. "It's just, her son misses her."

"Tough night?"

She nodded vigorously. "He didn't sleep at all. Neither of us did." She sighed. "This isn't her. Whitney would never, *ever* walk out on him. She was mad at me and Marko, so walking off makes sense, but refusing to return isn't something she would do."

"Why was she angry with you and Marko?" Jenkins asked.

Allee opened her mouth to answer, then closed it again. Her expression became thoughtful. After a long moment, she finally answered the question. "We kept something from her."

"Oh?" Jenkins asked. He hadn't begun to suspect Allee of any wrongdoing.

Bodies of Proof   265

"It was something with the business. We were trying to shield her from it, and she found out anyway."

"She found out through the execution of the search warrant?" Jenkins asked.

"No, the search warrant had nothing to do with it other than the fact that you all are way off track with that one. Way. Off. Track."

That was interesting. "Why don't you guide me to the track, then?"

"I can't."

"Why not?"

"I just can't," Allee said, her temper flaring. "Or Marko could lose his license and we could lose this business, and the whole world I have fought so hard to create over the last year will fall apart."

Lose his license? Jenkins wondered. Crimes were a cause for a lawyer to lose their license. Murder, especially. Was Allee covering for him to protect her business?

Allee shook her head. "I need to get to work. Will you promise to keep looking for her?"

"Absolutely." And he meant it.

Allee seemed to relax, and he walked away from Justice Bites, heading for the law enforcement center, where he remained for the rest of the morning. He felt like he was spinning his wheels. He had two dead women and a third missing. He had a primary suspect, one he was itching to arrest, but he still had to wait on forensics.

Shortly after noon, his phone rang. Mia's name showed on the screen. He snatched it off the desk and jammed it to his ear. "Tell me something good," he said by way of greeting.

"Are you sitting down?"

"I don't need to sit. Just tell me." Jenkins began to pace.

"It's a match. Bauer is your guy."

"Yes!" Jenkins pumped his fist in the air.

It was time to go get his man.

56

ALLEE

The entire evening had been a total disaster. Arlo had started crying the instant Allee had told him that, "Mommy isn't coming home tonight." He continued sobbing until he had no more tears left, and then he had moped.

This is exactly why people lie to children, Allee thought as she drove Justice Bites north toward Franklin. She should have told him his mother had gone on an unexpected work trip or something. But she was stupid and honest, and as a result, she'd gotten very little sleep. Her eyes felt gritty when she blinked.

Marko was asleep next to her. She'd arranged for Adaline to come over and watch Arlo so she could leave by six o'clock in the morning. She wanted to get to Franklin as early as possible so she could start searching for Whitney.

Allee picked up the phone and began dialing as she drove. She'd already talked to Lieutenant Davis at five-thirty that morning, before he'd gotten off work at six. He'd come up with nothing during the search other than the knowledge that Whitney had headed west before seeming to disappear into thin air.

Damn. There was no answer. Allee hung up and continued driving. When she got to the courthouse, she parked and spoke to Jenkins, then she did the only thing she could think to do. She started her morning as though

Bodies of Proof 267

it was any other day. She served customers, moving robotically, as her mind remained elsewhere.

Mid-morning, there was finally a break in the crowd. She shut the window and got into the cab of the truck, once again dialing her phone and bringing it to her ear. It rang three times, then a now-familiar, flat voice answered.

"Where is she?" Allee demanded.

"Where is who?" Innis replied.

"Is she still alive?"

"Are you okay, Allee? You sound crazy."

"Don't gaslight me, you little shit. I know you took Whitney, and I want you to bring her back."

"Bring her back? She's not a doll, Allee." His tone was infuriatingly calm. "She's not a ballerina."

The word choice was so oddly specific that it made Allee's skin crawl. She'd read through the search warrant repeatedly throughout the night, searching for signs that could lead her in the right direction. In the application for a search warrant, Jenkins had stated that they were looking for more music boxes with ballerinas or a receipt for them. He'd also described that Rebecca's body had been dressed as a ballerina. Allee hadn't heard that information anywhere outside the search warrant, which wasn't public knowledge unless she made it public, and she hadn't. No news outlet had reported on the ballerina angle, and that could only be because they didn't know yet.

"If you don't tell me—"

"Now why am I being threatened by my own attorney?" Innis asked.

"I'm not your lawyer. I'm his investigator." Allee glanced over at Marko. He was snoring and reeked of alcohol. He was going to have to receive inpatient treatment if he didn't get the reins on his addiction. And soon. For now, she had bigger concerns.

"Whatever. You do all the real work," Innis said. There was a smile in his voice.

"You set Marko up. Why?"

"See? I told you that you do all the real work. He probably wouldn't have put that together without you. Nobody would have. Not that you can do anything about it."

"I can tell law enforcement."

"No, you can't. Privilege," he said. "And I've got . . . help."

"Screw privilege," Allee growled.

She was over playing these lawyer games. She was willing to play by the rules when the world wasn't crumbling down around her, but now that Whitney was gone and Marko was off the wagon, she had no such desire. She thought of the tattoo running along her left collarbone, *Beware; for I am fearless, and therefore powerful.* When everything was falling apart, there wasn't much to lose, which made her fearless.

"Okay, fine," Innis said with an exaggerated note of disappointment. "I thought you might say that. Look, I chose your firm for a reason, of course. I think you suspected that from the start, but Marko was way too greedy to figure it out."

"Figure what out?" When he didn't respond, she pressed him. "Figure what out?"

She waited impatiently. He seemed to be thinking it over. "What the hell. Nobody will believe you. Not over me. You can scream from the rooftops that I'm the guy, but the evidence points to Marko."

Allee looked up as Innis uttered the words. Jenkins and five other officers were standing there, staring at her and Marko, who was still sleeping off the booze. Jenkins held something in his hands. She rolled down the window and Jenkins approached.

"I've got an arrest warrant for your boss," Jenkins said. He didn't sound excited or elated. He sounded almost apologetic, which Allee appreciated.

"Oh, good," Innis said into Allee's ear. "I get to hear him get arrested. This is really something."

Allee unlocked the doors, and Jenkins walked to the passenger side. He pulled the door open and caught Marko—who had been leaning against the door as he slept—as he fell out.

"What? What is going on?" Marko grumbled, still half drunk and half asleep.

"Where is she?" Allee hissed into the phone as she watched Jenkins get Marko to his feet and handcuff him. "She'd better be alive."

Bodies of Proof 269

"She's alive," Innis said. "For now."

An idea popped into Allee's head. One that she hoped would keep Whitney alive until Allee could find her. "You've miscalculated, Innis," Allee said.

"I don't think I have."

"Oh, you have."

"Tell me." She heard a note of concern creeping into his voice. "How exactly have I *miscalculated*?"

"Because if Marko is in custody, how can you blame him for Whitney?" she asked. "This blows your whole plan. You can't have bodies turning up while he's in jail—the cops will figure out they've got the wrong guy."

"I—"

"That's a problem, isn't it?" Allee said. "You've got a girl who was gonna be your third ballerina—because you can't stop. You killed Rebecca and Leslie because you are a psychopath and you can't control yourself. You got Woodford to help you. So what are you going to do now that Marko is in chains, you little prick?"

"You got just about all of it figured out, don't you?" he asked. "I think maybe she'll be found right where she is. Cops will assume Marko didn't get to her yet."

That might work, but she needed to give him doubt. "No, it won't," she said, putting as much venom behind her voice as possible. "You're screwed. The cops figured it out just a little too soon. You do anything to Whitney, and they'll know Marko had nothing to do with it, and the whole thing will come tumbling down, you freak."

"Don't call me that."

"I'll call you whatever I want," Allee said. "You took my friend and killed two innocent women. You hunted them; now I'm going to do the hunting. Watch your ass."

57

WHITNEY

Everything hurts, Whitney thought as she forced her heavy eyelids to rise. She was lying on her left side with her cheek, hips, and legs pressed against something hard and cool. *Cement.*

She used her hands to push herself up into a sitting position. They were bound together with zip ties. Her feet were bound together in the same way. *What is going on?*

She remembered walking away from Justice Bites, furious with Marko and Allee for keeping secrets. She'd made it to the trail, and then nothing.

Where am I? And how did I get here? Whitney wondered.

Looking around, she saw one bare bulb illuminated, creating a halo of light around what looked like a large freezer that hummed with electricity. The rest of the room was empty. A large, garage-style door was to her left and there was a door behind her. The lighting cast deep shadows in the corners of the room. Whitney's fingers brushed up against something small and round. She felt around and found several other similarly shaped objects. She grabbed one and brought it near her face, examining it in the dim light.

It's a music box, she thought. *How strange.*

She wound it up and listened to the familiar tune as the lid opened and a ballerina rose. The music came to a stop while she was trying to recall the

Bodies of Proof 271

name. Just then, the side door opened, and two men stepped into the room. The light was so strong it blinded her, but she could discern that one man was smaller, frail. The other was large and imposing. They were talking in hushed voices. Fortunately, the beam of light from the open door did not illuminate her, and she lay down quickly, feigning sleep.

"She's going to wake up any minute now."

The voice was familiar, but—like the music—she couldn't place it.

"I don't care; we can't kill her," the second man said. His words sent a shiver up Whitney's spine—it was James Innis!

Does this have to do with what Marko and Allee were shielding me from? Whitney wondered. She'd known it had something to do with Innis, but that was it. If so, they'd done a poor job of protecting her.

"We can do her in a different way and make it look like someone else did it," the first man said.

Whitney knew his voice, too. It was a client, for sure. She had talked to so many of them over the phone of late. She just needed to pinpoint him.

"Oh, yeah, that's real believable, Clint," Innis said, his voice dripping with sarcasm.

Clint Woodford!

"We've had no murders in Franklin for twenty years, and now, all of a sudden, there are two related ones and a completely unrelated one in a span of a few days," Innis said. "Do you even hear yourself? It'll screw up everything."

"We could make it look like an accident," Woodford suggested.

"We took her in the same way we took the others," Innis hissed. "And besides, I don't want to make it look like an accident. I want to make her a ballerina, too."

"You have a problem," Woodford said. "The ballerina stuff is weird."

"It wasn't my idea."

"Well, it wasn't mine!"

"Yeah, well, we're all in this together."

"I'm here for the money." Woodford shrugged. "That's it. I helped you guys move the bodies. That's it."

"You'll do exactly what we tell you to do," Innis hissed. "Or you-know-who will come see you."

"So, what do we do?" Woodford asked.

"I'm not sure," Innis said. "I need time to think."

Whitney tensed but forced her body to remain still even though she could feel their eyes on her.

"Leave her," Innis said. "There's nothing she can do even if she wakes up."

"What are you going to do?"

"I need to go see my lawyer."

58

MARKO

"Well, Marko, it doesn't look like much has changed, does it?" Shaffer said as he strolled through the door. He held a manila folder in his hands. "Marko Bauer drunk in a jail cell."

And your fat ass harassing me, Marko thought.

He was sitting in an interview room in the law enforcement center, *again*. A year ago, he'd sat in the very same room after Shaffer had arrested him for operating while intoxicated. He'd had a splitting headache then, and he had another now.

He shouldn't have been drinking. He knew that when he'd left the proffer and headed for Olde Bulldogs. Five or six double whiskeys and a couple of beers, and two hours later he'd stumbled back to Justice Bites to find his business ransacked by law enforcement and Whitney missing.

"This time things are a little worse, though, eh?" Shaffer approached the small table where Marko was seated and took the single free chair. He settled his large frame into it and stared coldly at Marko, apparently hoping for a response.

Marko didn't answer. Sure, his head hurt like hell, and he'd give just about anything to get out of this brightly lit interview room and to his next location, which undoubtedly would be a smaller, darker jail cell—but he knew better than to start talking.

If you didn't call them, don't talk to the cops. How many times had he given a client that advice? Nothing good ever came out of running your mouth, even if only to claim your innocence.

"Nothing to say?" Shaffer asked. He pushed back in the chair so the front legs were off the floor. "Let's try it this way. Do you know why you are here?"

Marko blinked. A long beat of silence passed.

"Let me help you out," Shaffer said. "Let's look at some pictures, shall we?"

He opened the folder and took out a blown-up photograph, sliding it across the table to Marko. Marko looked down to see Rebecca Calloway hanging from a tree. She was dressed and positioned like a ballerina. Her skin was ashen. Her face was . . . Marko looked away and tried to keep his expression even.

"She's dead there," Shaffer said, tapping the photograph, trying to get Marko to look at it again. "But you knew that already, didn't you?"

Marko pressed his lips into a thin line.

"Here's another one," Shaffer said, taking another photograph out of his folder and sliding it across the table.

Marko's gaze skated across the image, then darted away. It was Leslie Martin. She was dressed similarly, also hanging from a tree, but in a slightly different position.

"You gotcha some kind of ballerina obsession?" Shaffer asked.

Marko blinked again.

"You wanted to dance when you were a kid, but your mommy wouldn't let you? Is that what this is? So you hate women and you hate ballets, so you merge the two?"

While Marko hated to admit it, Shaffer might be onto something. Not with him, of course. He'd never seen a ballet in his life, and he never planned to go to one. But he recalled that Innis had come into their very first meeting complaining about his mother, and he was from a rich family, one that probably traveled to Chicago to go to ballets and operas and do the other things rich people did.

He couldn't and wouldn't share his thoughts with Shaffer, who wouldn't believe him anyway. If Marko started talking, Shaffer would twist his words

Bodies of Proof

and use them against him. It was precisely why Marko advised his clients not to talk to law enforcement. Even when they thought they were helping themselves, they were still digging a hole.

"You've got nothing to say about these women?" Shaffer leaned forward so he was closer to Marko. "Nothing to say to their grieving families?"

Marko blinked several times.

"Fine." Shaffer shoved back his chair and stood. "You can sit here and think about it. But know this: we've got your ass, Bauer."

Shaffer stormed out of the room, and Marko did nothing. He didn't shift his weight. He didn't sit back and relax. He kept as still as possible. Shaffer was gone for now, but the cameras were still rolling. If McJames later wanted to show Marko's interview to the jury, Marko was going to make it as boring as humanly possible so they'd lose interest.

He might be hungover, he might be under arrest and in chains, but he was still a lawyer—and a damn good one at that.

59

ALLEE

Allee was sitting in the truck, her hands gripping the steering wheel. When she glanced at the clock, it read 10:16. Marko had been perp-walked across the street to the law enforcement center fifteen minutes ago, probably to be taken to an interview room where they would start the interrogation process. She had a decision to make: see if there was anything she could do to help him, or try and find Whitney.

The storage shed, Allee thought. *That's where she has to be.*

She could go, of course, but how would she get inside? She didn't have a key. And what if when she got there Innis was there? And Woodford, if he was working with Innis. She couldn't overpower them both, and there'd be no telling what they'd do to Whitney if Allee tried to force her way inside and got caught.

Whitney needs me.

Marko was tired and hungover, but he was still a lawyer. Drunk, sober, or hungover, he'd know better than to talk to the cops about anything.

That's it, then, she thought. *Decision made.*

She was about to start the truck when she saw Innis jump out of the black limo and enter the law enforcement center. He had to be going to see Marko. She hopped out of the truck and jogged across the street, then took

Bodies of Proof   277

the stairs two at a time to the second floor. She approached the gatekeeper at the front desk. Margaret, according to her nametag.

"Can I help you?" Margaret asked, appraising Allee.

"Is Lieutenant Davis here?"

"Well, yes, actually. He works night shift and he's not normally around this time of day, but there was—" She stopped speaking abruptly, then chewed on her lower lip, thinking for several moments before she continued. "Well, he's here anyway. Would you like to speak to him, Ms. . . ."

"Smith. Allee Smith."

Margaret lifted the telephone receiver and brought it to her ear. "Give me a few minutes."

"Tell him it's an emergency."

Moments later, Davis exited through the secure door that led to the law enforcement portion of the building. Seeing Allee, he headed straight for her.

"What's going on?"

"Marko was arrested a little while ago."

"I know." He looked around himself, his expression wary. "I know he's your boss, Allee, but I can't interfere with—"

"That's not what I'm asking you to do," she interrupted. "Just listen. Please."

He was watching her closely. "Okay."

"James Innis just entered the building."

"Okay, yeah," he said uncertainly. "We've talked about him before."

Allee was watching Davis closely; he clearly had no idea where this was headed.

"He's gonna want to talk with Marko. Let him."

"What? I don't—" He shook his head. "Marko is being interviewed by Captain Shaffer right now. I'd have to ask him."

"Do it!"

"Why? What do you think—?"

"So you can hear what he says."

"But doesn't Marko represent him? We can't—"

"Innis isn't going to be talking about his OWI, I can tell you that."

"What will he be talking about?"

"I, uh, can't tell you that."

"Allee! For crying out loud!"

"Look, talk to Shaffer," she insisted. "Trust me."

Davis looked around. "Okay, you wait here," he said uncertainly. "I'll be right back."

While she waited, Allee reviewed what she knew of attorney-client privilege, but only for the OWI—not for anything else. With Marko in handcuffs, his and Innis's roles were essentially reversed. Innis was not in chains; he could come and go as he pleased. If Innis chose to say something on camera in an interview room, then that was his choice.

Davis had returned. "Why am I letting Innis talk to Bauer again?"

"Marko isn't talking, is he?" Allee asked.

"No," Davis admitted. "He's been infuriatingly silent. He won't even say he's innocent. He says nothing."

"Let Innis in," Allee said again. When Davis didn't move, she pressed him. "What did Shaffer say?"

Davis shrugged. "Can't find him."

"Dan," she pleaded. "I know that I haven't done anything to earn your trust, but just . . . trust me. Please. You want Marko to talk, this is how you do it."

"Fine," Davis said, running a hand over the stubble on his face. "It's probably gonna cost me my job, but fine."

"Good." Allee gestured toward the locked law enforcement door. "Show me where we can sit to watch."

"Follow me," he said.

Allee knew that Davis would not believe that Innis, the scion of the Innis family, was a cold-blooded murderer without seeing and hearing it for himself. Allee needed Innis on camera, and she had to hope that Marko would figure out what was going on and seize the opportunity.

60

MARKO

Marko had been sitting alone for at least thirty minutes, trying to relax and wishing his head would stop pounding when he heard the door open.

"Shaffer," he said. "I'm not going to say anything. Why don't you—"

"Hello, Marko," Innis said. He walked quickly across the room with his head held high and a slight smile playing across his lips, clearly enjoying the sight of Marko chained up and under interrogation.

Marko hadn't asked to see Innis, and even if he had, Shaffer wouldn't or shouldn't have allowed it. There was nothing in the law that allowed a suspect to talk to anyone outside of a lawyer after his arrest and before booking. Something was up.

"How did you get in here?" Marko demanded. "Who authorized it?"

"I dunno. Some lieutenant," Innis replied dismissively. "Doesn't matter. I'm your client and I need advice."

Oh, but it does matter. Where is Shaffer? "You want advice on your OWI case right now?" Marko asked.

"Not my OWI."

The contract that Innis had signed outlining the scope of Marko's representation only included the OWI. He'd been able to shoehorn his earlier confessions of prior murders under Marko's privilege umbrella only because he'd divulged his acts in private while seeking Marko's advice.

They were not in a private place anymore. They were in an interview room that was clearly and obviously recorded. Privilege would not apply to anything Innis said.

"I want you to understand something," Innis began.

"What's that?" Marko was trying to remain calm, but he could see it coming.

"I have something you want. Something you are very fond of. As long as you do exactly what I tell you, that something will be returned unharmed."

"You sorry bastard!" Marko seethed.

"Tsk, tsk," Innis clucked. "You haven't let me finish. Now my, er, associate Clint Woodford has made some rather surprising claims."

"None of which are true."

"Perhaps, but the deal is this: you will acknowledge every detail and admit to those acts, and in return I will return the item of yours undamaged." Innis allowed himself a thin smile that didn't reach his eyes. "Well, there may well be some minor damage, but I think you understand—"

Marko looked toward the one-way glass, hoping someone was watching. He laughed. It was a dark, mirthless laugh. "You're kidding, right?" He lifted his hands and jingled his shackles. "I'm here because of *you*. Do you really think I'm going to cooperate with you based on a promise?"

"What choice do you have? I have what you want."

"I'm not going to admit to killing those girls!"

"I'm not asking you to do that," Innis replied quietly. "I just need you to admit to writing the notes."

"That's the same thing, you idiot!"

Innis smiled as though he were speaking with a small child. "Indirectly, perhaps. But if you don't agree to my terms, then your item will not be returned."

"Listen to me," Marko said, leaning forward. "I want to know where you took Whitney! If you hurt her—"

"She's fine. She's . . . safe. At least for now."

"Why her?" Marko growled.

Innis shrugged. "Because she is beautiful. Just like the other . . . things. I don't know why I took the others, either. I just had to."

"You're sick, you know that?" Marko said.

Bodies of Proof 281

"Marko, I came here to make a deal that will benefit both of us and all you can do is abuse me?"

"How do I know she's okay?" Marko asked. "How do I know it's not too late?"

"Marko, have I ever lied to you?"

"Absolutely. You lied to me when you came to me with this bogus OWI case, you lied when you framed me with clues that pointed to me, and you're probably lying now."

Innis's eyes had narrowed. "I never actually lied to you, Marko. I'd say you heard what you wanted to hear," he replied quietly. "And now I'm telling you the absolute truth. The deal is this: your life for hers. You admit to what I tell you and I'll release . . . the thing I have that you want."

"You understand that if I go to prison, I'll be waiting for you to join me. And when you do—"

"Don't be melodramatic, Marko. I'm not going to prison. Not for any of these crimes." He forced a smile. "If anyone goes, it'll be Clint."

"Woodford?" Marko asked. "No one will believe that he was smart enough to pull all this off."

"Oh, he had help," Innis replied calmly. His voice had lowered to a near-whisper. "Professional help. Are you surprised?"

"No," Marko replied. "Can't say that I am. In fact, I'm not even sure I'm disappointed." He stared at Innis. "You know he'll turn on you. As soon as he realizes he's going down, he'll flip on you easy."

"No, he won't," Innis replied. "He's in too far."

"If you believed that, you wouldn't be here, trying to do a deal with me," Marko said. "On camera, by the way," he added, looking pointedly at the camera mounted in the corner of the room.

"The camera doesn't matter. They can't watch it. We have attorney-client privilege."

Marko laughed. "Privilege prevents *me* from telling other people. You admitting to a crime in full view of a camera is not a protected conversation, moron."

"But he told me it would be!"

"He who?" Marko asked.

Marko watched while Innis shifted his weight.

"If you get arrested and charged, which you probably will, your attorney will argue to keep the confession out of evidence at your trial," Marko explained. "But they won't be successful because you weren't seeking legal advice from me. You were extorting me into falsely confessing to a crime in return for your not killing Whitney. That's not a protected conversation."

"But no one knows that!" Innis said, standing. Gone was the arrogant boy.

"They are if they're listening."

"But they can't listen to our conversations—he told me so."

"Woodford's no lawyer," Marko replied, shaking his head. "By the way, I recorded our conversation. The one where he told me he was working with you." He was watching Innis closely. His eyes were wide, his skin was ashen, and he began to shake.

"Who?"

"Woodford," Marko replied. "Who else?"

"N—No one," Innis assured him.

"Well, no deal, son. You'd best be on your way. I expect there's probably folks listening now. You'd better hurry, because if Woodford harms a hair on her head, I'll see you in hell."

He wasn't finished speaking before Innis sprinted from the interview room.

Marko felt a degree of satisfaction. Innis's overconfidence and misunderstanding of the law would result in his arrest—and hopefully, Whitney's rescue. Allee and Marko couldn't say anything about the storage shed as it pertained to Rebecca and Leslie—Innis's unsolicited confessions for those murders were crimes previously committed and could never be revealed. But the effort to extort him and Whitney's abduction were ongoing crimes.

If he was still holding her, and if she was still alive.

Marko looked straight at the camera.

"You can take them to the storage shed now, Allee."

61

WHITNEY

I'm going to die, Whitney thought, *unless I do something now.*

Innis had left a while ago. Whitney guessed fifteen minutes had passed, but she couldn't be certain. She couldn't see her watch with her hands tied behind her back. Woodford remained. He'd been pacing at the other end of the storage unit. He hadn't approached her, and she wanted it to stay that way, so she remained still, pretending to sleep.

A phone started ringing. The sound came from Woodford's direction.

"Hey, baby," Woodford said. His voice grew sweeter, softer. "Hold on, I'm working. I'll step outside."

It was probably his wife or his girlfriend, and he didn't want to risk Whitney waking up and making noise. How would he explain the sound of her voice?

Disgusting. The man was truly disgusting. He worried about the woman in his life while simultaneously helping Innis take women out of other people's lives.

She remained still and silent until she heard the door open and close, and his muffled voice outside. Then she twisted and pulled at her wrists. The restraints bit into her skin, but they were slowly loosening. She tried the same with her legs, but they had been tighter from the start. She couldn't move them at all, so she focused on her wrists. She pulled and pulled until finally there was enough space for her to wriggle one of her hands out.

I did it! Whitney thought, elation spreading through her, but the excitement was short-lived. A moment later, the back door swung open. She dropped back to the floor and placed her hands behind her back to make it look like they were still bound.

"Get off the phone, Clint." It was a man's voice. Deep and bass. "We've only got a few minutes."

Not good, Whitney thought.

She needed a weapon, something to protect herself. She had the element of surprise, but that was her only benefit. She felt around her, and her hand closed around a small, circular object. A music box! Several of them were stacked near where she was lying.

She could hear his footsteps as he approached, the heavy boots on the concrete floor. Clint, she could tell, was still outside, finishing up his phone call. She ignored him and focused on the closest threat. The man was close enough now that she could feel the air around her change. He was standing right above her! His knees cracked as he crouched, and she could feel his hot breath on her ear.

"I only wish we had the time to play, my little ballerina," he said.

She was almost overcome with panic, as well as the smell of his sour breath. "But your coworkers have complicated things." There was a rustling sound. A plastic bag, maybe?

Oh my God! He's going to suffocate me!

It was not going to end for her like this. No way. She'd been through too much. She forced herself to remain still until he drew near again, then she sprang up and bashed him on the head with the music box.

He issued a small cry of surprise. As she continued to hit him, the music box began to break apart in her hand, but she didn't stop. She hit him for herself. She hit him for Rebecca. She hit him for Leslie. She hit him for all the women and girls he'd no doubt bullied and victimized throughout his life. She hit him like she was in a trance. She hit him until shouting voices cut through her daze.

She looked up at the door. Where was Woodford? She used a broken shard from a music box to cut off her leg restraints. Then she grabbed another box and prepared for a second assault. In the dim light, she looked down at her attacker, who lay on the ground, unmoving, blood dripping from various spots on his face, neck, and head.

Serves him right, Whitney thought. Dead or knocked out, she wasn't sorry. He deserved it.

Her hand dripped blood, but she wasn't sure if that was her own or his. It was probably a little of both. She listened closely, taking deep breaths and trying to count the number of voices.

Three. Possibly four. Then she heard another. She was in trouble.

62

ALLEE

Allee could feel Davis's body tense as they sat in a small room, watching the live-stream of the conversation between Marko and Innis.

She watched as Innis jumped to his feet. "But no one knows that!" she heard him say.

"They are if they're listening."

"But they can't listen to our conversations—he told me so."

He?

Allee was thinking it through when she heard Marko ask Innis, "Who else?"

"Oh, my God!" she cried. "We need to go! Now!"

"Shit! There's an accomplice!" Davis said, jumping to his feet. "We've got to get there before he does!"

"What about Innis?" Allee asked.

"I'll call for backup to take Innis into custody."

"Good. I think I know where the accomplice is going!" Allee said, her gaze remaining on the video feed. "Follow me." She ran to the door and wrenched it open.

She burst into the hallway, sprinting toward the door with Davis following hot on her heels. When they made it to the stairwell, there was one other person headed down the stairs. Jenkins.

Bodies of Proof 287

"What's happening?" Jenkins asked. "Why the rush?"

"Follow us," Allee said as they passed him. "Whitney needs help!"

"You found her? Where is she?" He was running now, too, but he was older and couldn't move as fast as Davis and Allee.

"I'll explain on the way," Allee said.

When they made it outside, Davis motioned to Jenkins and Allee. "Get in my car. It's right here."

They all piled into his white Franklin PD SUV. Davis backed out before Allee could buckle her seatbelt.

"Where to?" he asked.

"Kum and Leave Storage, unit 31," Allee said.

Davis put the vehicle in gear and screamed down the street without turning on his lights or sirens.

"You were right," Jenkins said, his tone cowed. "I had it wrong with Bauer."

"You can apologize later," Allee said. "I don't care about any of that until I know that Whitney is okay."

They took a quick corner and turned in through the storage facility's gates.

"Which way?" Davis asked. There were several different aisles of storage units and they weren't clearly marked.

"Left," Allee said.

Davis turned and continued following Allee's instructions until they pulled up to the end unit. Woodford was standing outside talking on the phone. He looked up when they pulled up. His eyes widened and he hung up the phone.

Jenkins and Davis were on the run almost as soon as the vehicle came to a stop.

"Stop right there, Woodford!" Davis shouted.

The men rushed toward Woodford, handcuffing him, but Allee's attention was focused on finding Whitney. She ran past them and tore the side door open.

"Whitney!" Allee shouted. "Are you in here?"

"Yes." Whitney sounded tired, but her voice was strong.

Allee relaxed until she saw that Whitney was covered in blood. "Are you okay?" She rushed toward Whitney. "Do you need an ambulance?"

Whitney looked down at her hands, moving slowly as though she was in a daze. "I don't think the blood is mine."

"You what?" Allee asked, then she noticed the crumpled, bloodied figure lying in front of Whitney. "Who is that?" The lighting was poor, and his face was so battered that it was difficult to make out his features.

"I'm not sure."

"Is he alive?"

Whitney kicked him, striking him in the stomach.

Shaffer groaned.

63

MARKO

Marko waited in the interview room. Thirty minutes passed and nobody came for him. The door wasn't locked, but he was in belly chains and cuffs. He'd been arrested for murder, and the arresting officer had treated him according to standard operating procedure.

So he waited and alternately prayed and cursed, drumming his fingertips on the table. He tried not to look at the clock or think about his splitting headache. He tried not to worry about Allee or Whitney. He tried as well not to think about the one thing that would quickly erase all of his cares—booze.

Twenty minutes later, a heavily perspiring Jenkins came through the door. "I'm too old for this shit," he huffed. "Give me your hands," he instructed Marko as he withdrew a key. "You're getting released. And I owe you an apology."

"How about that?" Marko said. "Law enforcement who knows when to apologize. I never thought I'd see the day."

"Yeah, well, I can admit when I'm wrong," Jenkins said. "I . . . followed the evidence, you know. I mean, between the note—"

"That was a lie."

"And the pen—"

"Planted."

"The DNA—"

"Of course."

"Well, it was solid there for a while. And every time I had doubts, well . . ." He looked around furtively. "I was actually looking at Shaffer. I just didn't have anything."

"Speaking of which, will I be getting an apology from Shaffer?"

Jenkins laughed. "Don't push it," he said. "Besides, he may not make it."

"Make it?" Marko asked.

"Whitney roughed him up pretty good."

"Oh yeah?"

"Yeah," Jenkins said. "She might be a little tougher than you and Allee give her credit for." He opened the door and motioned to it. "The prosecutor is filing a dismissal of all the charges, with prejudice. You're free to leave. Get out of here."

Marko slowly rose to his feet, then took Jenkins's hand.

"Thank you."

Jenkins nodded. "Go. There are a couple people out there waiting for you."

When Marko reached the hallway, he found Whitney and Allee sitting side by side, watching the door. Their faces split into wide grins when they saw him. Whitney looked tired and she either lost a lot of weight or she was wearing some of Allee's spare clothing, because her clothes hung off her.

He walked up to them and stopped, then cleared his throat. "I suppose 'I'm sorry' wouldn't be sufficient." He was the one who had brought Innis into their lives. He was the one who couldn't see past his greediness. He was the one who had turned to the bottle when he should have been helping them solve the problems he'd created.

"No," Allee said. "It wouldn't."

Marko's shoulders drooped. This was it. He'd taken things too far and they were abandoning him. They'd have to dissolve the businesses and start all over again. He didn't think he had the strength to do that.

"But an apology plus a month of inpatient treatment followed by extended outpatient treatment would do it," Whitney said.

Marko nodded. "That's going to be expensive."

"That's the bad news," Allee replied. A grin spread over her face. "The

Bodies of Proof

good news is, the guy who framed you and attacked Whitney just happens to be stinking rich."

"And from a powerful family," Whitney added.

"A family that will be desperate to make this story go away," Allee said, finishing the thought. "Do you know someone who could file a lawsuit for damages, emotional and physical, caused by Innis?" she asked.

"I know just the guy," Marko said, grinning for the first time in days.

EPILOGUE
WHITNEY

Six Months Later

Whitney, Allee, and Marko stood in front of a refurbished brick building in downtown Franklin, across the street from the courthouse and the law enforcement center.

"Why are we doing this outside?" Marko asked. "I'm freezing my ass off."

"Then hurry the hell up," Allee said.

"Yes!" Whitney shook her head. "Let's just cut the ribbon and get inside!"

A crowd of locals had gathered, and all eyes were on the three partners —Allee with her prison tattoos, Marko with his law degree and newfound sobriety, and Whitney, the former teacher who was still trying to find her new lot in life.

Their lawsuit against James Innis had been successful. Marko had gotten a call from their legal staff shortly after he had filed the complaint and arranged for service. The offer was one million dollars apiece.

Marko had laughed and said, "Go pound sand."

"What do you want?" the Innis family legal representative demanded.

Bodies of Proof 293

"I know what your family is worth. Make that one a five and we'll talk. Until then, I'm prepared to release a statement—"

"Five million. Fine."

"Each," Marko said. "Five million each, fifteen million total."

Whitney had gasped when she heard Marko's counter. One million dollars was more than she could fathom as a recently divorced, single mother. Five million dollars seemed too good to be true.

"Fine," the Innis legal representative had said.

When Marko had hung up the phone, he'd said, "I should have asked for more."

"Are you going to cut the ribbon or not?" Allee said, her voice cutting through Whitney's memories.

Whitney shook her head and held the large shears up to the golden ribbon. She sliced through it and announced, "Justice Bites Law Firm and Eatery is now open!"

The crowd cheered and streamed inside.

She followed and kept an eye on Marko while Allee poured the champagne and served finger foods. The last thing they needed was to see Marko relapse yet again.

They had plans.

Their little food truck had grown into a full-blown business. Now independently wealthy, Whitney had already decided to take some of her money and apply to law school. If everything went as planned, in three years she'd be one of *two* attorneys working at Justice Bites.

The Final Appeal
Smith and Bauer Book 3

The jury convicted him. The evidence tells a different story.

Small-town lawyer Marko Bauer and sharp-tongued associate Allee Smith aren't eager to risk another courtroom disaster—especially not for Byron, a convicted kidnapper swearing innocence from his jail cell.

But when a waitress at the Justice Bites restaurant brings them Byron's plea, something doesn't taste right. A sketchy voice ID, a basement crime scene that doesn't exist, and a detective nursing grudges deeper than the county's riverbeds. Marko and Allee soon realize Byron might actually be telling the truth—this time.

Crafting a bold legal strategy, the duo pushes forward with a post-conviction relief hearing, hoping to secure Byron's release. But freedom might unleash a darker side of Byron. His angry, entitled, and volatile demeanor is leaving those around him to wonder if they're freeing an innocent man— or releasing a ticking time bomb.

Marko and Allee soon confront a troubling realization: some clients should never see daylight again.

**Get your copy today at
severnriverbooks.com**

30% Off your next paperback.

Thank you for reading. For exclusive offers on your next paperback:

- **Visit SevernRiverBooks.com** and enter code **PRINTBOOKS30** at checkout.
- Or scan the QR code.

Offer valid for future paperback purchases only. The discount applies solely to the book price (excluding shipping, taxes, and fees) and is limited to one use per customer. Offer available to US customers only. Additional terms and conditions apply.

ABOUT JAMES CHANDLER

Wall Street Journal bestselling author James Chandler spent his formative years in the western United States. When he wasn't catching fish or footballs, he was roaming centerfield and trying to hit the breaking pitch. After a mediocre college baseball career, he exchanged jersey No. 7 for camouflage issued by the United States Army, which he wore around the globe and with great pride for twenty years. Since law school, he has favored dark suits and a steerhide briefcase. When he isn't working or writing, he'll likely have a fly rod, shotgun or rifle in hand. He and his wife are blessed with two wonderful adult daughters.

Sign up for James Chandler's newsletter at
severnriverbooks.com

ABOUT LAURA SNIDER

Laura Snider is a practicing lawyer in Iowa. She graduated from Drake Law School in 2009 and spent most of her career as a Public Defender. Throughout her legal career she has been involved in all levels of crimes from petty thefts to murders. These days she is working part-time as a prosecutor and spends the remainder of her time writing stories and creating characters.

Laura lives in Iowa with her husband, three children, two dogs, and two very mischievous cats.

Learn more about Laura Snider's books at
severnriverbooks.com